I0748796

War Becomes Her
An Alexis Snupperdoom Novel
Book 3

JD BROYHILL

DISCLAIMER:
THE CHARACTERS, PLACES, EVENTS, AND ITEMS PORTRAYED AND DEFINED IN THIS WORK ARE FICTITIOUS. THIS BOOK IS THE WORK OF THE AUTHOR. ANY SIMILARITY TO ACTUAL DEFINITIONS LISTED IN THE BOOK IS BY COINCIDENCE AND NOT INTENTIONAL. ALL ARTWORK IS THE PROPERTY OF THE AUTHOR. THE AUTHOR HOLDS ALL COPYRIGHTS TO THE ART DISPLAYED IN OR ON THIS BOOK.

ISBN: 9798992673289

LIBRARY OF CONGRESS CONTROL NUMBER:
2025904795

PRINTED IN THE UNITED STATES OF AMERICA

DEDICATION

To my beautiful and imaginative children—
keep dreaming and believing.

To Rick—I love you more, period, stop…

CONTENTS

THE BEGINNING

"Mom, choose a side. You must pick your allegiance. I'm sorry, but you have to..." Zandorah agreed. The time had come. There would be a battle and potentially war. The Battle Rounds were the perfect time to get in shape and sharpen the skills needed for combat. She did not believe Alexis, nor was she intimidated by her.

"I will not choose a side. You cannot ask me to do that. I refuse! You are my daughters, and I love you. You two, work it out. I plan to find my son-in-law, Armbruster, and tell him what is happening. I suggest you talk this through before doing something rash that will affect all of Alstromia and Iriss." Lorthana walked away, leaving them alone on the Landing Deck. Their backs were turned to each other, neither talking nor moving.

Alexis spun around and faced Zandorah. "Mom made her decision. It is fine with me. I have no issue with Mom staying out of this or staying neutral. You and I are finished. I am tired of you and your blatant inability to recognize what happened on the mountain. You want to believe, Dad, that is fine. I will see you in the Battle Colosseum. I cannot wait to destroy you! We will see who makes it out of the *'battle zone'* and who doesn't. I tell you what…let's not play games. We both know what this really means."

Zandorah glared at Alexis, knowing the answer before she even said it. "Absolutely, Alexis—it means WAR!!!"

CHAPTER 1

Alexis felt there was nothing worse than an incomplete conversation. It left so much to the imagination, and she hated it. *'Why does Zandorah believe she can threaten me? She is not that powerful. Her planet and its Clan members are not warriors. They are humble and kind but far from war-ready.'*

Most residents lived on Iriss because they were either weak or non-confrontational Witches, Wizzards, or Warlocks (W3s). They preferred to live a quiet and peaceful life.

Alexis doubted Zandorah could turn any of her Clan members into strong leaders or warriors. They could not match the army Alexis established on Alstromia.

Long ago, Alexis prepared her army for war, placing Andreh Darkhill in charge since he was an excellent trainer, recruiter, and warrior. Andreh ensured he only enlisted strong, elite Warlocks ready to fight and support the cause.

The Army of Elite (*AoE*), the best and most powerful team, was hand-selected by Andreh with the help of Armbruster and Pauto. Without a doubt, the AoE was ready to face war at any time, in any climate or environment. With 500 members, the team is divided into two groups, and each group trains once a month in the southern region of Troficcah, where the hot and tropical climate poses a significant challenge. This training serves as an excellent preparation for battles and requires immense strength and endurance.

The AoE was not the only team Alexis planned to use in case of war. She also had 1,500 other members, known as the Standard Army of Warriors (*SAoW*), on standby. They trained monthly in the far eastern region of Draffenite. Its dry and barren desert serves as a useful survival training environment. They also practiced with the AoE every six months to ensure readiness for hand-to-hand combat and Magical Exchange (*ME*)—the Battle of the Ceptres and Wands.

Alexis had no doubt her planet, Alstromia, would withstand war and emerge victoriously. She hoped it did not come to that. The horrific thought of the destruction of her beloved home and planet made her cringe. Alexis was also concerned about the commoners. Most were ill-prepared for battle. She planned to meet with Andreh and Pauto to implement a plan to arm the commoners in the event that war broke out on Alstromia.

Zandorah turned in her bed within the Castle of Zandor, drawing the covers up and snuggling deeper into the cozy blanket. She wasn't quite ready to rise. Instead, she gazed out the window, pleased to see it was a splendid day. The sun beamed down brightly, illuminating the sky adorned with soft, pink clouds. The ambiance on Iriss always had a delicate lavender hue during the day, transforming into a deep purple as night fell. As she reflected on her mother, a wave of longing washed over her, and she found herself hoping for her mother's visit soon.

Zandorah sat up in bed and looked around her room, almost ready to get up. She felt melancholy. Ever since Gardone, her father, disappeared, she has experienced difficulty sleeping. She wished to know where he was hiding. Most of all, she hoped he was okay.

During her last conversation with her mother, she swore she did not know where Gardone was currently hiding. However, Zandorah found it difficult to believe. Nonetheless, she refused to argue with her mother about the subject since she was not doing well emotionally and appeared fragile. Zandorah disliked the effect on her mom, who usually acted stoically under most circumstances.

Gardone vanished immediately after Alexis was rescued from the cabin on Tullah Mountain. Since Gardone was responsible for kidnapping Alexis, his daughter, he knew it was safer to disappear instantly, without a trace. Many wondered how he managed this vile act against his child. Others contemplated why. What would make him want to harm his daughter? It seemed unthinkable. Nevertheless, Gardone managed to do so and made enemies in the process. He became a wanted Warlock, and many tried to locate him.

Alexis was quite vocal about telling her side of the kidnapping story. She shared details of the event with anyone who would listen, claiming she was the victim of torture and abuse. Sadly, the more she told it, the more she embellished her account of the event. It became more violent and blown out of proportion. Many stopped listening to her outrageous tale altogether. But Zandorah listened intently, looking for flaws in her story and web of deceit. She knew there was more to what she was telling everyone and, without a doubt, figured Gardone was a victim, too.

Zandorah's security team informed her that someone spotted Gardone on Zarkher Mountain, on the northern side of Dorleenah, near the capital of Iriss. Eager to find her father, Zandorah sent several scout units to determine if the information was factual.

Unfortunately, the scouts returned without any evidence of his existence or whereabouts. The lack of new information about her father disappointed Zandorah even more. She assumed Gardone might have taken refuge on Iriss, hoping he would be safe. She vowed not to give up so quickly and planned to continue searching for Gardone independently. Her father meant the world to her, and she wanted to hear his side of the story about what had occurred at the cabin with Alexis. She would give him the benefit of the doubt, at least for now.

Grudgingly, Zandorah chose to face the day. She wanted to speak with her Head Council

Staff about the upcoming Battle Rounds on Alstromia. Three of her Elite Guards wished to enter the contest, especially when they heard Zandorah had already entered her name into the competition, ready to battle against Alexis once more.

Following Zandorah's harsh encounter with Alexis on Alstromia, she realized a battle was inevitable, and this was likely only the start of their conflict. It appeared to Zandorah that Alexis was seeking a war. She was overly aggressive and downright taunting her, pushing her toward battling. Zandorah recognized she was ill-prepared to face Alexis in a war, especially an interplanetary war. Even so, she would do what was necessary to protect Iriss.

Alexis and her AoE, known throughout Clans and planets as the best of the best, were a vast and daunting challenge. Zandorah felt her team and army were unprepared to face such opposition. That is why she planned to meet Rammadar, her Second-in-Command, this morning in the Command Chamber. He would know what needed to be implemented to assemble an elite team ready to fight Alstromia and Alexis.

Zandorah dressed in a hurry, wanting to head toward the Royal Planning Chamber to discuss the protection of her planet and the Clan. Alexis would, without a doubt, start a war without any notice. She would most likely sneak onto Iriss at night when most Clan members slept, catching them off guard. Zandorah did not fear for her own life.

Instead, Zandorah worried about others. She was a kind and loving leader, always protecting the most vulnerable. Now, she contemplated their fate with apprehension. *'How can I protect them? Can I enable a spell to save the planet, keeping Alexis and the AoE away? Probably not.'* It was inevitable she would face Alexis after the Battles. Unfortunately, that left little time to prepare for war.

On Alstromia, Alexis sat in the plush, dark brown chair in the Battle Planning Chamber (*BPC*), the most secure room in the Palace. Andreh, Pauto, Armbruster, Aerianna, and others sat around the large oblong table, waiting for Alexis to begin the conversation. Aerianna fidgeted with her pen, a present she had bought on Earth long ago.

Aerianna still preferred to write on paper with a pen rather than use a Docu-Tab—a magical tablet that floated silently next to the person owning it. It recorded all conversations and translated them into writing to be read like a book and stored for later retrieval. Aerianna liked the magical tablet but preferred the old-fashioned method of writing on paper with a pen. Aerianna placed the crystal-encrusted pen on the table next to her notepad. She looked up and smiled. Pauto reciprocated by giving her a wink with a coy smirk. Next to him, Andreh stared at Alexis, looking strange. Aerianna glared at Andreh and wondered what he was thinking and why he was so close to the Queen. Everything about their relationship seemed very suspicious.

She overheard Armbruster hollering at Alexis a night ago, hearing Andreh's name mentioned more than once. Armbruster insisted on finding out what was going on between Alexis and Andreh. The incident on Tullah Mountain during Alexis' rescue still made Armbruster furious. He felt Andreh had no reason to be there. Even more, he was irritated to see Alexis run into his arms after she was rescued and not his, her husband's.

"What exactly is happening between you and Andreh?" Armbruster yelled, looking at Alexis as she sat on the bed in her chamber the night before.

Alexis retorted adamantly, "Absolutely nothing! You are making a big deal over a friendship. Andreh is a good friend and confidant. I have been instructing him on potion-making because he is a gifted Warlock. I knew under my guidance, he would grow. He can become a successful potion-maker. It is a rare gift."

Armbruster did not believe her explanation and was tired of fighting with her. Angrily, he pounded his fists on the chamber door, exiting quickly. Armbruster left disgusted, assuming she was having an affair with Andreh. The two glanced at each other all the time in an odd yet comforting way. Armbruster planned to put an end to the affair. He felt it harmed the Queen's image and ultimately hurt the Clan. The Queen's reputation would take a hit if their romantic entanglement were revealed, and Armbruster did not want that.

He decided to head to Yarlen's chamber to talk with him about this. He knew he would come up with a solution. Alexis had graciously allowed Yarlen to resume his previous post and job as Head Seeier after he helped rescue her. After a brief trial, all earlier charges against Yarlen were dropped. He was allowed to stay at the Palace, aiding the Queen. Ultimately, it all worked out for him, thanks to Alexis acting civilly and forgiving for a change.

Two months after his trial, Sonia returned to Alstromia as well. She moved to the other end of the Palace and stayed in her chamber, still not fully trusting her husband, Yarlen.

Hopefully, they could resume their life as husband and wife before too long. Though Sonia wondered if she could be happy not working on Iriss with Zandorah. She missed her good friend and the power she was given on

Iriss. Sonia did not trust Alexis and speculated if she still held a grudge toward Yarlen. Sonia feared that, in time, Alexis would find a way to get rid of Yarlen again. She seemed spiteful and unscrupulous. Sonia only truly trusted Armbruster. He was honest and forthright. She never worried about him. He kept Alexis in check most of the time and seemed fair in his dealings with others.

In the Battle Planning Chamber, Aerianna spoke up. "Alexis, should we prepare to fight Iriss and Zandorah? You know she is not ready and cannot match our AoE. Her army is pathetic. Why should we even bother?" Aerianna said with a chuckle.

"I will fight and destroy her in the Battle Rounds. After that, we will see how things progress. However, I am tired of her shit. If she wants war, she can have it. I have no doubt we will be victorious and annihilate her. I have held back because I know how this will affect my mother, Lorthana. Also, it is still my opinion that Zandorah is hiding my father, Gardone. Since he is ultimately responsible for my kidnapping, I want him found. I believe if I force war, Zandorah will turn him over. If for no other reason than to save her Clan and planet," Alexis remarked, standing with her hand on the table, glaring at the others.

Pauto stood up and began clapping. Andreh joined him and bowed to Alexis out of respect. Aerianna rose as well, looking at Armbruster, who appeared livid.

Armbruster shook his head in disagreement. A war was extreme at any level, and he did not want to destroy what they had worked so hard to accomplish on Alstromia. He felt Alexis was acting out of spite and overreacting. It was apparent that she wanted to prove to her sister that she was the more powerful of the two. It made him sick to his stomach. He spent hours the night before pleading with Alexis to drop the threat of war. He informed her that he supported confronting Zandorah in the Battle Rounds but felt war was unnecessary. He could not condone such actions. Alexis objected to his comments, clarifying she did not care what he thought. She was in charge and would decide her next step based on facts.

The fact remained—Zandorah felt Alexis was indirectly responsible for the kidnapping. This was an absurd notion to Alexis. *'Surely, Zandorah is kidding?'* Alexis thought.

Unfortunately, Zandorah was not. She still believed Alexis drove Gardone to kidnap her and attempt to overtake her monarchy.

Regardless of what others believed or wanted, Alexis was ready to confront Zandorah and her weak army. Alexis felt prepared, ready for war. She would win, and if need be, Iriss would be destroyed. Alexis was okay with that. She no longer worried about the Witches, Wizzards, or Warlocks on Iriss. Most left Alstromia to live on Iriss because they despised Alexis or her vision for Alstromia. So, it was okay. They could perish. It was of no loss or consequence to her at all. At this point, she did not care. Alexis motioned for everyone to sit down. Once the Queen was comfortable in her chair, she folded her hands and placed them on the table. She stared out the window, daydreaming of her Torrin, wishing she could fly to relieve the mounting stress.

Andreh noticed her blank stare and knew what she was thinking. He smiled, ready to head to the stables to retrieve the Torrins. Andreh planned to accompany Alexis back to the cabin on Tullah Mountain, this time to be alone with her.

Alexis stood. "I am retiring to my chamber. There is nothing else to discuss. I request that the Harvest Festival Team meet in the Planning Chamber tomorrow. I ask you, Aerianna, to ensure everyone is there. If you need me, I will be back by tonight." She walked out without another word. Andreh excused himself and headed toward the stable, assuming she would show up shortly.

Armbruster meandered toward the window and gazed out, admiring the valley below. It looked peaceful and beautiful. He loved this time of year. He could not wait for the Harvest Festival, which started with the biggest event of the year, the Battle Rounds. It would be good to see many of his close friends from other planets, including Earth, participating in or watching the event.

★ *. ★ *. ★ *. ★ *. ★

Arriving at the stables, Andreh asked Essten to prepare his Torrin as well as the Queen's. Essten did not think that was an odd request, given the fact that Andreh was security. He figured he would accompany her on the flight. Andreh sat on the large stone bench outside the stables, waiting. He looked at his dirty boots and wondered why he had not polished them. If Alexis saw them, she would say something. She did not like anyone on her staff to look messy or dirty.

Within five minutes, Alexis appeared wearing her flying outfit. She looked stunning in her snug, black pants tucked into her boots. A short cape was draped over her shoulders. The Wand of Grimleah was tucked in the wide, black belt. Alexis did not fly with her heavy Ceptre. It was too bulky and uncomfortable. Instead, Alexis chose the wand given to her by Lorthana, her mother.

The Wand of Grimleah belonged to Lorthana's mother, Grimleah Magicca Snipperdoom. When Alexis became the Queen of Alstromia, Lorthana bestowed her the wand.

It was the most powerful wand known to exist. It held powers that Lorthana and Alexis still did not fully understand.

They spent months researching its power and history. Many believed Grimleah received the wand from Drexxlie Vandzinderling, her ex-fiancé. He had been an extraordinary Wizzard, having studied under the great and powerful Vizzork - the most formidable Wizzard and Warlock ever to exist. Vizzork also created the *Vizzork's Advanced Magical Exchange 1 - (VAME 1) School for Witches and Vizzork's Advanced Magical Exchange 2 - (VAME 2) School for Wizzards and Warlocks.*

Most Wizzards attended the *VAME 2* to learn the *'good magic,'* while the Warlocks hoped to acquire the *'dark'* and more evil magical abilities. Vizzork taught both.

Many feared Drexxlie would become more commanding than Vizzork. Perhaps that is why everyone questioned his mysterious and swift death. As a result of his demise, Drexxlie faded into the *Eternal World of Guidance,* becoming even more influential than ever predicted. Now, he could inspire and guide many, and one of his favorite new students happened to be none other than the talented and beautiful Alexis Snipperdoom!

Alexis smiled the moment she spotted Andreh, though she was surprised to see him.

'How does he know me so well?' Alexis speculated.

"Why are you here, Andreh?" she inquired.

"I knew what you planned to do when I saw you staring out the window, gazing at the sky. I know you all too well. Do not forget that," Andreh teased, standing before her.

"I suppose you are right," Alexis replied.

"Shall we?" he asked as he took her hand, leading her toward the flying beast. The two mounted their Torrins and headed to the field to take off for the flight. The sky was clear, and the late afternoon was crisp. The wind picked up, and Alexis shivered lightly, snuggling down onto her Torrin for warmth. She took off first, soaring into the sky, her long black hair whipping around behind her. Andreh followed quickly, not wanting to be left behind.

Essten smiled as he watched them fly off. He walked back to the stables to secure the building for the night. He would stay in the main office awaiting their return, missing dinner at home. Marittaz, his wife, would be upset. Nonetheless, she understood his responsibilities, and this time, it was the Queen he had to wait for before going home. Essten had no choice. Duty before anything else!

If Collan were still alive, he would have stayed behind. Essten and Marittaz still missed him every day. His brutal murder was forever in their minds, making their lives miserable.

Alexis flew like no other, an incredibly gifted Torrin rider. She knew how to handle the beast and could do things in the air with her that no one else would attempt. Since its inception at the Battle Rounds, Alexis won the Battle Flight every year for the last ten years. Andreh was still amazed, watching her zoom through the sky, laughing and looking joyful. When Alexis was on her Torrin, her world was complete. She felt utter freedom, and it was apparent watching her. Andreh wished he could kiss her.

His heart melted when he saw her happiness. Alexis headed in the opposite direction of the cabin on Tullah Mountain, perplexing Andreh. Andreh pondered, *'Where is she going?'* shaking his head. Eager to know her plans, he flew up beside Alexis, their Torrins almost touching.

"What is our destination? I thought we were heading to the cabin?" he shouted.

"Why would you think that?" Alexis replied as she pushed her Torrin forward, heading toward Highgrove Mountain on the other side of Alstromia. Andreh reluctantly followed her toward the mountain range, curious as to why she wanted to fly there.

Life with Alexis was never easy. Armbruster knew this better than anyone. Most days, he tolerated her nonsense because he loved her.

Other days, he wanted to strangle her, though he would never actually harm her. Armbruster paced in front of Yarlen, his boots making strange clicking noises as he walked around. He held his Ceptre in his right hand, moving it back and forth. Yarlen watched him in silence, noticing how nervous Armbruster looked. Yarlen could also feel the tension in the air.

Apparently, Armbruster was not capable of hiding his feelings or displeasure. After a few minutes, Yarlen became exasperated, watching Armbruster walking around aimlessly, and decided to speak up.

"Armbruster, sit down. You will wear out the tiles under your feet. For goodness' sake. Sit down, Sir!"

"Oh, right," responded Armbruster, annoyed with himself. He sat on the fluffy, old chair by Yarlen.

"So, why are you here, Armbruster? You seem agitated. What happened? Why did you come to see me today?" asked Yarlen with great curiosity.

Armbruster relaxed and decided it was time to fill Yarlen in on Alexis' plan for Alstromia and the potential war with Iriss and Zandorah. After a lengthy conversation, he stared at Yarlen, awaiting a response. Yarlen looked bewildered.

"Well, that is a scary thought, Armbruster. Are you certain she plans to wage war against Zandorah and Iriss? It seems silly, considering they are family. Also, how does Lorthana feel about this?" Yarlen figured something was wrong. There was no way Alexis would consider engaging in war unless there was more to the story. What was Armbruster not telling him? Armbruster was famous for leaving out pertinent facts, and Yarlen knew that all too well.

Yarlen heard the rumors of war and details about the fight between Alexis and Zandorah on the Landing Deck at the Palace. Supposedly, Lorthana was present, but she left the two to work it out on their own. She did not want to get involved in their differences.

After a long talk, the sisters decided to fight it out in the Battle Rounds after the Harvest Festival. If Alexis did not like the results, she promised to initiate a war with Zandorah to prove her superiority.

Again, this seemed childish and senseless to Yarlen. Confused but curious, Yarlen watched Armbruster, and he slumped down in the chair. He looked exhausted, neglecting his appearance. His hair was messy, and his cloak was stained. It was very unlike Armbruster to forgo his hygiene.

It took some time, but eventually, Armbruster spoke up. He wanted Yarlen to understand the repercussions that would come from the possibility of war with Iriss.

Armbruster had already met with the security team and the AoE Commander, Steffen Starleight, to determine where they currently stood and if they were prepared for war. Steffen informed Armbruster that the AoE was one hundred percent ready for battle. Their training this cycle was complete, and most Clan members sensed war coming. The entire Clan on Alstromia knew about the differences between Alexis and Zandorah.

Unfortunately, rumors about Alexis and Zandorah's rift also made their way back to Earth, causing many to head back to Alstromia to prepare for what they believed would become a battle of the planets. Steffen assumed the end of the Battle Rounds would signal the beginning of the war. He informed his Second-in-Command, Sheillah Hexxon, to prepare the first team—250 warriors ready for battle and war. She acknowledged his request, ensuring their readiness. Steffen had received his orders directly from Alexis, though she did not get directly involved in the day-to-day operations of preparing the teams.

Instead, Alexis allowed Steffen to decide how to deploy the units. She was not interested in the small details, ultimately demanding results. Steffen listened attentively and accepted his responsibility.

The late afternoon was magnificent as Alexis touched down swiftly by Cosmett Lake, an oval, deep-blue body of water nestled at the foot of Highgrove Mountain. This lake was famous for its unique residents—Draghoons, large, scaly beings that combined features of dragons and giant fish. They could often be spotted soaring above the surface or, at other times, plunging below, swimming gracefully beneath the water.

Most Draghoons, however, favored the water-filled pools within the moist caves near Cosmett Lake. Alexis had a deep affection for Draghoons. She had a secret pet named Trixxie, a large purple one. Trixxie resided in the largest cave by the lake. Alexis intended to visit her, and she hoped that Andreh would be excited to meet the extraordinary creature.

CHAPTER 2

Alexis smiled as she entered the musty and dark cave. Andreh walked behind her, wondering why they were in a smelly cavern. Suddenly, Alexis cast an *Illumination Spell*, and the space lit up in a bright, warm, white light. Andreh jumped back when he saw the fierce creature. The Draghoon stared at them. Her gills flapped on the side of her neck while her scales glistened. The beast stood tall, nearly 12 feet.

Her two small arms hung down on the side, touching her enormous, round belly. She stood on her two long, muscular legs. Her lacy-looking wings were tucked behind her and folded in a non-combative way.

Alexis extended her hand toward the massive beast. As Trixxie moved forward, her big forked tail flicked about, producing unusual sounds on the sandy floor of the cave.

"Hello, my love. How are you today, Trixxie?" Alexis asked, now standing before the Draghoon, petting her oval, purple head. Trixxie rubbed her head gently against Alexis, almost causing her to fall over. The beast was quite strong.

"Umm, what is this?" asked Andreh nervously, watching the interaction between the beast and Alexis.

"This is Trixxie—my pet Draghoon. No one knows she is hidden in the cave. I want her to remain free and enjoy her life. I come to visit her every few weeks. We are actively training for the Battle Flight. I plan to use her on the Flight and Fight portion of the competition. Zandorah is predictable and will use her Braggli. I don't think the wings on the Braggli can compare to those of the Draghoon. The Braggli's are such non-impressive beasts, and their wings are weak and thin. I am confident Trixxie will outfly any Braggli," Alexis stated adamantly, giving Trixxie an Ordall, a fruit similar to an apple and orange combination found exclusively on Alstromia. Trixxie devoured it, shaking her head.

Andreh knew about Braggli's but had never seen a Draghoon in person since they were solitary beasts. Andreh knew most Braggli's were no bigger than 7 feet tall. They were known to be speedy, but their smaller and delicate wings could not keep up with the more powerful Draghoon's wings, or so he heard. Also, Braggli's died young. Most live for only about five years. After the first few years of life, they became lazy and spent the remainder of their lives sleeping. Zandorah would be at a disadvantage using her Braggli.

Utilizing Trixxie could undoubtedly help Alexis. Andreh smirked, feeling proud of Alexis for being a pioneer, ready and willing to develop a new way to win.

Andreh approached Trixxie cautiously. The sizeable purple beast blinked her enormous, round, amethyst-colored eyes. She slowly lowered her head, allowing Andreh to pet her. Alexis stood next to Trixxie, observing. The creature was unaccustomed to strangers in her cave, and Alexis worried she would become aggressive toward Andreh. However, Trixxie seemed fond of young Warlock, passively lying before him, which she only did when she felt comfortable with someone.

"Wow, she seems to like you, Andreh. That is fantastic," marveled Alexis, grinning.

"She is adorable. So, where do you train her?" Andreh asked, mystified.

Alexis shared the routine, which typically began with her guiding Trixxie to the lake. Once they reached the water, they practiced take-offs and landings on both the surface and the ground. Afterward, Alexis climbed onto Trixxie's back, wrapping her arms around the beast's long, scaly neck. Despite Trixxie's thick neck, Alexis was able to grip the rough scales along the sides. She considered using a specially designed saddle and reins that had been crafted for Trixxie. Although the Draghoon wasn't particularly fond of having it on her, she would sometimes accept it.

Trixxie, ever so gentle and conscious of Alexis on her back, was protective. She flew in such a manner as to protect Alexis at all times. She never allowed her to slip off her back. The two shared a unique bond.

Furthermore, Alexis described to Andreh how Trixxie learned to dive quickly, slamming her massive wings tightly against her body and shooting like a bullet to the ground. "Just as she is about to crash, she fully opens her beautiful and webbed wings, like a parachute, gently landing," Alexis clarified, beaming with pride. The two perfected the dives, hoping to outmaneuver the other contestants in the battle flights. Alexis knew it would be epic!

"That's quite interesting," Andreh replied. "But, aren't you worried that Trixxie will be the only Draghoon in the competition? No one has ever entered a Draghoon." Andreh thought it was terrific but wondered how others would react.

"No, that is the whole point. I think it will be magnificent. I cannot wait to see everyone's response." Alexis giggled, snuggling up against Trixxie. Andreh watched the two in wonder, excited about the possibility of their impending victory at the Battle Rounds.

In the Palace of Snipperdoom, Aerianna sat on her bed, pouting and feeling restless. She pondered the recent changes in Alexis's behavior. Typically impulsive, Alexis had started picking fights with everyone, which was unlike her. Aerianna sensed that something was off. She couldn't understand why Alexis wasn't opening up to her and instead seemed to be keeping her distance.

Aerianna looked at the list on her notepad and read the comprehensive notes. Alexis and Aerianna picked the team for the Harvest Festival. Everyone on the list was assigned a specific job. As the official overseer of the event,

Aerianna was now in charge of ensuring everything would run smoothly.

In the morning, Aerianna planned to assemble the group to complete the finishing touches of the event. Most of the days were already planned. The Harvest Festival lasted a total of six days. The seventh day was the Celebration Event Day (*CED*), the most attended day. Aerianna had a few surprises in place and could not wait to show Alexis her ideas.

Armbruster informed Aerianna that he wanted to be left out of the planning of the Harvest Festival this year. He would be a spectator and not a participant, feeling exhausted. The last year had been too stressful.

Over numerous meetings, Armbruster downright begged Alexis to cancel the Battle Rounds, but she stubbornly refused. Wizzards, Warlocks, and Witches attended the annual week-long event, coming from all over. It was the most significant and celebrated occasion. Alexis was a great entertainer, and this event made her shine. She would not allow the spotlight to be taken off her or Alstromia.

Aerianna placed the notepad on the table and walked to the window, her red cape dragging behind. She untied it and allowed it to drop to the ground, leaving her dressed in a grey, slinky gown that clung to her curvaceous body. She stared into the distance, watching the darkening sky. The twin moons glistened brightly, illuminating the Valley of Grandu below. She wondered if Alexis had returned to the Palace.

Earlier, she had witnessed Alexis heading to the stables, assuming she had planned a flight on her Torrin. Aerianna was eager to get to the bottom of why Alexis was acting strangely. She planned to visit Alexis, and hopefully, she would speak with her. Aerianna absentmindedly gazed at the valley, admiring the land's beauty and noticing the flickering lights in the huts below. The lights looked magical, twinkling brightly in the darkness.

Not far away, Armbruster waited patiently for Yarlen to speak. As usual, he said very little. He tapped his index finger on his right cheek, staring at the tall, stone ceiling. After a few minutes, Armbruster's patience was gone.

"Will you speak already? What will we do about Alexis?" he screamed, startling Yarlen.

"Sir, the last time I did what I thought was right, I turned your wife into a ghostly apparition. That did not work out well. She almost ended my life. I prefer you to inform me of what you believe we should do. I will consider helping you."

"If I knew what to do, I would not be asking for your guidance. I am well aware of what happened before. You will not make the same mistake twice. Now, should we speak with Aerianna and find out what she knows? I want to inquire about what is going on with Andreh. Am I paranoid? Please, Yarlen, be honest. Give me your feedback." Armbruster finished his sentence and looked directly at Yarlen. It was an uncomfortable moment as Yarlen rolled his eyes and looked away, making Armbruster wonder what information he was hiding about Andreh and Alexis.

After what seemed like an eternity to Armbruster, Yarlen spoke up. He informed the king that he was unaware of what was happening between Andreh and Alexis. He could only assume they were good friends. Yarlen also begged Armbruster to drop the inquisition and let things go. He also reminded him that starting a fight with Alexis right before the Harvest Festival was a horrible idea. Ultimately, Alexis would retaliate, and nobody needed that drama before the event.

Armbruster contemplated Yarlen's advice. Though it was not what he hoped to hear, he reluctantly agreed. He knew it was in his best interest to stop harassing Alexis about her relationship with Andreh. If and when she was ready, Alexis would discuss it with him.

In the meantime, Armbruster intended to stay vigilant and encourage others to keep an eye on the pair when they were together.

He suspected that there was more to their relationship than met the eye.

On the other side of Alstromia, Alexis and Andreh stood beside Trixxie by the lake. Trixxie tolerantly waited for instructions from Alexis. The second Alexis jumped on her back, Trixxie instinctively knew what to do. The two took off and flew over the water, Alexis giggling the entire time. Andreh stood below, watching. He was thrilled Alexis was having so much fun. It amazed him how graceful the ginormous beast was, diving down quickly and accelerating into the darkening sky.

After some time, Alexis asked Trixxie to land, and she obliged. Trixxie hunched down, allowing Alexis to slide off her back and land on her feet. Once Trixxie saw Alexis walking away, she raised herself and followed her.

Alexis strolled up to Andreh, Trixxie not far behind. "So, I suppose we should be heading back to the Palace? It is almost entirely dark. Thank goodness for the beautiful moons that helped illuminate the lake. Shall we escort Trixxie back to the cave?"

"Sounds good to me," responded Andreh, eager to return. He was hungry and tired.

In the cave, Alexis spoke to Trixxie lovingly. Andreh chuckled, amused. He felt it was funny that Alexis talked to Trixxie as if she were a

Witch or Warlock, understanding every word. Strangely, it seemed Trixxie did understand Alexis. She nodded her big head several times and looked as if she was smiling while a tiny, playful Cayley encircled her head, dropping pink, iridescent dust from its glittery wings, causing Trixxie to sneeze. The forceful sneeze blew Alexis to the ground. Instead of getting angry with Trixxie, she laughed, looking at her sparkling pants. Andreh dashed toward Alexis, worried about her tumble, though she was already standing by the time he reached her, swatting away the annoying Cayley. Andreh was astonished. Trixxie was not bothered by it at all.

"Trixxie has a great disposition. I am surprised she did not snap at the Cayley. It is such an annoying creature," remarked Andreh, noticing that the Cayley was watching him from afar, taunting him.

A Cayley, a tiny being resembling a fairy, fluttered around the cave like a butterfly. This particular Cayley was a Cave Cayley, preferring the darkness. The small, black-colored being's head resembled a cat, without whiskers, furry and soft. The ears of a Cayley were small and pointy, though the Wilderness Cayley's ears appeared rounder.

The Wilderness Cayley was also the most common, identifiable by their white and tan coloring. All Cayleys had fur-covered hands with four tiny fingers. Wilderness Cayleys preferred living in the open, building small nests in tall trees, or residing in miniature huts inside dead Trimber trunks deep in the forest.

The Striped Cayley, often referred to as the Mountain Cayley, was known to inhabit forested regions. Its distinctive fur features tiger-like stripes in shades of orange and brown. While Cayleys could be somewhat bothersome, many preferred to have them around, especially Witches and Warlocks. Most Witches, Wizzards, and Warlocks welcomed Cayleys into their homes. These creatures made excellent house guests, as their sparkling dust was commonly incorporated into magical mixtures. This dust was recognized for its potency as a compound that could enhance speed or strength, frequently utilized in potions.

Alexis secretly kept a Moonerling Cayley in the basement of the Palace of Snipperdoom. This rare Cayley only produced silver sparkling dust, granting levitation abilities to lift the heaviest objects.

All Moonerling Cayleys are predominantly black with silver hands, feet, and ears, though the tiny creature's nose is a bright, hot-pink color. Its beautiful wings are also vibrant pink.

Alexis patted Trixxie on the head and walked toward the cave entrance. "Are you ready?" she asked Andreh as she turned around one more time to watch Trixxie head back into the deepest part of the cave, barely visible except for the glittery glow from the Cayley encircling her. Alexis felt miserable leaving Trixxie. Then it hit her. She came up with a brilliant idea.

'What if I prepare a place for Trixxie closer to home? Maybe in the Palace's dungeon?' The dungeon under the High Tower had a large entrance leading to the River of Miccay. *'That would be perfect!'* Immediately, Alexis decided she would look into the possibility of housing Trixxie at the Palace. Feeling enthusiastic, she planned to ask for Andreh's input.

Back at the Palace, Lorthana appeared unannounced. She was in a foul mood, having returned from visiting Zandorah on Iriss, begging her to make up with Alexis. Unfortunately, Zandorah was inflexible and told her *"no."* She vehemently informed Lorthana that Alexis had sealed her fate. The two would proceed as previously agreed—first, the Battle Rounds, then potential war. Lorthana could not believe her daughter. The one who usually agreed to keep peace seemed to want war. *'What is happening to my family?'* Lorthana wondered, shaking her head in shock.

Lorthana strutted up to the main gate, her head held high, wearing her Cape of Dismay. Wearing the cape signaled that the Witch,

Wizzard, or Warlock was in crisis. The cape, constructed of woven Trimber material, is dark navy with tiny black and silver crystal teardrops encrusted on the bottom. Lorthana wanted Alexis to see her wearing the Cape of Dismay, hopefully asking her mother why she was under duress.

Lorthana planned to explain that the rumors and threats of war reached Earth and that the Clans were in upheaval, unhappy about the decision. Lorthana hoped it would convince Alexis to stop the crazy talk of war against her sister. Lorthana swiftly marched toward Alexis' chamber, ready to confront her daughter, hoping to negotiate peace.

Alexis and Andreh landed safely near the stables. The Torrins slowed down and trotted quickly toward the building. The beasts were exhausted from the long flight. Essten was already outside the structure, waiting for the pair. He took both Torrins and wished the two a good night. He wanted to place the creatures in their stalls and head home to Marittaz, ready to eat dinner and relax.

As the two returned to the Palace, Alexis abruptly stopped on the gravel path. She grabbed Andreh's left hand, pulling it close to her. "Listen, we must stop seeing each other for a while. There are a large number of eyes on us.

Many are starting to suspect something. Armbruster is furious, and I am tired of his inquisition. I hope you understand." She grudgingly released his hand and kept on walking, focusing on the path ahead.

"Of course. Whatever you desire, Alexis," he yelled, sprinting to keep up with her. Without warning, she stopped and pushed him backward, almost causing him to fall.

"No, please do not accompany me. Allow me to enter the Palace, and then you can follow in a while. I do not want anyone to see us entering the building together. I mean it!" She snapped at him, turning around and heading hastily down the trail toward the Palace.

Andreh stared at her, offended. He knew this day would come. After all, he was not deaf. The rumors and speculation about their constant contact made every topic of conversation. Andreh realized it was best to steer clear of Alexis unless it was a meeting he should be attending. Alexis kept walking, and he hurried to catch up to her briefly, kissing her on the cheek.

"Go ahead. I get it. You know where to find me." Andreh turned around and marched back down the steep, rocky path away from the Palace, leaving her alone. He was disappointed and frustrated.

Off in the distance, Armbruster observed Alexis approaching as he looked down from the small balcony off his chamber. He also witnessed Andreh kissing Alexis on the cheek, which turned his stomach. He wanted to kill Andreh. However, Armbruster realized Alexis was to blame, too. Exasperated with Alexis and Andreh, he decided to confront her. He was done pretending nothing was going on between the two.

Earlier, Yarlen informed Armbruster he planned to stay out of the situation between Alexis and Andreh. He finally managed to get on Alexis' good side again and was unwilling to jeopardize making her angry and potentially having to deal with her wrath all over again.

Armbruster figured he had to handle the situation independently, which was okay with him. He had no problem whatsoever dealing with his cheating wife. She would hear what he had to say. Most of all, she would disclose what was transpiring between them. Armbruster planned to use a *Revelation Spell* before speaking with her, forcing her to reveal the truth. He was prepared. Alexis would not have time to counteract his spell, which was precisely his intention.

★*.★*.★*.★*.★

On Earth, Gardone met with several other Warlocks. They sat quietly around an old, round table in an inconspicuous hut deep in the woods of New England.

Eyes closed, Gardone fidgeted with the Ring of Stainnard on his middle finger. The other Warlocks impatiently watched him, hoping he would divulge his new plan.

After several minutes of silence, Gardone finally stood up, but seconds later, he shook his head and sat back down. The others looked on, perplexed. Korbin sat next to him, wondering what he was doing. Gardone was usually prepared for meetings, taking the reins and forcefully in charge! Korbin gently pulled on Gardone's sleeve, trying to get his attention. However, Gardone swiped away his hand.

"Listen, everyone. As many of you know, my daughter has scouts searching for me. Our efforts to take the kingdom failed. Kidnapping Alexis backfired as well. Unfortunately, she has been rescued and is back in the Palace, sitting on the throne, probably gloating. Now, Korbin and I are fugitives. I appreciate all you have done for me. But I have reluctantly decided to move to Iriss to live with my other daughter, Zandorah. I do believe she will take me in. In the meantime, please do not tell anyone what I am planning. Once I have a strategy on how to proceed with taking power away from Alexis, I will reach out to you." Gardone stood, and the others clapped and cheered.

Korbin grinned, feeling proud of Gardone. He remained hopeful that Gardone would allow him to accompany him to Iriss. After all, he had helped him with Alexis before and planned to be right by his side this time!

The evening was dark and quiet on Alstromia. Most of the commoners in the village were already in their huts, sleeping soundly. Aerianna dressed in her navy blue and silver sleeping gown. Seconds later, she crawled into her warm bed. The fireplace blazed, filling the room with warmth and light. She snuggled deeper under the covers, feeling secure and happy. She drifted off to sleep, thinking about Pauto, wondering why she had not seen him earlier.

A few doors down, Alexis approached her chamber, tired and smelly. She was sweaty from her flight and training with Trixxie and eager to shower quickly. She opened the chamber door, stripped off her clothing, and walked toward the bath chamber.

"Well, well, aren't you sexy?" commented Armbruster, sitting by the window, watching her. He had been patiently waiting for a while for her to appear. He smiled as he saw her standing there, basically naked, only clothed in black, lacy underwear. Armbruster still wanted Alexis. Seeing her in her undergarments made him sweaty, and he could hear his heart racing with desire for her.

Infuriated, she grabbed her cape and wrapped it awkwardly around her waist. "What the heck are you doing here?" she screamed. "I would appreciate it if you announced yourself. I do not like coming into my chamber and finding someone here unexpectedly, especially as I take off my clothing."

"Oh, really? Or is it just ME you do not want to find here? Maybe it would have been okay if it had been Andreh?" He stood up and walked toward her, noticing she squinted her eyes. Alexis fiercely gripped the cape as her long, blood-red nails deeply embedded in the material.

Alexis backed away but immediately changed her mind, deciding to face him. "You know what, Armbruster? You are crazy! What is your obsession with Andreh? Why are you feeling so damn insecure?" she shrieked, turning away swiftly and heading toward the shower.

Before she got too far away, Armbruster managed to snatch her cape and rip it from her body. Incensed, she spun around and slapped him hard across his face. Dumbfounded, he stared at her, speechless. Alexis smirked, feeling victorious, and removed her underwear, dropping it on the ground. She marched toward the bath chamber without a care in the world, swinging her hips, teasing him.

Flabbergasted, Armbruster released her cape, watching her walk away from him butt-naked. He wanted to follow her and continue their conversation, but realized she was uninterested in speaking with him. He would wait for another time. Armbruster chose to leave the chamber, slamming the heavy door and marching toward his room. He was outraged and fuming over Alexis's lack of answers. Plus, he could not believe she had slapped him!

As usual, Alexis had been brilliant and careful in the words she chose when answering him. She said nothing to incriminate herself. Armbruster's *Revelation Spell* would have made her tell him the truth, but she ended the conversation before she could lie. *'Very clever, indeed!'*

Alexis swiftly closed the bath chamber door behind her, wondering if Armbruster would wait for her to finish or if he planned to leave her chamber. He had not appeared in her room unannounced in a very long time. She giggled, thinking about the look on his face as she strode off, wiggling her butt, taunting him. She enjoyed their games.

Finally, alone inside the shower, she turned on the hot water, allowing it to soak her tired and aching body. Her long, black hair became wet, flat, and stuck to her back. Alexis washed her hair using an exquisitely smelling floral potion, thinking about Andreh and contemplating his whereabouts. She wished he were there with her.

Freshly showered and reenergized, Alexis brushed her hair, standing before the fireplace, desperately attempting to warm up. She was cold, shivering, and furious with Armbruster. She wondered why he was so adamant about confronting her regarding the relationship she shared with Andreh. *'What does he think he will gain by doing so?'* She shook her head and walked to the bed, placing the brush on her nightstand.

Sleep was her priority, and everything else could wait. Alexis needed to regain her energy for the upcoming Battle Rounds. Lastly, Alexis thought about her plan to sneak Trixxie into the dungeons of the Palace. Exhausted, Alexis pulled the heavy blanket up to her neck, feeling her eyes become heavy. The curtains to her rooms were open, and she could see the twin moons off in the distance behind Tullah Mountain.

Suddenly, there was an unexpected, commanding knock on the chamber door. She sat up, irritated, assuming it was Armbruster returning to finish their earlier conversation.

"Enter," she yelled.

Lorthana entered the chamber, perplexed as to why Alexis sounded so annoyed. Nevertheless, Lorthana forced herself to smile as she walked into the room, hoping to start their conversation non-confrontationally. Alexis remained in bed, staring at her mother, interested in finding out why she chose to show up in her chamber at this time of night.

"Why are you here, Mother? What is wrong?" Alexis quickly asked, hoping to get right to the point.

"I need to speak with you. I refuse to wait until the morning. Every day that goes by, we are one day closer to catastrophe. Alexis, please…hear me out," Lorthana begged as she sat on the edge of Alexis' bed, wringing her hands in frustration.

"Fine, Mother. What is it now? I have had an unusually long day, and I am beat. I prefer sleep over this conversation. So, why are you here? Please, do tell."

"Alexis, this volatile situation between you and Zandorah has accelerated beyond what I had hoped. I wish you and your sister would find a way to resolve your differences without making life hell for everyone else. The entire Clan on Alstromia is upset. Clans on Earth and Iriss are scared. Is this what you want your legacy to be remembered for–War? Conflict? Please, you are too smart for that," pleaded

Lorthana, observing her daughter's reaction.

"I see. So, you are here to make me change my mind. You probably have already spoken with Zandi, and she did not budge, so now you want me to do so? Am I correct? NO! It is not going to happen. I promise you—we will fight it out. We will start at the Battle Rounds. Mom, you must understand. It is the principle. I do not want war. But I will go that route if she fails to recognize my position and perspective. She took Shawnatar away from me, and now she wants to steal my happiness and reputation by saying I am responsible for my kidnapping. What the heck? What is wrong with her? Mom, you must force her to see what she is doing."

"Aha, so it is about Shawnatar? Or is it just revenge you seek? Be honest, Alexis," demanded Lorthana, now standing in front of her daughter with her arms crossed, fuming.

"No, Mom. It is not just about Shawnatar. She is never held accountable for her actions. She continually gets away with everything. Everyone always feels sorry for poor Zandorah. Come on. This has to stop. I am going to be the one to put an end to it, like it or not!" Alexis yelled.

"So, there is going to be war? Yet, you claim you still love your sister? But… you want war? Love and War? I don't get it, Alexis. I really don't," Lorthana shouted, wishing there was a way to reason with Alexis.

"Mother, please—it is not just about the lies, love, and war. It is a fact that you and everyone else incessantly give Zandorah too much leeway. You protect her like a delicate Bloomitz. I am sick of it. Why can't you love us equally?"

Alexis jumped out of bed and stood before Lorthana, chewing on her lip and trying to stay calm. "Mom, you have to choose a side. Zandi is correct. Now, please leave. I am tired and not in the mood to deal with you or this situation further. I am tired of the drama."

Frustrated, Alexis crawled into bed, turning her back to her mother. Sadly, Lorthana realized there was no way to fix the current state of affairs.

As she left the chamber, Lorthana informed Alexis she would stop interfering and allow the sisters to resolve their differences. She was tired of trying to be the peacekeeper. Lorthana slammed down her Ceptre in the hallway and transported herself back home, hoping to sleep and forget about the mess her two daughters had created.

After his discussion with Alexis, Andreh waited quite a while before finally walking toward the Palace. He wanted to allow Alexis ample time to get inside the building without him nearby. Once he entered the structure, he reluctantly shuffled toward his chamber.

Unfortunately, he noticed Armbruster standing by his door as he approached his room. Andreh's heart skipped a beat, feeling frightened. He knew what was coming, and he felt ill-prepared. There was no way to escape. He took a deep breath, ready to hear what the King had to say to him.

Andreh approached Armbruster. "Sir, what are you doing here? How may I be of assistance?" stuttered Andreh, afraid of Armbruster's words.

"I suggest we step inside your chamber. I wish to discuss some things with you. Private matters. Do you understand?" The King responded, watching Andreh. Armbruster folded his arms, refusing to let Andreh sidestep the conversation this time, demanding the truth.

Andreh nervously fidgeted with his cloak, and that was precisely how Armbruster liked it. He enjoyed watching the young Warlock squirm.

"Of course, please." He opened the chamber door, allowing Armbruster to enter first. He quickly followed, closing the door and hoping for the best.

Armbruster strode toward the window inside the tiny room, finding a rickety chair. He expeditiously plopped down, staring at Andreh, who sat on his bed near him.

Apprehensively, Andreh chose to begin the conversation, hoping to expedite things. "Sir, what may I do for you? What things would you like to discuss? I assume the Harvest Festival or perhaps the Battle Rounds," he boldly asked.

"Hell, no! I am here to discuss the Queen. Specifically, your relationship with my wife." He flexed his jaw, looking mad.

There it was. It was precisely what Andreh feared he would say. He had no idea how to respond. He nodded and immediately decided it was best to tell the truth…as much as possible.

"Sir, the Queen and I are good friends. She taught me potion-making and has helped me with my Spellcraft. I have learned so much and am grateful for her time and confidence in me. I am not sure what else there is to say." Andreh felt confident in his answer for about a second. Then he noticed Armbruster's scowl and knew he was not out of the woods.

"Right, the spell thing. But that is not what we are talking about, is it, Andreh? I am talking about you kissing my wife a little while ago, Alexis running to you after her rescue, not me… and more. How do you explain all those things? Please, do clarify. I am not ignorant. I am interested in discovering exactly how stupid you believe I am." Armbruster was pissed and refused to allow Andreh to keep up the charade.

Andreh knew it was best to choose his words wisely if he wanted to see another day. He took a deep breath and closed his eyes briefly. Then, he calmly placed his hands on his lap and began talking while Armbruster listened intently to every word spoken.

Morning arrived too soon for Alexis. Her chamber became bright, and she hated it. On days like this, she wished she had not agreed to make the environment more like Earth's to appease the commoners and inhabitants of Alstromia. However, Armbruster begged her relentlessly, informing her it would make her look like a gracious Queen and help her stay in power. So, begrudgingly, she agreed.

Unfortunately, now, looking at the sunny day, she seriously regretted her decision. Eager to start her day, she stretched and slipped out of bed, her feet hitting the cold stone floor. Shivering, Alexis sprinted to the bath chamber to take a quick hot shower before dressing and heading to the Planning Chamber. Alexis wanted to stay positive and work on getting Trixxie relocated to the Palace.

After an emotional and challenging night, Andreh woke up later in the morning and immediately thought about his previous conversation with Armbruster. The two spent a long time talking.

Armbruster began the conversation very abrasively, but in the end, he seemed calmer. Andreh hoped he had convinced Armbruster that his relationship with Alexis was platonic.

He stood in front of the mirror, feeling like a traitor. He lied to Armbruster, someone he greatly respected. The truth of the matter was that he loved Alexis, not as a friend. He craved spending time with her, loved touching her, and, yes… he loved kissing her.

Andreh wanted more but realized it would never happen. Alexis would never give up her rein or territory for him. He was a nobody, and she was royalty…a Queen! Andreh spent many restless nights tossing and turning, contemplating how the two could be together.

Each scenario always ended the same—Alexis with Armbruster. He could not compete. Andreh recalled Alexis telling him she was ready to have another baby. She wanted to expand her family to leave a legacy. The more he listened to her, the more he noticed that the legacy did not include him.

Yet, when they were together, Alexis acted like she could not live without him, implying their relationship would continue. Andreh felt confused by her contradictory actions and words. He concluded it was time to chat with Alexis and find out where they stood in their relationship. He did not want to waste his life chasing after her if she planned to stay with

Armbruster. Part of him still thought about leaving Alstromia and heading back to Earth. Maybe it was the best idea and in his best interest. His departure would allow Alexis to try to rebuild her marriage with Armbruster without his presence or interference. Andreh had much to contemplate. Many options were available. Sadly, he disliked most.

When Armbruster opened his eyes, he felt more frustrated than before. He experienced horrible nightmares about Alexis and Andreh, causing him to wake up with a pounding headache. Still irritated, an hour later, Armbruster entered the Security Command Chamber. He decided to hunt down Andreh, feeling dissatisfied about how their conversation had ended. Armbruster believed there were too many loopholes in Andreh's story.

Another point that infuriated Armbruster was the statement Andreh made. He was pretty vocal about his strong feelings for Alexis, though he did not outright say he loved her. This annoyed Armbruster to no end. Since Alexis refused to speak with him, his only choice was to confront Andreh again and dig deeper for more information. Armbruster planned to cast a *Respect* or *Revelation Spell* to force Andreh to tell him the truth. First and foremost, Armbruster deserved to know the extent of their relationship.

The Security Command Chamber was empty when Armbruster arrived. It was quiet, and the windows were closed. No one was working. As Armbruster was about to leave, Pauto entered with a pile of old Spellbooks overflowing in his arms. Pauto looked surprised to see Armbruster opening the windows. Pauto carefully placed the books on the long conference table and approached Armbruster cautiously.

"Sir, I am surprised to see you. Is there something I may help you with today? Did we have a scheduled meeting? Are you looking for someone?" he smiled apprehensively, hoping he did not forget about an important appointment.

"Yes, I am searching for Andreh. Have you seen him? I am afraid I must discuss a few items with him. Also, what time is the Harvest Festival Planning Committee meeting? I have a few things I would like to bring up." Armbruster appeared angry to Pauto.

"Sir, Andreh is holding the meeting with the others in a while. I do believe they are conducting it at the Lodge on the other side of the grounds. Would you like me to inform him that you need to speak with him?" Pauto offered.

"Oh, no, do not bother. I will find him. Thanks, Pauto." Armbruster left the chamber, eager to locate Andreh. He was tired of waiting for answers. Armbruster was an easy-going Warlock, but his patience dwindled quickly.

It occurred to Armbruster that he knew very little about Andreh. Armbruster realized he had to learn more about the young Warlock, specifically his relationship with others and his family background. Armbruster decided it would become his new priority. He would enlist Yarlen for help.

Yarlen was well-versed and knew everything there was to know about most staff members. With his latest plan, Armbruster felt empowered and happy. He strolled down the long corridor, whistling happily, walking past the tall, open windows, not noticing Alexis and Andreh holding a conversation in the courtyard below. If he had seen their interaction, he would have been furious.

CHAPTER 3

Alexis knew it was imperative to find a way to appease Armbruster and stop his suspicions. Keeping Andreh away from her was probably the best solution, but regrettably, it also saddened her. She would be miserable without him and knew he felt the same. Alexis understood that Andreh was someone she refused to live without.

Though he was younger, he knew her better than anyone else. Andreh was keenly aware of when to give her space or be a source of comfort. It is why she ran into his arms after her kidnapping rescue and not Armbruster's. She wanted to feel Andreh's body against hers, making her feel secure. Now, she considered what their relationship would be like in the future. Alexis still loved Armbruster, but the passion was gone, for the most part. Alexis considered rekindling the relationship with Armbruster for their daughter's sake. Other than that, there was no reason to do so.

Selfishly, Alexis preferred to end her marriage and go public with her feelings for Andreh, though she feared it could cause her problems. Andreh would likely become an unwanted target as well. That was something she dreaded. So, as she stood by the window, surveying her kingdom, Alexis decided to keep Andreh away for now and attempt to salvage her relationship with her husband, Armbruster.

Alexis washed her face and dressed for the day. She planned to attend the Harvest Festival Committee meeting, ensuring the event would go off without a hitch. Alexis would make a point of speaking with Andreh and explaining the future of their relationship, something that made her nervous. She knew they needed to talk. Andreh would be hurt.

Alexis remained hopeful that he would understand and concur with her plan. She headed to the Lodge across the Palace grounds, ready to face the day.

It seemed like fate that they ran into each other on the way to the meeting. They stood awkwardly far apart, though Alexis finally decided to speak, grabbing his arm and moving him closer to her. She knew this was the perfect time to tell Andreh to stay away. But she noticed a few security commoners approaching and quickly released Andreh's arm. She suggested the two head to the meeting, worried Armbruster or Pauto would find them together and assume they had been doing something they shouldn't.

Alexis chose to walk ahead while Andreh sauntered behind. He knew she was right. Keeping their hands off each other was in their best interest, especially in public places. The guards and commoners were nearby. If they witnessed the two together, it could elicit more rumors and idle chit-chat.

Unexpectedly, Aerianna approached. "Hey, you two! We are waiting at the Lodge. I wondered where you were hiding. We need to begin the planning. Come on…" she urged, turning to head toward the Lodge. Reluctantly, Alexis and Andreh followed, keeping their distance the entire way.

Aerianna sounded chipper, talking with Yarlen as they discussed the upcoming events entering the Lodge. Andreh wondered if she was planning her Ceremonial Exchange with Pauto. The two looked happy and in love. Andreh felt a twinge of jealousy because he could not display his feelings toward Alexis, fearing the consequences.

Finally, the Harvest Festival committee was able to complete its planning. The event was quickly approaching, and everyone wanted it to be a successful and memorable time. The meeting took quite a while, but many great ideas and suggestions were shared.

Alexis fiddled with her hair, listening to Armbruster. She wondered why he chose to attend. Looking at him made her furious. She wished he had stayed away as he promised.

Armbruster sat beside her, watching Andreh like a hawk. It was pretty obvious his newfound interest in the Harvest Festival Committee had everything to do with keeping an eye on Alexis and, more specifically, Andreh.

Alexis chuckled as she thought about how ridiculous Armbruster acted. She shook her head and wished the meeting would hurry up and end so she could return to her chamber to rest. The meeting was boring for her.

On Iriss, Zandorah woke up eager to speak to her mother, Lorthana. She pulled open the drapes in her room and smiled. Fluffy clouds graced the sky, making her feel hopeful and happy.

Zandorah planned to attend the Harvest Festival and stay at the Palace with Alexis. She worried about how that would go over with her sister. Their feud was still ongoing, and she knew there would be more tension.

Nonetheless, she planned to attend the festivities and visit with family and friends. Strutting down the Castle's corridor, she wondered where her husband, Shawnatar, was hiding. She had not spoken to him for two days and missed him dearly. But it was not unusual for him to be gone, usually visiting with friends and other Clans on Earth.

Shawnatar was a restless soul. He did not like to stay in one place for too long. He had wanderlust. It was okay with Zandorah. Long ago, she had accepted his behavior and realized it was part of his identity, something she could not change. Zandorah's goal for the day was to speak with her mother and find out if anyone had spotted her father, Gardone. Zandorah had many unanswered questions and wanted clarification before facing Alexis on Alstromia.

Waiting for the meeting to finish on Alstromia, Pauto and Aerianna sat side by side, listening to Alexis barking out orders. Aerianna noticed Andreh looking drained. He remained quiet, avoiding eye contact with Alexis. He also did not look at Armbruster. It was an awkward moment for everyone in the room.

Armbruster sat between Alexis and Aerianna. He half-heartedly smiled at Aerianna, listening to Alexis ramble on about the event. He appeared annoyed with squinted eyes, looking at Yarlen sitting across from him, his hands folded.

"So, does anyone have questions?" Alexis asked. Her eyes darted from one individual in the room to the next, wondering if anyone would speak. After a minute of silence, Armbruster stood up.

"I am sure we all agree that the planning is complete. There is nothing left to discuss. Aerianna and Pauto have done an outstanding job handling all the details this year. Thank you both!" Armbruster sat down again, wishing to end the topic.

"Agreed. I am delighted with all the plans and feel confident we will provide a memorable festival this year to all attendees," Alexis chimed in. "So, if there is nothing else,

I am leaving. Oh, Andreh, may I please speak with you for a moment?" she commented, giving Andreh a pleading look. He acknowledged her request and followed, exiting the chamber.

Armbruster almost lost his temper, his eyebrows raised, and his lips pursed. His right eye twitched uncontrollably. He wanted to chase after them and speak with Alexis, but knew better. It would only start another fight, and he was not in the mood.

Instead, he stayed behind in the Lodge, discussing Clan issues with Yarlen. Aerianna and Pauto quietly left the chamber as well, hoping to avoid any further inquisitions by Armbruster about Alexis and Andreh.

The stable grounds were beautiful. Much of the scenery had changed in the last few weeks. It was Fall on Alstromia, and the colors of the leaves on the Trimbers were glorious. Essten stood by the main doors at the stable, supervising the recently hired commoners. They were inspecting and grooming the Torrins, following Essten's instructions.

Essten turned his head and looked up at the Palace, excited about the upcoming festivities, which typically brought a lot of business for his wife, Marittaz. She sold various shapes and sizes of beautiful pearls from the Sea of

Miccay and made an assortment of jewelry. Marittaz was famous for the extraordinary, shimmering powder that she created from crushed pearls. This powder was worn as makeup by the wealthier Clan members. All festival vendors were allowed to have booths to display their wares. The Festival was an excellent way to introduce new goods and services.

In the Village of Miccay, a large group of Clan members worked feverishly along the river, decorating the main street with flowers, arches, garlands, and other décor to make the Village look festive. Most visitors stayed at various Inns to attend the Festival. W3s, Blud-Trackers, and Hunters came from Earth, Draekidell, and even Xeagadale for this epic event.

For the Battle Rounds and those planning to stay longer, they usually rented huts along the river. The wealthier commoners owned multiple properties and usually turned them into Inns for special occasions.

As leaves swirled on the ground and the brisk wind brought chills to Andreh, he halfheartedly followed Alexis onto the Landing Deck. He was not happy about her request to join him. Andreh knew Armbruster would question their meeting. Alexis chose to sit on the stone bench facing Tullah Mountain. Andreh plopped down next to her, waiting to hear what she was about to say to him, assuming she wanted to call off their relationship. After meeting with Armbruster, it was clear to Andreh that he would insist that Alexis and Andreh cease meeting or at least not be seen in public.

Alexis smiled, turning to look directly into Andreh's eyes. She gently took his hand into her own. He knew what she was about to say and felt the urge to puke. He tasted bile coming up his throat. Andreh forced himself to swallow hard, trying to push it back down. Alexis noticed and glanced at her lap, instantly feeling guilty.

"Andreh, I want you to know how much you mean to me. I believe you know this, but I wanted you to hear it from me. I also want you to know that I will continue to teach and instruct you on potion-making. However, on a personal level, we must cease all communication and time spent together. Armbruster is unhappy, and I must keep our family together…for now. I wish things were different, but they are not. With the Festival upon us, all eyes are on me. I cannot afford anyone getting suspicious about our relationship."

She took a deep breath, watching his reaction. "I love you! I really do. You and I have a unique bond. I wish things were different. I hope you and I could be together. Right now, that will not happen. I am sure you understand this?" Alexis announced regretfully. Her eyes were watery, and she held back from sobbing. Her heart ached, and she desperately wanted to kiss him, feeling his soft lips on hers.

"Trust me. I knew this was coming. I saw it on your face today in the Lodge. I do not blame you. I know you need to ensure Lilah's family is complete. I will miss you terribly and hope to continue working together in the laboratory. I wish to continue to learn from you. You have been an extraordinary teacher, and I am grateful for your tutelage. I will miss you every second I am not near you. I love you and hope to be someday able to kiss and hold you in my arms again."

Andreh pulled his hand away from Alexis and stood up. She started to stand, and he shook his head. Andreh did not want a goodbye hug or any physical touch, realizing it would make the situation unbearable. He bravely mustered a smile and walked away before she spoke again.

Alexis placed her head between her hands and cried. She felt a tremendous loss, worse than she predicted. She was angry, not ready to give up Andreh, but knowing it was best for her family. Alexis remained on the Landing

Deck for a while, crying, wiping her tears, and attempting to stand. Her legs felt rubbery, and she felt drained. After some time, she returned to her chamber to nap, hoping to temporarily forget what occurred.

Feeling glum, Andreh figured it was best to work, mindlessly meandering toward the Security Command Team Chamber. With his heart crushed, he instantly felt abandoned. Regardless of the massive hurt, he was determined to act as normally as possible, hiding his deep sorrow. Andreh planned to treat Alexis as his boss, a member of the Royal Family, and perhaps, in time…he would learn to live without her. It was all he could do.

Armbruster stared at Yarlen. He fidgeted with his long beard, deep in thought. Yarlen had an idea of what Armbruster wanted to discuss, but honestly, he was tired of the Alexis and Andreh conversation. Everyone was keenly aware that the two were having some kind of affair. No one knew how deep their relationship was. The rumors ran rampant and even reached Earth. Many Clans on Earth were displeased to hear about the drama, wondering why Alexis would cheat on Armbruster. He was a catch. Many Witches would be proud to have him as their mate.

Still, the fact remained that Alexis was becoming increasingly unpopular, and Armbruster's reputation was steadily increasing. After Alexis was rescued from her kidnapping ordeal, her reputation was stellar. Many felt extremely sorry for her and believed she bravely fought for her freedom. Now, however, after the torrid rumors emerged, all that changed.

Witches gossiped, calling Alexis awful names, stating she was an adulteress and should be forced to step down, allowing someone else to run the kingdom. Many Wizzards and Warlocks felt the same, though most still admired Alexis and said very little.

"Yarlen, for goodness' sake. Are you planning to speak or play with your beard all day?" bellowed Armbruster with annoyance.

"Sir, I know what you wish to discuss. I have no answers. I believe the Queen and Andreh are in a relationship. What kind of relationship? Who knows? The Clans are not happy. It is causing problems on Earth. Our spy on Earth, Senior-Scout Cinderillah Winterbloom, has relayed newly acquired information about a potential uprising and protest. We will have to see what happens with that unrestful situation. I am concerned that drama may erupt at the Harvest Festival. Some Clan members, especially the higher-ranking, older ones, demand answers. How are you planning to address this?" replied Yarlen.

Armbruster could not ignore the issues at hand. Too many senior W3s insisted that the Royal Staff find them answers. Armbruster contemplated Yarlen's remarks. Sadly, Yarlen was correct. Some members would love to see Alexis fail. They would push for answers using the courts, maybe even demanding she step down as Queen if necessary. Armbruster was not sure how he felt about that. A small part of him hated that she had put the kingdom into this position in the first place. Another part of Armbruster wanted Alexis out of office if she planned to continue her affair with Andreh. It was disrespectful to him, the Clans, and the entire kingdom!

"Yarlen, I know. I hear what you are saying. I have listened to the rumors and complaints. I have no idea how to proceed. I plan to speak with the Queen and outright ask her if their intimate relationship is over. She must decide how she wants to continue. Alexis cannot remain in an affair with Andreh and run the kingdom as its ruler. It sends mixed messages."

Armbruster slumped in the chair, looking defeated. He pondered the options and considered Alexis losing her position as Queen of Witches. It would open up the spot for someone else. Naturally, he would be the first in line unless the royal name was too tarnished by her infidelity.

On the other hand, maybe it would make him look like an innocent victim, which would be great for him if he chose to run for the position of the kingdom's new ruler. Armbruster smiled, realizing not all news was bad. Perhaps this would allow him to shine and bring the Clans back together in unity. He figured it was time for a change.

"Listen, Yarlen. I have one more favor to ask of you. Could you find out more about Andreh? I want to know about his family, any friends or family on Earth, and anything you can find out in general. I want to know what makes Andreh click. Plus, it would be great to know why Alexis is so attracted to him," Ambruster stated.

"I will find out what I can. In the meantime, do not lose sleep over Andreh. He is insignificant compared to you. Alexis is probably in lust, not love. He is young and good-looking. There are many younger Witches after him. However, he is not interested. Hmmm, maybe he is after Alexis because she is the Queen? Do you think he could be using her to gain something? That is an interesting thought, no?" Yarlen announced, feeling like he had just solved a piece of the puzzle.

"Yarlen, I do not know Andreh's motives. I am unaware that he has any. He seems genuine. However, I do not know him well enough to judge for sure. That is why I ask you to dig deeper and discover everything you can about him. I would love to find out what he is hiding."

Ambruster excused himself and left the room. Yarlen remained standing, rubbing his beard and looking out the window. He knew Cinderillah would be a great source of information. Yarlen planned on paying her a visit on Earth. He would also ask her to discover everything she could about Andreh Darkhill and his family. The young Wizzard and Warlock had previously lived on Earth for a while. Perhaps he had left behind some secrets? Yarlen grinned.

CHAPTER 4

The next few days passed quickly. Everyone was busy preparing for the Harvest Festival. The excitement was felt all around. The Village of Miccay looked festive. Women dressed in their best cloaks and gowns, even while out shopping. The town was ready to welcome guests. The farmers had their stands out, displaying and selling goods, hoping to add to their income.

The Harvest Festival was very lucrative for most Clan members. Yes, Clan members were Wizzards, Witches, and Warlocks, but they still had to make a living.

The Queen did not allow any Clan member to remain idle. She expected everyone to contribute value to Alstromia and demanded that everybody work. In return, she provided all the food and entertainment for the Harvest Festival for everyone's enjoyment.

Alexis spent most of her spare time before the Harvest Festival at the Battle Colosseum, training with Pauto for the upcoming Battle Rounds, hoping to keep her mind off Andreh. At night, she returned to the Palace, bruised and tired.

Alone in her bed, she thought about Andreh and cried herself to sleep, wishing he were there. Alexis missed him more than she could ever imagine. She wanted to run to his chamber and see him, missing their time together. His smile warmed her, making her feel something she had never felt before meeting him.

Something about him made her heart flutter with excitement the day she met him. She had been on her way to a meeting. Andreh approached, bowing respectfully, then lifted his head, flashing his perfect, white teeth. His eyes sparkled, and she instantly felt warm all over, making her blush. Embarrassed, she quickly ran away, heading to the meeting chamber. Perplexed, Alexis wondered who he was and why he made her feel that way. Later in the day, he appeared at a meeting. Pauto introduced him as his assistant—Second-in-Command. Looking at Andreh, she knew her life would never be the same.

Now, years later, she jumped out of bed, feeling restless. Alexis wondered if Andreh thought of her and missed her as much as she missed him. Lonely and sad, Alexis wandered into Lilah's room and saw her sleeping peacefully in the crib. Her baby girl was getting so big, almost two years old now. She wished to have another baby before too long, giving Lilah a brother or sister. Then, it hit her hard. She realized she wanted a baby with Andreh and not Armbruster. She started crying as she rubbed the baby's back.

Quietly, Alexis exited the room and returned to her chamber. She crawled into bed, drawing the covers over her head, crying, and reminiscing about her lover and friend.

The night was bright, with both moons fully out, not a cloud in the sky. The Village of Miccay was well-lit by tall, black Ozar lanterns lining the cobblestone streets. Music blared from huts lined along the River of Miccay. Clan members started celebrating early, eager for the annual event to begin. At Henrii's Potions & BrewHaus, the excited Clan members indulged by drinking brews, Porting Wine, and eating roasted Rue, a favorite snack. Along the riverbank, many Witches, Warlocks, and Wizzards sat around large blazing bonfires, drinking potions and wine, laughing, and enjoying the beautiful night on Alstromia.

Not everyone was celebrating and having fun. In the Palace of Snipperdoom, Pauto reclined in a small Trimber chair in Aerianna's room. The two shared a delicious meal, enjoying the quiet in the room. Pauto wanted to tell Aerianna about his day at the Colosseum with Alexis, but figured it was best to keep any Alexis comments to himself. Aerianna was tired of hearing about Alexis and her escapades. After the meal, Pauto initiated the conversation to avoid any awkward silence.

"So, I was thinking. Maybe we should start planning our Ceremonial Exchange Celebration? I know how much you love Winter. We could hold it soon, maybe during the WinterFrost Festival? What do you think? It would be good to have something wonderful to look forward to right now. I am sure Alexis and Armbruster would permit us to hold it here, at the Palace?" Pauto smiled, hoping she would concur. He could not wait to marry her and begin their new life together.

Aerianna thought about his suggestion, feeling loved and grateful that he wanted to marry her before too long. She adored Pauto.

"Pauto, I believe we should start planning it. However, the WinterFrost Festival is a time Alexis cherishes more than most of us. I do not want to hold our special event then. It would be better to hold it during the Bloommitz Fest at the end of the First Season. How do you feel about that? Would that be okay?" she responded, hoping he would agree.

The First and Second Seasons were by far her favorite. Aerianna loved the idea of holding their special celebration when the Palace grounds were colorful and filled with Bloommitz in every shade. The thought made her happy, and Pauto noticed her big smile immediately.

"I think that is a fantastic idea. Also, it gives us enough time to figure out what we want to do, who we want to invite, and exactly where we want to hold it. The first Season is beautiful, and I cannot wait to become your mate." Pauto kissed her gently and then let her go. He saw a small tear running down her face. Feeling nervous, he stepped back. "Is it something I said, love?" Pauto worried.

"No. Absolutely not! I remembered that I would not have any family at the event. My parents are dead, and I am an only child. The only real family I have had for a long time has been Alexis and Armbruster. I suppose I just realized how much I miss my family."

She reached for him and pulled his body tightly against hers, quivering as she sobbed. He rocked her, whispering into her ear that she would never be alone again.

Hours later, Alexis awoke to a brightly colored sky. She yawned, stretched like a cat, and frowned at the radiantly glowing sky. She wished it were raining and gloomy, tired of the cheery environment. Alexis frowned as she dressed in battle attire, screaming at Karita to bring her breakfast. Once Alexis had food before her, she looked out the window while eating, thinking about heading to Tullah Mountain for the day.

Another long day of training was planned out. Alexis felt excited and loved this time of year. Unfortunately, she found out the hard way that she was terribly out of shape. On the first day of training with Pauto, he knocked her out a record six times, which had never happened before. He did not gloat, but she noticed the slight smirk on his face. He probably assumed he would defeat her in the Battle Rounds. *'Ha!'* Alexis thought. *'Hardly.'* She was out of shape because of her previous pregnancy, but determined to make an incredible comeback. Now, she would work twice as hard to get back into shape. She planned to meet with Andreh to help her train before Pauto arrived. It would also allow her to see him without drawing unwanted attention or raising any suspicions.

Yes, Alexis was wise. She knew she would devise a *'logical reason'* to meet with Andreh. Armbruster knocked on her chamber door and entered. He looked disheveled.

"What may I do for you, Armbruster?" Alexis snapped as she stood up. Irritated with his presence, she moved the food Trillay away, pushing it toward the fireplace, gawking at Armbruster.

"I would like to discuss the Festival briefly. Also, I want to talk about a serious, personal matter. Please, sit back down," he insisted, looking glum. He pointed to the chair, demanding she sit.

Alexis frowned but obliged, intrigued. She assumed he was there to discuss Andreh. Armbruster had been keeping his distance, not bringing him up. Their conversation about what was happening between Alexis and Andreh had never been completed. Alexis figured he wanted to set the record straight about their relationship status.

"As you know, there is much talk about you and Andreh. I am tired of hearing about this. If you cannot stop the rumors and your relationship with him, I will!" he shouted at Alexis, standing before her and looking down. She looked up at him, batting her eyes as if she did not care what he said. Watching her act so callously made him even more furious.

"Furthermore, I expect you—the Queen—to know better. You are putting all of us in an awkward position to defend you and your lover, Andreh. Maybe we should discuss sending Andreh back to Earth? I believe it would be a brilliant move while reducing the temptation between the two of you! Yes, I know you are having an affair. I am not blind or stupid. You are disgusting. I thought you had enough common sense to realize you are hurting our royal name, family, and your birth family's reputation. Is that what you want? To throw away everything you worked so hard for ...for a worthless, young Wizzard? Wow, I cannot believe you, Alexis!"

Exasperated, Alexis stood up. She had had enough of his accusations, constant badgering, and belittling. She bravely faced Armbruster, sucking in her bottom lip, deciding to choose her words wisely.

"Oh, so now I am a wicked home-wrecker, am I? A worthless Queen to boot? Really, Armbruster? Is that all you got? You better have more up your sleeve. You are NOT going to remove me from my position or threaten me. Andreh will not return to Earth, and you… have no say whatsoever! Get it? Yes, I adore Andreh. There it is! He accepts me unconditionally. Unlike you, he does not try to mold me into someone or something I do not want to become! Sadly, I still love you, too. I know you don't believe it, but I do. I am trying to figure everything out and do the right thing. I have informed Andreh that I could only see him for official Clan, Palace, or potion-making business. He accepts the terms and has stayed away. So, back off, Armbruster," she hissed indignantly.

Alexis sat down, anxiously twirling a long strand of her hair, watching him, waiting for his response. Surprisingly, he backed away and chose to sit on the bed. Armbruster looked at her, feeling awful that their lives had become so uncomfortable.

Armbruster recalled a time not too long ago when they were happy together, laughing, and in love. It was the day Alexis gave birth to Lilah. He was there, holding her hand, brushing her sweaty hair away from her face, encouraging her through the painful screams of childbirth.

Afterward, Armbruster remembered holding Lilah and gazing lovingly at Alexis, so proud of her and feeling lucky to be her husband. Now, he observed her and felt pure emptiness. The betrayal was too much for him to bear. He had no clue if he could ever forgive her or get over this awful feeling in his stomach. He waited patiently for her to talk. Alexis sat in silence, staring into the abyss. She refused to speak. After a while, he realized their conversation was over. She would not respond or elaborate on the subject.

Grudgingly, Armbruster rose from the bed and walked toward the chamber door, planning to meet with Yarlen. As he reached for the door handle, Alexis finally spoke.

"Armbruster, I am sorry. I will fix this. I promise. Give me time." Distraught, he walked out the door, leaving her to think about her actions and the words spoken, which could not be reversed.

It was the day before the kick-off of the Harvest Festival. The Palace was lively. The locals worked hard to finish decorating for the upcoming Gala. Alexis stood before her clothes closet, hoping to pick out the gown she planned to wear to the Gala. Nothing appealed to her. One of the local dressmakers, Contezza, sent a few new dresses and cloaks to the Palace for Alexis to consider wearing for the event. Alexis did not see the clothing in her closet. Frustrated, she summoned Karita, who appeared within seconds, standing at attention.

"Yes, My Queen. What may I do for you?" Karita nervously asked.

"You can find out where the new gowns and cloaks are that Contezza sent to the Palace for me. I do not see them. I am attempting to pick out my gown for the Gala tomorrow. Please find the missing clothing and let me know when you have them. You are dismissed," Alexis waved her hand, turning her back to the commoner. Immediately, Karita bowed, quickly escaping the chamber to search for the missing garments.

Alexis shuffled toward the window and stared at the top of the mountain, thinking about today's training with Andreh and Pauto. She smiled, thinking about having one-on-one time with Andreh, hoping he would show up.

On Earth, Gardone sat in a circle with several other Warlocks in a hut deep in New England's Forest. He planned to head to Iriss to live with Zandorah, but first wanted information on some rumors brought to his attention. The story was about his daughter, Alexis. Supposedly, she was having an affair with a younger, lesser-known Wizzard.

Shocked, Gardone immediately sent out two scouts to gain information. Within a day, he received word that Bartin and Korbin wanted to meet him and others in the hut to discuss the report. As Gardone listened to Bartin and Korbin, he smiled at the news relayed to him. He finally had some ammunition to use against Alexis and was ready to implement it immediately. Gardone was tired of running and wanted his life back. Perhaps he could use her indiscretions against her and attempt to take the kingdom away. It probably was Gardone's last chance, and he was more than willing to try.

Armbruster and Yarlen sat around a large table in another part of the Palace, waiting for Pauto to appear. He was tasked to provide his final security analysis to Armbruster before the upcoming event.

Andreh entered the Security Command Team Chamber and immediately took a seat, looking down at his lap and ignoring Armbruster and the others. Pauto requested that he attend the meeting, which was not unusual, though Andreh hoped to avoid any contact with Armbruster.

Pauto briefed Armbruster and excused himself to meet with Aerianna. Later, he would meet Alexis in the Battle Zone to train. Armbruster stayed in the chamber talking with Yarlen. When Andreh walked toward the chamber door to leave, Armbruster stopped him unexpectedly by cutting off his path.

"Andreh, may I please have a word with you?" Armbruster asked politely but quite sternly. He felt the need to confront him and clarify his position about the affair.

"Of course, Your Majesty," Andreh replied, reluctantly sitting back down. He became annoyed at the constant demands.

Armbruster began his conversation with Andreh, making it clear he was aware of his relationship with Alexis. Andreh remained quiet and listened, pretending he was not worried. Armbruster paced around the chamber while he spoke, seemingly unable to stay still. Andreh followed him with his eyes, remaining attentive. After a few minutes of talking, sometimes rather loudly, Armbruster finally sat beside Andreh.

"Do you have anything you wish to say to me, Andreh? I have always respected you. It seems you are a nice enough guy, hard-working, on time, and always ready to lend a hand. That is why I am so confused about your relationship with my wife. Please tell me what I am missing. Something is just not right. You cannot be so dumb as to have an affair with my wife, the Queen!" Armbruster bellowed.

"Sir, I am not sure what you wish for me to say. Your wife and I are very close. She has made it clear I am to stay away from her unless it is work-related. I promised to obey her wishes. As for you, I deeply respect you. I am sorry our close relationship has caused so many rumors and speculations. Please know, for that, I am genuinely sorry." Andreh awaited Armbruster's response.

Instead, Armbruster stood up, placed his right hand on Andreh's right shoulder momentarily, and then left the room. Andreh remained in the room, alone and utterly confused. He had no idea how to take that response from Armbruster. Rather than making himself crazy, attempting to read between the lines, he chose to head to the Colosseum. Andreh refused to be late for his training with Alexis. He planned to inform her about the meeting with Armbruster and seek her advice on what his response could mean. Andreh felt flabbergasted. The meeting was strange, to say the least.

On Iriss, Zandorah finished meeting with Rammadar, her Second-in-Command. They discussed possible war scenarios with Alstromia, in the event that things did not turn out well at the Battle Rounds between Alexis and Zandorah.

Rammadar, though always an optimist, felt war with Alstromia would be catastrophic for Iriss. He was keenly aware of the AoE Alexis had established on Alstromia. Some of his best friends were part of the elite warrior team. Rammadar also knew there was no way to prepare for war with Alstromia on such short notice. It was nearly impossible. They would be unable to find enough warriors to train and prepare them for hand-to-hand combat. Everyone knew the rules.

Magic could be used during the war, but it had to fall under the War Guidelines established by the *Council of Peace & War* on Earth. This meant warriors were limited in what kind of harm they could inflict on the enemy physically or magically.

So, Rammadar knew time was short. He ordered his Second-in-Command to recruit villagers and immediately train the currently enlisted warriors.

"Rammadar, before I head back to meet with Shawnatar, are you sure we can recruit at least 1,000 new recruits to begin the intensive training?" Zandorah asked nervously.

"Zandorah, I have already enlisted 1,000 members. I am hoping for 500 more before tomorrow. Do not worry. Let me handle it. It would be helpful if Shawnatar spoke with the commoners and got them excited about the prospect of joining our new mission. It will be easier with his help. He has a great rapport with the heads of the Village. I will report back to you tonight if that is okay?" Rammadar excused himself, heading to the War Planning

Chamber and his office.

Zandorah knew Rammadar was correct. She had to convince Shawnatar to enlist more help from the villagers. Without them, they stood zero chance against Alexis and both her armies. Zandorah felt sick to her stomach. The idea of fighting against her sister in a war was overwhelming. Just as she was about to leave the room to find Shawnatar, he entered the room, smiling, looking ever so handsome.

Shawnatar approached Zandorah and kissed her on the cheek. She smiled, wrapping her arms around his neck and kissing him. He happily reciprocated until there was a loud, uninvited knock on the door. Annoyed at the interruption, Zandorah shouted, "What is it?" Rammadar entered with two other warriors.

"Zandorah, I must speak with you immediately. We have a problem." He glanced at Shawnatar. "Please stay, Shawnatar. I believe you need to hear this as well."

Twenty minutes later, Rammadar left the chamber with his two warriors. Zandorah leaned back in the oversized chair, speechless. Shawnatar marched around the room, flailing his arms.

Seeing how frustrated he was, Zandorah decided to speak up. "Do you think it is true? How should I handle this? Please help me decide what to do. Should I contact Mom? I am at a loss." She arched her back in the chair, hands interlaced behind her neck, moving her head around. Her skull ached, feeling as if it was about to explode.

'How does Gardone believe he can just show up on Iriss without my knowledge? Why would he plot revenge against Alexis? He is in no position to get himself into any more trouble,' Zandorah believed. She assumed and hoped he had learned his lesson from before. It never occurred to her that Gardone would dare to be so unreasonable. In her mind, she thought he would contact her and ask permission to reside on Iriss and provide him refuge.

Zandorah was even willing to do that until now. If Gardone wanted revenge against Alexis for escaping, she could not condone his actions. This newly acquired information also made Zandorah wonder if maybe Alexis had been telling the truth about her kidnapping.

The thought instantly made her puke. She jumped off the chair and attempted to run to the bathroom, but never made it there. She dropped to her knees, covered in vomit, crying. Shawnatar rushed to her side, reassuring her everything would be okay. He planned to investigate the information further to see what he could discover on his own.

Zandorah felt ill. She decided to head to her chamber to bathe and crawl into bed. She was done with the day and sick of all the dramatics and stories surrounding her father, Gardone. After all, Gardone was technically the reason Alexis and Zandorah were at odds, willing to enter into war. It was all too much. Zandorah somehow managed to get back on her feet, then dashed to her chamber, leaving Shawnatar alone.

A wicked smile surfaced on Alexis' face as she stared at the top of Tullah Mountain. She stood inside the Battle Colosseum when she noticed Andreh's advance. He wore black, snug-fitting pants, a blue shirt, and tall leather combat boots, and his wand was tucked into his narrow black belt. Suddenly, she noticed Andreh looked glum as he approached. She wondered why, assuming he would be ecstatic to see her.

Standing before her, he bowed formally and then backed away quickly, not allowing her to touch him. Perplexed, she glared at him, speculating why he acted so strangely.

"Hi, handsome. Thanks for coming to meet me. I missed you, " Alexis walked toward him, Andreh continued to back away from her, wishing she would engage and battle.

"What are you doing?" Alexis snapped, becoming irritated.

"Your Majesty, I am here to train with you as requested. Shall we begin?" He entered the

Battle Zone, hopeful she would follow. But that would not happen.

Shocked, Alexis stood in place. She refused to move. " Excuse me," she yelled as Andreh remained in the center of the ring. Stubbornly, he looked away, pretending he did not hear her. Alexis finally ran after him, harshly grabbing his arm. "What is your problem, Andreh?"

"Alexis, stop. I mean it. I am here at your request, acting professionally. You wanted our relationship this way. Please, let's train. If not, I will return to the Palace. There is much I can do there."

Alexis shook her head in disgust. "Whatever! We can train instead if you do not want to talk with me. That is fine! I thought you wanted to spend time together." She stomped off toward the large, red circle in the middle of the Colosseum, ready to engage. *'If he wants to train, let's go,'* she thought.

Andreh hated having to appear aloof toward her. However, he knew it was in his best interest, especially after his last conversation with Armbruster. It was better to keep his emotions in check.

Alexis entered the circle and waited for Andreh. She pulled out her Wand of Grimleah from her belt. She aimed it at Andreh. Instantly, he jumped into the ring, drawing his wand. They faced off.

"What will you do, Andreh?" she teased. She quickly flicked her wrist. The wand produced a painful bolt that zapped Andreh in the leg. He winced in pain, getting angry. He rubbed his ankle, surprised she used painful magic against him.

"What the hell, Alexis? I was under the impression we were training, not battling?" Instantly, Alexis hit him with another bolt from her wand. This time, he felt the burning heat radiate up his leg. He dropped to the ground, looking up at her in disgust.

"Alexis, stop! What are you doing? Why are you so angry?" He managed to stand up, placing his wand back into his belt loop. Andreh raised both his hands. "I am not fighting you if you are using magic. I am here to train physically. You are acting vengeful, and I am not interested." He turned his back on her.

"Do not walk away from me, Andreh. I mean it." She ran after him and forcefully grabbed his shirt, almost ripping it. He stopped immediately and spun around.

"Alexis, do you want to train or not? I came here because you asked me to, and I respect you. Now, you are acting rudely. I am getting upset." Andreh stared at her, feeling frustrated. She looked crazy. *'Her nose is flaring like an angry Torrin,'* he thought, squinting his eyes.

"I am sorry. I figured you understood. I used the *'training'* as an excuse to see you. Pauto is on his way to prepare me for battle. I wanted you here to spend some time with me. I miss you. I cannot stop thinking about you, and I know we must be careful. I assumed this was the best way to see each other without raising suspicion. Please, do not be mad at me," she pleaded, on the verge of crying.

Andreh moved toward Alexis, taking her wand and gently placing it into her belt loop. He pulled her against his body, embracing her. He kissed her passionately, running his hands down her spine and pulling her close to his chest. His hands were intertwined with her long, black hair. He heard a noise and spun around.

Pauto entered the Battle Zone, perplexed. His face was scrunched up in anger. His bottom lip was puckered as he shook his head, pointing his finger directly at Andreh.

"What is going on here? Andreh, step away from the Queen!" Pauto screamed, ordering Andreh. Pauto's wand was drawn and aimed at his subordinate. He was stunned at seeing Andreh with Alexis, blatantly displaying their unbridled love for each other.

Nervously, Andreh released Alexis and backed away from her as he cautiously approached Pauto. Alexis remained in the middle of the circle, watching the two interact.

"Pauto, I am leaving. You can train with the Queen. We are done with our meeting," replied Andreh, pretending it was a casual get-together.

"Not so fast, Andreh. That was no meeting. You must think I am stupid. I hoped the rumors were fabricated. Tell me you are NOT involved with our Queen? Are you insane? Why would you do this?" He viciously punched Andreh in the stomach, causing him to double over.

Alexis remained standing in place, not meddling in their fight. Cautiously, she continued to observe their interaction.

"I could bring you up on charges. You realize this, right?" Pauto yelled, threatening Andreh, all the while feeling his blood boil with anger. He was disgusted that someone he trusted would betray the kingdom by having an affair with the Queen!

"The Queen and I share a special bond. That relationship is none of your business, Pauto. I am sorry. It is private. I will not justify it to you or anyone else." Andreh insisted.

"You do what you need to do. Honestly, I don't care." Andreh started to walk away, turning his back on Pauto.

"Well, well…isn't that special? You and the Queen share a special relationship? Bullshit! You are having an affair. It would be in your best interest to stop immediately. I am warning you, Andreh. Armbruster is not happy. I have had plenty of discussions with him about you. He is tired of the bullshit. You do not want to face him. Armbruster will destroy you. You have no idea who you are messing with."

Alexis approached, listening to Pauto threatening Andreh. She had finally had enough. Forcefully, she pushed Pauto, ensuring he knew she meant business.

"Knock it off, Pauto. I can handle my business. Stay out of it. If Armbruster hired you to keep an eye on us, then you do not need to be here. I trusted you to be on my side. So, pick a side. What will it be?" Alexis asked sarcastically, her hands on her hips.

"You do not understand, do you? I am on your side. That is why I am telling Andreh to back off. It is in everyone's best interest. Don't you two get that? Come on. You are both intelligent. You know Armbruster will not tolerate this indiscretion. Eventually, he will lash out and destroy Andreh. Is that what you both want? I do not think so." Pauto rubbed the side of his head, feeling exasperated. He was also totally disgusted by what he had just witnessed.

Andreh half-heartedly agreed with Pauto. It was best to keep his relationship with Alexis formal. He attempted to do that today before she started acting out. Andreh knew her outburst was a way to gain his attention, much like a misbehaving child. He desperately wanted to see Alexis and spend time with her, but quickly realized the need for the distance between the two. His continued contact with her was causing too many problems, especially with his job. His career was something he cherished, and he was not willing to give up. So, Andreh knew the only reasonable choice would be to avoid Alexis as much as possible in the future.

"I am heading back to the Palace. You two, feel free to start your training for the Battle Rounds. I concur with Pauto. It is better if I take my leave. This situation is out of control. Alexis, we can talk later." Andreh walked away, heading toward the rein pole to retrieve his Torrin.

Andreh wanted to fly back to the Palace and figure out what to do with the rest of his life. The run-in with Pauto made him realize things were getting too complicated and risky.

After watching Andreh depart, Alexis believed it was time to make amends with Armbruster. She was happy to make him think she had given up Andreh and was working on repairing their marriage. She planned to make a move later in the day when she returned to the Palace to seek out Armbruster. If need be, she could be quite the convincing actress. It was the best option at the moment, and her mind was made up.

Alexis and Pauto did not discuss the Andreh situation further. Instead, they began training, concentrating on preparing Alexis to face Zandorah in the Battle Rounds. Their focus remained on making Alexis the victor, regardless of the drama surrounding her marriage to Armbruster.

Pauto kept his mouth shut the rest of the day, though he planned to call Andreh into his office later to formally charge him with insubordination. He hated to do it, but he realized it was imperative to show others he did not play favorites. Everyone knew that Pauto and Andreh were great friends. Pauto also planned to reach out to Head Legal Counsel (*HLC*) Jamessihn Shorttar to inquire about what other potential charges they could bring against Andreh for his actions.

Once armed with more information, Pauto would speak with Armbruster and ask if he wanted to proceed with those charges. Pauto did not believe Armbruster would do so, as it would complicate his already volatile relationship with Alexis. However, Pauto felt convinced he had to do something. If for no other reason than to cover his own butt in the event things went sour later. The last thing Pauto wanted or needed was Armbruster accusing him of shielding Andreh.

CHAPTER 5

Andreh swiftly arrived back at the Palace. He reminisced about Alexis and the fight in the Battle Zone on the flight. He felt nervous, wondering if Armbruster would approach him again or if something worse would happen. He understood Pauto was correct when he said Armbruster was someone he should not challenge in any way.

Armbruster was known to be a fair Wizzard and Warlock. Most believed he was an even-tempered individual. Andreh had never experienced issues with him in the past. Obviously, their relationship changed after Armbruster accused him of having an affair with his wife.

Armbruster waited for Alexis after hearing she was on Tullah Mountain training with Pauto for the Battle Rounds. He commended her on her efforts, considering how out of shape she was after giving birth to Lilah. He wanted to share interesting news about her father, Gardone, that had been relayed to him. He hoped she would not overreact.

Hours passed, and Alexis finally entered her chamber to find Armbruster sitting on her bed. Instantly, she became enraged. "I thought I made myself clear the last time. I do not appreciate you just showing up unannounced. Why are you in my chamber?" Alexis interrogated.

"First off, how was your training? You look tired and sweaty. Is that a cut on your forehead? How did that happen? I thought you were training, not going to war?" he joked.

Alexis was not amused. "Funny. What do you want?" she retorted. "There was a little incident at the dome today, but it is nothing for you to worry about. Anyway, tell me why you are here. I need to shower." Alexis tapped her foot with impatience.

"Hmm, the vision of you naked is enticing," Armbruster playfully responded. Though he wasn't teasing, he missed making love to her. Armbruster enjoyed seeing her naked the other day. She still had an alluring figure and a round, tight butt. He also loved her voluptuous and perky breasts. Armbruster missed feeling her warm body next to him in bed.

"Forget it. I am going to take a shower. You obviously are not here to hold a discussion." She started to undress. Armbruster grabbed her arm and pulled her against him. He kissed her, though she just stood there. No emotion whatsoever! Kissing her was like smooching a dead fish. He cringed, rolling his eyes.

Embarrassed and feeling rejected, he released her and sat on the bed. "Fine, I get it. You don't want me. However, I am here to share newly acquired information you will find interesting."

"Oh, do tell," Alexis snidely replied, standing half-naked in front of him, her arms crossed, pissed off at the audacity of the kiss.

"Your father is pulling some royal shit. He is spreading more tall tales. He is aware of your affair with Andreh and is now asking the courts to remove you as Queen. How do you feel about that?" Armbruster announced, feeling powerful. "However, no one knows exactly where Gardone is hiding." Armbruster stared at Alexis, awaiting a response.

Alexis threw her clothes on the floor next to her bed and proceeded to take a seat by him. She was ready to let Armbruster know she was tired of his constant badgering.

"I already told you—I do not see Andreh except for Palace business. What else do you want from me? I have not seen him in his chamber, nor has he come to mine. We are in public together, but nothing is going on. I am doing everything I can to keep things casual. It is not my fault that my father, the kidnapper, is trying to start a new round of trouble. Let him go whining to the courts. He must first provide adequate proof. Good luck with that. It is all hearsay." Alexis rose from the bed and walked to the bath chamber, slamming the door. All Alexis wanted was to shower. She was tired of Armbruster and her disloyal father.

Alexis allowed the hot water to soothe her aching body, which also helped to clear her mind. She was furious. *'Why does Gardone still try to cause me harm after everything he has already done? Does he want to get caught?'* Alexis pondered. *'Without a doubt, he is hiding on Earth or Iriss.'* Again, she felt the need to speak with Zandorah about Gardone.

Two days prior, Lorthana informed Alexis that Zandorah was planning on staying at the Palace for the Harvest Festival. Zandorah would arrive either that evening or early the following day. She would probably be staying in the chamber next to Lilah's room. It was the chamber that Zandorah considered her room in the Palace. It was a large room with an enormous balcony and a breathtaking view of the Valley of Grandu. Alexis felt it was good news that Zandorah planned to stay at the Palace. It meant Zandorah would be close by, allowing for a much-needed conversation.

Alexis dressed in her favorite long, white gown. She sprawled on her bed, closing her eyes, thinking about the day. Pauto had been rough during their training. It was the first time in a long time she had beaten him. It felt amazing—she was back, good as ever. Still, she was upset at the interaction with Andreh. She had not expected him to act the way he did. He seemed cold and uncaring. It was very unlike him.

Alexis rubbed her forehead. The blow to her head, which caused a gash, was now throbbing. She thought about casting a *Healing Spell,* but changed her mind. As crazy as it seemed, she enjoyed feeling the pain. It reminded her she was alive and training for the best competition of the year.

It was getting late when Andreh entered his chamber. Exhausted, he opted for a quick shower. His stomach still ached from the punch by Pauto. Feeling fatigued, he dressed in a sleeping tunic. The day had not gone as expected. Pauto showing up when he did was worrisome. Their confrontation would change everything between them. Andreh hated that. He wondered if Pauto had informed Armbruster about what he had witnessed. He hoped not. It would infuriate Armbruster.

Andreh started feeling sleepy. Reluctantly, he closed his eyes, covering up, shivering. He dreamt about Alexis. She was beside him in his dream, kissing and rubbing him gently. He moaned lightly in his sleep, believing she was there.

★ ★ ★ ★ ★

A thunderstorm hit just before midnight. Zandorah arrived minutes later at the Palace of Snipperdoom, accompanied by Rammadar and six others. They entered the Palace and were expeditiously escorted to their chambers by the Security Command Team.

Once in her room, Zandorah thought about the Harvest Festival and facing off against Alexis. She contemplated whether Gardone was on Alstromia, hoping he was not. After unpacking and getting comfortable in her room, she walked down the hallway to check if Alexis was still awake.

Rammadar entered the Security Command Chamber. Instantly, he was greeted by Pauto. "Sir, we were expecting you. I have a team assembled. I thought it would be a good idea if we could meet before the Harvest Festival kick-off tomorrow." Rammadar smiled at Pauto and his efficiency. He liked the young Warlock.

The fact that he greeted him so quickly and was willing to work together showed him there would be cooperation, which was the best Rammadar could hope for, given the current circumstances.

It was nice to see Alexis had a great staff. Everyone was welcoming and kind. It made Rammadar realize how much he missed his friends from Alstromia. Two of his friends entered the chamber. They heard of Rammadar's arrival and were eager to say hello.

Immediately, the three Warlocks started talking, laughing, and having a good time, just as before. Rammadar contemplated whether he could remain on Alstromia, leaving Zandorah and relinquishing his position to Juannah Ogarstan. She was capable and brilliant. Rammadar loved Alstromia. He planned to see how he felt this next week and then decide. He assumed Zandorah would feel betrayed, but he missed his family and friends. Most of them resided on Alstromia. Living without them was becoming miserable and challenging.

While relaxing on her bed, Alexis mindlessly gazed out the window, admiring the bright flashes of lightning. It made her happy. She loved the roar of the thunder and the heavy rain pouring out of the sky. There was nothing better than a powerful storm. Alexis heard a knock on the door, forcing her to sit up in bed. Taking a deep breath, Alexis prayed it was not Armbruster ready to start another round of arguments.

The chamber door opened, and Zandorah appeared, looking drawn. Her long hair was braided and draped down her right shoulder. She wore a sleeping gown but entered the chamber barefoot. Alexis greeted her cordially.

"Hello, Zandi! I see you made it. How are you? Are you settled into your room?" Alexis inquired, urging Zandorah to sit on the chair near the fireplace.

"Alexis, I wish to thank you for allowing me to stay at the Palace. I appreciate it. I will be gone as soon as the event is over. I just wanted to let you know I plan to attend the Harvest Festival Breakfast tomorrow. I hope that is okay?" Zandorah asked meekly.

"You are my guest. Of course. No matter what is happening between us, we are still family. I hope you know that. I will see you in the morning," Alexis responded, hoping Zandorah would get the hint and head back to her room.

"I stopped by quickly to let you know I had arrived. See you at breakfast. Maybe we can talk later in the morning after we have eaten? I have a few things I wish to discuss with you. Goodnight, Alexis."

"No problem. Sweet dreams," Alexis said, rolling over, now extremely tired. Zandorah left the chamber and headed to her room. She was elated that Alexis acted civilly toward her.

Alexis could have been nasty, but chose to be kind. It was a small step in the right direction. Zandorah noticed the beautiful moons shining in through the window in the dark chamber now that the storm had subsided. She contemplated whether she could beat Alexis at the Battle Zone competition. She had trained for six months straight.

Alexis was probably not in the best shape since she became a mother and had stopped training. Zandorah wondered if she trained with Pauto. Many vied for his time and expertise, but Alexis was the only one he committed to training. Nervous about the upcoming event and eager to rest, Zandorah crawled into the tall, fluffy bed, feeling comfortable and happy.

Pauto left the chamber, allowing Rammadar time to catch up with his friends. He did not wish to intrude. He hoped to find Aerianna awake and inform her about the situation between Alexis and Andreh. He could not wait to hear what Aerianna had to say about the matter. Pauto was tired of keeping his mouth shut about the subject. Aerianna needed to know all the details. She had to learn how close Andreh and Alexis were. Though Alexis would not be happy if Aerianna confronted her, Pauto thought it was time.

Aerianna had suspected something was happening between Andreh and Alexis for a while. Though she chose to mind her own business, she now urgently wanted to speak with Alexis and face her directly. The two needed to have a candid conversation about the affair. As the Second-in-Command to Alexis and her friend, Aerianna felt blindsided by the lack of communication from Alexis.

'Why has Alexis refused to confide in me? I have always been her ally. What reason could Alexis

have to keep this hush-hush?' Aerianna felt betrayed by Alexis and would make a point of letting her know. Alexis did not always realize how hurtful her actions were to others.

The night turned to day, and trumpets blared from the Valley below, waking Alexis. Irritated, she rubbed her eyes. It was a beautiful morning on Alstromia, not a cloud in the sky. Alexis jumped out of bed, dashing to the shower and dressing.

The day had finally arrived—the kick-off for the Harvest Festival. Lorthana should have arrived last night, too. Alexis wondered if Zandorah was already in the Hall waiting for the Harvest Breakfast to begin. Roughly 150 Witches, Wizzards, and Warlocks would attend this event. It was the beginning of the monumental occasion.

Thereafter, there would be a casual Meet and Greet in the garden so visitors could mingle. Later in the day, the event would move to the Manor on Tullah, where a ribbon-cutting ceremony would officially open the event.

In the evening, a glamorous gala was held for a limited number of guests, primarily VIPs. The night would end with fireworks over Tullah Mountain.

As Alexis arrived at the Hall, the double doors were wide open, and loud chatter came from the room. W3s enjoyed themselves immensely, engaging in conversation, sharing laughs, and sipping on brews and various potions. It brought a smile to Alexis's face to witness such a joyful crowd.

Aerianna approached, looking beautiful in an icy-blue, strapless, short dress, showing off her long, sculpted legs. It was unusual for her to wear such a petite dress. Alexis was immediately jealous that she had not chosen a similar outfit.

Holding her head high, Alexis entered the room wearing a long, red, slinky dress cinched at the waist. The plunging neckline exposed her full breasts, peeking out. Her voluminous, long hair was curly and cascaded down her back, almost touching her tiny waist.

Andreh's jaw dropped when he saw Alexis enter the room. His heart started beating fast, and he felt his hands become sweaty. He had to force himself to look away to avoid becoming aroused.

Pauto stood beside him and gave Andreh a stern look, noticing his facial expression and evident restlessness. Two security commoners walked before Alexis, and two others followed, ensuring her safety. She approached the long table where she would sit beside Armbruster and Aerianna.

The room became hushed as the Queen approached the table and expeditiously sat down. Once the Queen was seated, everyone else quickly took a seat, observing her. Armbruster stood up.

"Warriors and Friends. Welcome to our beautiful Alstromia and the Palace of Snipperdoom! Thank you for your participation in this monumental event. Alexis and I are grateful you have come to attend the Harvest Festival. We realize some of you have traveled a long way to join the event. We are grateful and excited to begin the event by hosting this breakfast. Please, enjoy!" He sat down next to his wife. Alexis nodded approvingly to the wait staff to start the food service.

Within minutes, the room was filled with staff pushing Trillays that were overflowing with food and potions. The delicious smells permeated the area. The hall was an elongated room with three, tall windows overlooking the valley below. An exquisite crystal chandelier hung in the middle, flanked by two smaller light fixtures.

Ever since Alexis saw a chandelier in an old, deserted estate in New England, Alexis has fallen in love with the look of crystal light fixtures. After moving back to Alstromia, she filled the Palace with various chandeliers, all of different styles and sizes. Some had clear crystals, while others boasted colored gems. The food and potions were a great success with the guests, and Alexis felt content with the menu choices Aerianna made. The time came to conclude the breakfast and allow the guests to rest a while before the Meet and Greet took place in the lavish garden by the enormous pond.

After the guests were dismissed, Alexis and Armbruster joined Pauto and Aerianna at the round table at the end of the Hall. They briefly discussed the Meet and Greet, including the special opening act by the famous Witch and musical star—Viollah Grackenbone. She had the most beautiful voice and would be opening the event with a song from her new collection of Chants and Songs. Everyone looked forward to seeing her perform in person.

"Well, it seems like the breakfast was a hit with our guests," Aerianna announced, smiling.

"I agree. The crowd was lively, and I heard many wonderful compliments about the foods and brews," added Pauto.

Alexis nodded, choosing to remain quiet. She was still mad that Andreh had left in the middle of breakfast. She saw him walk out the side doors. Tempted as she was to follow him, Alexis knew she could not do so. Instead, she pretended to enjoy the morning and the food festivities. Feeling restless, she excused herself and headed back to her chamber.

Ambruster watched her walk away, looking distraught. He wondered where she was headed. It had been a great start to the day, and he felt it could only get better. Armbruster shrugged his shoulders, leaving the hall, wishing to change into a different outfit before meeting up at the next affair, starting in two hours.

Aerianna and Pauto remained seated. Yarlen, who had been standing by a window, turned and exited the room, following Armbruster. Aerianna and Pauto were left with the wait staff.

"What do you think is happening with Alexis? She left rather quickly. I thought the breakfast was fun. Everyone mingled, and it was fabulous to see so many familiar faces from Earth and other Clans," Aerianna added.

"I believe Alexis is still pouting. She knows she must stay away from Andreh, and I think it is proving to be more difficult for her than originally expected. Plus, Andreh hurried off in the middle of the food service. I should head to his chamber to see if he is okay. Do you mind if I do that, honey?" Pauto asked.

"Of course not. I will change my outfit and meet you later. The Meet and Greet is by the pond. Don't forget!" The two walked out of the hall, heading in opposite directions.

Andreh stretched out on the bed, his legs dangling off the end. He flung off his boots and closed his eyes. Seeing Alexis at breakfast made things more awkward for him. He did not realize how much things had changed. It was becoming almost impossible for him to be in the same room with her.

Suddenly, he realized what he needed to do. He knew it was the right thing, given the current situation. Though it would make him miserable, it was all he could do to change the circumstances.

After the Battle Rounds and the Harvest Festival Grand Finale, he would depart Alstromia and head to Earth to relocate. His good friend Alexx VonHorner would happily allow him to stay at his residence. They were still in constant contact.

Alexx refused to move to Alstromia because he had a child with a human named Vaneza Smith. Many of the Clans highly frowned upon their mixed marriage and Non-Magical Child. The Clan of Tarbo was more lenient and accepted the family into their circle. Thus, Alexx chose to live on Earth in New England.

Alexx begged Andreh to return to Earth many times before. However, Andreh remained resolute—he loved Alstromia and did not want to leave. He visited Earth several times but never had the urge to stay. Now, it seemed like his only option, given the circumstances. Alexis would be furious once she found out what he did. By the time she realized he was gone, he would be living on Earth with Alexx and his family. Hearing the loud knock, he sat up, wondering if he should answer. Andreh became nervous, wondering if it could be Alexis. Then, he listened to the voice and felt instant relief.

"Andreh, it is Pauto. May I enter?" he asked loudly, pounding on the metal door. Andreh opened the door and stepped aside so Pauto could enter. The two sat on his bed beside each other.

"So, what happened today? You left abruptly. Are you okay? Are you not feeling well?" Pauto asked him, concerned. He noticed Andreh's pallid complexion.

"Yes. I am fine. You know the situation. I cannot be in the Queen's presence. Just seeing her is becoming a problem. I have to start thinking about how I can continue to stay here. She is constantly trying to see me. It is an enormous problem. I am aware that I made the situation what it is, but still, it is not easy. I am attempting to rectify it." Andreh took a deep breath and locked eyes with Pauto.

"I know you are trying. I have noticed your effort. You may want to think about moving away from Alstromia. I am not telling you to do so. Given how things are turning out, I am unsure if you can stay. Armbruster is livid. I have not seen him like this in a long time. You should be frightened. Andreh, you know we are friends, and I am here for you. But, as your friend, I have to tell you, I think you are crazy for allowing yourself to get involved with our Queen. Please consider what I have said. Also, I need to speak with you about the charges. I am forced to write you up for insubordination. I talked to Head Legal Counsel Shorttar. He believes three other charges could be brought against you if Armbruster decides to do so. I just wanted you to be aware of pending actions. Leaving for Earth would be a great way to avoid the legal problem." Pauto explained.

Andreh felt betrayed. He could not believe Pauto would go to such lengths to make a point. He thought he was his friend and confidant. Now, he knew better.

Pauto and Andreh talked a bit longer. Pauto had no clue that Andreh had already contemplated leaving Alstromia. Andreh was tired of the pressure and the rumors, as well as the strange looks from the W3s. Andreh knew it was happening, and it was making him sick.

Twenty minutes later, Pauto left Andreh alone and chose to head to his chamber to change attire for the Meet and Greet. He also wanted to find Rammadar and discuss a few issues pertaining to the Harvest Festival. Rammadar had become a close friend and ally, and he wanted his feedback on some recently discovered problems with a few Security Guard of the Command staff. It would be good to get a new perspective.

Andreh considered skipping the Meet and Greet. It was another opportunity to be near Alexis. He was not interested in seeing her or others watching him intently. It would probably be better to attend the Ribbon Cutting Ceremony later in the evening. He would do whatever it took to stay away from Alexis.

In her chamber, Alexis reluctantly changed her clothing again. Karita helped her into the new outfit. It was sure to bring attention to her. It was a black pantsuit made out of glittery material from Earth. It was spellbinding. The bottom of the legs had tiny grey pearls sewn along the edge. The top had a stand-up collar encrusted with clear crystals and pearls. The high-heeled shoes matched. Alexis stood before the mirror, admiring herself and smiling at the reflection.

"My Queen, you look stunning! Everyone will surely notice," announced Karita. "Here is your lipstick." She handed Alexis the makeup item and quickly backed away.

Alexis rubbed her lips together and grinned, showing her pearly white teeth. The dark reddish plum-colored lipstick looked almost black. Alexis hardly wore any makeup. She was naturally stunning and did not need to apply potions and lotions to her flawless face.

"Would you like me to fasten your shoes, My Queen?" Karita asked, noticing the high heels were not on her foot all the way, nor were they secure.

"Yes, please do that. I do not want to bend over." She chose the dramatic outfit to make a statement and hoped Andreh would approve of her choice.

Without a knock, Zandorah appeared in the chamber. "Hello, sister. How are you? OH MY! Don't you look breathtaking? Where did you find that amazing outfit? Do tell," teased Zandorah.

Alexis smiled but said nothing. She looked at Zandorah. She wore a magenta-colored dress with a black cloak. *'Very boring,'* thought Alexis.

"Well, you look…ummm, very official. Why did you not dress up, Zandorah? That outfit is quite frumpy. You are such a pretty Witch. Why not emphasize your looks?" Alexis said, feeling annoyed at Zandorah's lack of caring. For some strange reason, Zandorah did not enjoy dressing up or accentuating her beauty. Alexis felt this was senseless.

"Honestly, I did not know we should dress up for this event. Do you want me to change? I brought plenty of other things I could wear." Zandorah asked, now feeling self-conscious. She saw the way Alexis frowned when she entered the room.

"Don't bother. You look fine. Anyway, is there a reason you are here?"

"I wanted to speak with you about a few things. Specifically, Dad. I know you are busy, but do you have a few minutes to spare?" Zandorah asked cautiously.

"I will not discuss our father tonight. Really, Zandorah! This is not the place or time. We can discuss the previous issues with Dad after the Harvest Festival. I do not want to think about him right now." Alexis fumed. She was furious with Zandorah for bringing up Gardone. *'How dare she?'* Alexis wondered.

Zandorah saw the expression and how quickly Alexis changed the subject. Now, Zandorah wished she had not brought it up. But it was too late. Alexis was already upset. She knew it was best to leave her alone. Zandorah excused herself and expeditiously left the chamber, heading to the room next to hers. Lorthana was probably getting dressed for the Meet and Greet. Lorthana did not attend the breakfast, which was unusual.

Zandorah wanted to ensure her mother was okay and hoped to chat with her.

Alexis looked out the large window in her room. She saw carriages and Torrins flying up the Landing Deck, delivering Witches, Warlocks, and Wizzards. She was happy things were progressing smoothly so far. Now, she wondered why her mother had been absent from this morning's breakfast. It was not like her to miss out on a food event. She loved to eat and spend time with her family. Instantly, she felt an odd sensation in her stomach. *'I hope Mom is okay,'* she said to herself, wringing her hands.

CHAPTER 6

Alexis believed you could tell a lot about someone by how they handled themselves at events. That is precisely why she chose to observe everyone and say very little. It was interesting how phony many of her friends acted when they thought they were the center of attention. It made Alexis sick. She was getting tired of all the fake smiles and backstabbing.

She caught a glance of Armbruster chit-chatting with Yarlen and two of their close friends from the Clan of Tarbo.

Alexis also noticed Zandorah laughing with Shawnatar near the pond on the other side of the grounds, having a good time. Shawnatar looked handsome, dressed in his battle uniform. Alexis still did not know what he saw in her sister. She was pretty, but could be so much more. Zandorah chose to be average, not emphasizing her good features. Alexis felt it was a waste. Her sister could be drop-dead gorgeous if she wanted to be.

Shawnatar was still as good-looking as ever. He was muscular, tall, and had that boyish charm about him. Many of the single Witches outright flirted with him. However, he never seemed to care. His eyes were always focused on his wife. He was loyal to the core. However, there was a time when he loved Alexis.

Shawnatar was a free spirit, yet he was devoted, which was exactly what Alexis desired and needed at that time. She nearly had a panic attack when she found out he was interested in Zandorah. How could he not be drawn to her and instead be infatuated with her sister, Zandorah? It was simply beyond her understanding.

Zandorah had played coy and pretended not to notice his apparent attention. It infuriated Alexis. Yes, she was dating Armbruster on the side, but she never thought the two would get married. She hoped to keep her relationship with Shawnatar until that fateful night.

Alexis planned to visit Shawnatar. The two had previously discussed potentially having dinner together, though they had not spoken in days. Alexis arrived at his hut to surprise him on Earth, bringing a basket overflowing with food and wine.

As she approached the hut, she heard laughter. Curious, she peeked through the front windows and saw Zandorah sitting on a couch beside Shawnatar. They were sipping Porting Wine, and she was barefoot, looking sassy and free. It turned her stomach. After minutes of watching them, she decided to knock on the door, confronting the pair.

Shawnatar appeared, looking confused and surprised. "Oh, hi! What are you doing here?" he nervously asked, stepping outside and closing the door behind him.

Alexis was furious. "We had a date. Or so I thought. I guess I must be mistaken. I see you have company." She hissed with annoyance.

"I did not hear from you and assumed we had no date. Your sister showed up with Porting Wine. So, I am having dinner with her. I am so sorry. Can we see each other on another night?" Shawnatar swallowed hard, noticing the scowl on her face. He could tell Alexis was about to scream.

"What makes you believe that I ever want to see you again? You are a cheater! I thought you loved me. What the hell? We are DONE!" Alexis yelled as she slammed down her Ceptre and disappeared.

Zandorah overheard their conversation. She was shocked, not realizing Alexis had been dating Shawnatar. When he returned inside, Zandorah faced him and decided to clear the air about their relationship. She outright asked him about it. He did not deny his love for her, but also shared some other news.

Shawnatar informed Zandorah that he knew Alexis was dating Armbruster simultaneously. Many other single Wizzards had shared that information with him. One Clan member even told him that Alexis would be engaged soon and planned to marry Armbruster. Alexis also wanted to be Queen of Alstromia, and Armbruster would help her accomplish that lofty goal.

Shawnatar was heartbroken. He loved Alexis and believed they would have a future together. He thought they would have children and raise them on Alstromia.

It almost destroyed him when he heard that Alexis had met Armbruster at the Annual

Meeting of Power and that everyone believed they made a powerful couple, approving of their union. Shawnatar knew they would be married someday. Then and there, Shawnatar decided to end things with Alexis and let her begin her new life with Armbruster, vowing to step aside. That is why he had not called on her and ignored any communication from Alexis. He honestly did not believe she wanted to date him anymore.

Zandorah was charming, comforting, and beautiful. Shawnatar was naturally attracted to her. At first, he did not want to date or see her because he feared what her sister, Alexis, would think. But now, he did not care. He was falling in love with Zandorah and her natural beauty. She loved him back, the way he needed. He moved forward with his relationship with Zandorah and erased Alexis from his life as quickly as possible.

When Alexis and Armbruster announced their engagement, Shawnatar knew he would marry Zandorah. It all worked out the way it was meant to, or so he thought.

On the day of the nuptials, the Ceremonial Exchange, Alexis had never looked more stunning. She wore pure white, like most Earthly wives. The ceremony was held on the seashore in Maine. She looked beautiful and sexy. Her long hair and white veil whipped around in the breeze on the shore, with the ocean waves making comforting splashing noises in the background. Shawnatar's heart ached as he witnessed Alexis exchange Ceremonial Rings with Armbruster. Zandorah sat next to Shawnatar, holding his hand. She could see his eyes well up with tears. Zandorah pretended not to notice, but she felt betrayed. *'How can he still want her?'* she wondered, angry and frustrated.

Zandorah dropped his hand, staring at Alexis and Armbruster as they walked hand in hand down the pathway leading to the gazebo, where they would greet guests before attending the celebration to follow.

It was a horrible day for Shawnatar—a day filled with mixed emotions and confusion. However, he was happy for Alexis, hoping she was truly in love with Armbruster. Later in the evening, when dancing with Zandorah, he knew she would become his mate. She loved him, and he wanted to love again. He committed to taking care of her and marrying her soon. Shawnatar proposed a few months later at the Harvest Festival. He began his new life with Zandorah.

Once married to Zandorah and living on Iriss, he never regretted letting Alexis go. She was better off with Armbruster. They were a perfect match. Armbruster's connections aided Alexis in becoming Queen, just as she had planned.

Years later, Alexis approached Armbruster and their guests on Alstromia. The visitors bowed to the Queen as she stood before them. Alexis mingled and chatted with many acquaintances. Half an hour later, Armbruster walked to the podium and loudly announced a warm welcome for all attendees of the upcoming events.

"Welcome again, friends and family. We are honored to host this annual event. Alexis and I are thrilled that so many of you have chosen to partake in the Battle Rounds. Alexis and her sister, Zandorah, will be contestants again this year. Please, let's give them a round of applause." Ambruster clapped, setting the mood. Soon, everyone stood at attention, clapping.

"Also, let us not forget the other formidable warriors among us. They, too, will be battling. Please, welcome them as well." Armbruster clapped again. Unexpectedly, the Queen approached. Armbruster looked perplexed. Earlier, they did not discuss her speaking at this time.

"I wanted to thank everyone for making this such a great turnout. I am excited to kick off this event tonight at the ribbon cutting on Tullah Mountain. Please be sure to arrive early. Thank you, and enjoy the snacks, potions, and Porting Wine." Alexis left the podium and approached Shawnatar and

Zandorah, hoping to speak to them. She wanted to ensure everyone had the opportunity to see her dazzling outfit. After all, it was the main reason she attended this little, late afternoon soirée. Nearing Zandorah, Alexis noticed the disapproving frown on Shawnatar's face. He did not look happy to see her.

"Why so glum, Shawnatar? Are you not enjoying yourself? It is nice to see you and Zandorah." Alexis managed to say without sounding too awful. She tried to sound upbeat, though she wished Zandorah were not there.

"Hello, Alexis. Zandorah and I are pleased to be here. Thank you so much for inviting us to stay at the Palace. We are grateful," Shawnatar stated.

"Well, where else would you stay? The Lodge? I think not! You are family. Of course, you will stay at the Palace. Has anyone seen Mother? I have not seen her yet. I am becoming concerned."

Zandorah thought it was odd that she had not seen her mother yet. The room next to hers was still empty.

"Mom is not here. I have no idea why she has not yet arrived for the events. I tried to summon her twice. I do hope she is okay. Should we send out a hunt team?" Zandorah joked. Her mother was usually punctual, and her absence was highly worrisome.

"I will ask Armbruster to find out what is keeping her. She must be back on Earth if she is not here. I can always send Pauto or Andreh to retrieve her. She knows how important this day is to you and me, Zandorah. I assumed she would want to be here." Alexis shook her head with disgust, getting irritated. Deep inside, she fretted. She hoped all was okay with Lorthana.

Armbruster overheard the conversation. He tapped on Pauto's shoulder and informed him to search for Lorthana. He felt it was a bad sign that she was not already at the Palace. She vowed to be there before any of the events started. Now, she missed the Harvest Breakfast and the Meet and Greet. It was unlike her. Armbruster had a horrible feeling, one he planned to hide from Alexis. He did not want her to know he was concerned.

Instead, he playfully wrapped his arms around her waist and said, "Care to dance with your loving husband?" Whisking her off to the outdoor dance floor.

Though there was no music, he spun her around while she laughed, pretending to enjoy the spontaneous dance. Others watched, believing the two to be deeply in love. The fake display of affection convinced most that they were still in love. Hopefully, it would help dispel rumors of her illicit affair with Andreh Darkhill.

The late afternoon turned quickly to dusk. It was getting dark, and the crowd dispersed. It was almost time for the ribbon cutting at the Manor. Alexis was back in her chamber, changing into her formal gown with Karita's help. It was by far the most exquisite gown she had ever seen. It was a deep purple color embellished with thousands of tiny pink sparkling crystals. The stones were randomly scattered at the bodice, and then they swept down the entire length of the gown's full skirt, adding a magical and glittery effect that resembled pink fog when she walked.

The plunging neckline showed off her large breasts. Alexis would turn heads, and that was her main goal. She craved attention. Sadly, it seemed like the only attention she sought was from Andreh, and he avoided her like the plague.

Andreh sat on the tall, Trimber stool inside Henrii's Potions & BrewHaus, in the Valley of Grandu. He skipped the Meet and Greet and figured he would make an appearance at the Gala, but not until much later. He planned to avoid Alexis at all costs. As he sipped his tall jug of Henrii's WickettBrew—a strong drink for which Henrii became famous, he listened to Alexx bragging about his son, Ethann. Alexx was a proud dad and was thrilled his son was walking and talking. Andreh was happy for him, but listening to him speak about his rambunctious child made Andreh's heart ache. He wished for a child of his own.

"I am so happy for you and Vaneza. It sounds like Ethann is a spirited young man. So, tell me, honestly—are you sure you are okay with me moving in with you until I figure out what I want to do? Right now, I am still attempting to put my life in order. I know it is asking a lot, but I could not imagine living with anyone else," Andreh asked his friend, grateful for his offer.

"You know you are always welcome. Vaneza is excited about the prospect of having someone else around to help out. Did you know we have expanded the Inn? It is much bigger now. We currently have twelve guest rooms. I never thought I would help run a bed-and-breakfast in America, on Earth. We love it, though. It is fulfilling. I still attend a few Wizzard and Warlock meetings, but not as much as I did in the past. I am becoming accustomed to living like a human. It really is not so bad. Sometimes, I wish Ethann had magical powers because it would be amazing to teach him, but now, I have to accept that will never happen."

"As long as you are happy, friend," Andreh interjected as he ordered another Henrii's WickettBrew, but this time the blue one, which had a more robust flavor. He hoped to get more drunk so he could forget about Alexis.

"You better slow down, friend. Those blue Henrii's WickettBrews are no joke. You may not be walking so well later, ha-ha," Alexx cautioned Andreh, chuckling. He slammed down another Brew and smiled.

Andreh was fully aware of the dreaded consequences of drinking too much. He didn't care. It would help him cope with Alexis and the shindig at the Manor later. Since deciding to reside on Earth, he knew his time on Alstromia was quickly ending. After the Harvest Festival Grand Finale, he planned to inform Pauto of his exit. Pauto would understand but still be angry at Andreh's expedited departure. It could leave the Command Staff in a lurch. Andreh hated doing that to Pauto but felt forced to move from Alstromia. There was no way he could remain on the planet with Alexis. Maybe one day, he could return. In the meantime, he planned to live a normal and uncomplicated life on Earth with good friends.

Alexis stood shivering by the fireplace. It was a chilly night. She asked Karita to find the shawl matching her gown. Alexis wrapped it tightly around her shoulders, wondering why her mother was still not at the Palace. She was becoming more and more worried. Hopefully, nothing was wrong. Even Armbruster stated he could not locate Lorthana. No one had seen her in three days, which was quite alarming.

On top of Tullah Mountain, the celebration area was brightly illuminated. It was already quite lively. Most guests were congregated at the Manor, anticipating the Queen's arrival.

Alexis waited for her carriage. She planned to use it to fly up the mountain for the Gala. Armbruster, Aerianna, and Pauto would accompany her in the lavish, Torrin-drawn carriage. Alexis knew how to make a grand entrance, landing in front of the Manor for all to see. A loud knock on the door interrupted her thoughts. She turned around as the door opened. Her mother, Lorthana, entered. She looked beautiful, wearing a dark green dress and a golden, iridescent cloak over her shoulders. Her long hair was pulled up and showcased colorful crystal flowers. She wore long, golden, cascading earrings that glistened. Alexis approved.

Alexis quickly walked toward her mother, embracing her. "Mom, where have you been? I have been so worried about you." She hugged her mother almost too hard.

"Child, calm down. I am okay. I will tell you all about it later. I am here. Are we almost ready? The guard outside said your carriage is on the Landing Deck. Shall we head there now?" Lorthana asked, deflecting Alexis's inquisition.

"Sure, then you can fill me in on why you were missing for three days," retorted Alexis, refusing to drop the subject.

"Alexis, let us enjoy the night. We have plenty of time to discuss this further at another time. You look absolutely stunning, my child. WOW! Turn around. Let me see the back of the dress."

Alexis turned around so her mother could see the back of the dress. Her bare back was exposed from the shoulders down to the waist. It was a very sexy dress from the back.

"You will certainly turn heads, my daughter," Lorthana teased, gently pushing her child out the door and toward the hallway to head to the Landing Deck below.

"Well, Mother, you look terrific. Very classy and gorgeous, as always. Too bad some handsome Warlock or Wizzard has not swept you off your feet, " Alexis responded, teasing her mother. She hoped her mother would date again now that her father was gone and out of the picture. Hopefully, Lorthana would want to find a new mate. She was a great and talented Witch and would make an excellent companion for some lucky Wizzard or Warlock of her choosing.

The two arrived on the Landing Deck. Armbruster, Pauto, and Aerianna were already seated and waiting for Alexis. Everyone was thrilled to see Lorthana. Once in the carriage, the commoner pulled back on the reins, and four majestic Torrins lifted off and guided the wagon toward the mountain's top.

The night was extremely chilly, but two warm, furry blankets were in the carriage for Alexis and Aerianna. Since Lorthana sat next to Alexis, they shared the cozy throw, keeping warm. Armbruster placed his arm around Alexis' shoulder, hoping to add warmth as he could feel her shaking. Aerianna cuddled closely next to Pauto. Their flight was spectacular.

The moons glistened in the cloudless sky. It was a perfect night. As the Torrins approached the Manor, Alexis sat up. She wanted to look regal. A large crowd assembled outside the building, awaiting her arrival. The Security Command Team arrived first on their Torrins to secure the perimeter.

Once they signaled to the carriage driver, he knew he could land safely, delivering the Queen and others on board. The crowd cheered as the carriage touched down in front of the Manor, the regal beasts coming to a complete stop. Armbruster exited first, helping Lorthana leave the golden carriage.

Pauto jumped down next from the carriage, helping Aerianna. Armbruster approached and put out his hand to help Alexis step down. She grasped his gloved hand, smiling and looking ever so stately. She stepped out of the carriage and quickly released his hand so she could wave to the spectators, calling out her name. She waved, nodding, happy to see so many friends and loyal followers.

The Royals entered the Manor, followed by Lorthana, Aerianna, and Pauto. Once inside, they were quickly ushered to the Ballroom in the back, overlooking the extensive Race Track. The ballroom was already decorated and festive. The enormous room was filled with 30 round tables decorated with bright red and orange tablecloths. Glasses with various drinks and brews were carefully placed on tables with exotic foods—local and imported from Earth.

Five chandeliers hung down from the 20-foot-high ceilings, adorned with fall foliage and Bloomitz. Floating candles illuminated the back of the room. It was a spectacular sight. The high-back chairs were decorated with iridescent orange and black ribbons.

The entire room looked enchanting. A concoction's bar was located in the room's rear with a row of seven cauldrons, operated by the best Ale and Brewmasters provided by Henrii Snubberly and his wife from Henrii's Potions and BrewHaus.

The wait staff, mostly commoners, wore their best uniforms: black shirts, pants, and highly polished shoes. They were ready to serve the guests. The hushed crowd waited patiently as Alexis was escorted to her seat at the main table with Armbruster.

Aerianna and Pauto joined her, as did Lorthana and Zandorah. However, Shawnatar was absent without an explanation.

Once the Royal couple was seated, the room became lively with chatter. Everyone was thrilled to attend the dinner. More importantly, the next day would be the start of the year's most anticipated event.

In the meantime, the attendees planned to enjoy the night, consume too much potion and ale, and hopefully reconnect with old friends.

"Ladies and Gentlemen…We ask for your silence, please!" Yarlen shouted to gain the attention of the lively group. "Please help us welcome the Royal couple and her mother, Lorthana, sister—Zandorah of Iriss, and Aerianna—Fanna of Alstromia. We are thrilled you are here to help us kick off this monumental yearly event. Please enjoy the night! The Queen and Armbruster extend their gratitude for your attendance!" Yarlen sat down, and the crowd clapped and stood as a sign of respect and honor. Yarlen blushed, uncomfortable at the attention.

Armbruster had appeared in Yarlen's chamber the night before and asked him to make the opening remarks. Armbruster felt that with everything that was happening, it was best if someone other than royalty made the grand announcement.

For once, Alexis concurred. Reluctantly, Yarlen agreed. He did not enjoy making such speeches, but understood why Armbruster chose him.

The wait staff immediately began service. The crowd was hungry and eager to enjoy the night's festivities. Alexis sat quietly by Armbruster's side, surveying the area. He noticed her wandering eyes and assumed she was searching for Andreh, which instantly fueled him with anger. He scowled at the thought, wishing Andreh would disappear forever! But he hated the fact that it would probably never happen.

In the City of Miccay, Andreh sobered up enough to return to the Palace to change his attire. It was getting late, and he realized he should head to the Manor. Alexis was probably livid that he was not there. He yearned to see her. Andreh also wanted to speak with Alexis and let her know he planned to leave Alstromia. But then, maybe he should not tell her anything. It would probably be better if he departed for Earth without an explanation. He remained conflicted about how to proceed.

Half an hour later, Andreh dressed in his best battle uniform and headed to the stables to fly to the Manor. He wanted to experience the brisk breeze on his face, hoping to feel more awake. He glanced at the valley below as he flew through the air on his Torrin, admiring the scene.

It was a beautiful sight. Seeing it made him sad, realizing he would soon be back on Earth. He loved Alstromia, and more importantly, he loved Alexis. It would be challenging to start a new life away from the one he loved. However, his mind was made up. He decided to depart Alstromia, hoping his absence would help Alexis resolve issues she faced over the relationship with him. Everything he planned was aimed at helping her, and he wanted only the best for Alexis. He prayed she would be happy with Armbruster on Alstromia.

His presence was complicating everything, and Andreh felt he deserved a fresh start, too. As Andreh landed the Torrin, he looked around. The Manor was filled with W3s, and he could hear their boisterous laughter. He wondered if Alexis enjoyed the night and could not wait to see her.

Andreh knew it was best to avoid Armbruster and the rest of the Command Staff. His relationship with Pauto was strained. Pauto was still furious with him for maintaining an apparent flirtatious relationship with Alexis. Pauto had not treated him the same since their nasty confrontation at the Colosseum.

Andreh was heartbroken about the situation but realized there was nothing he could say or do to remedy it. Instead, he promised himself to steer clear of Pauto until he departed for Earth.

Alexis spotted him the moment he entered the room. Her heart skipped a beat, feeling a rush of adrenaline take over. She wanted to stand up and walk toward him, but assumed it was best to remain seated beside Armbruster.

Within a minute, Andreh approached the main table and bowed respectfully before the Queen and King, then quickly walked away toward another table to be seated at the other end of the room.

Armbruster grabbed his wife's arm and shook his head, indicating she was not to follow him. Everyone was actively watching her every move. Armbruster refused to give anyone ammunition to use against Alexis in the future. His main goal was to keep her and Andreh separated for the night. He spoke with Pauto earlier to ask that he and his staff ensure Andreh stayed away from the Queen.

Alexis removed Armbruster's hand with a stern glare. She was tired of being handled by him and his staff. Alexis knew what he was doing, and it infuriated her. She pretended to enjoy the night, sipping her bubbling brew, giggling, and chatting with her mom, Lorthana. Alexis also wondered why Shawnatar was absent and thought about asking Zandorah, but she quickly changed her mind. She remained unwilling to discuss Shawnatar with Zandorah. It was a subject best left unspoken and a heated topic of conversation.

Andreh chose to sit with a few acquaintances from Earth. He was surprised Alexx was not present, as he had received an invitation. However, considering he was married to a human, he figured Alexx decided not to attend because his wife was not invited. It was a strained situation, and Alexx managed it in a way he felt was best for his family.

A few hours later, the evening finally began winding down. Dinner was finished, potions were still being served, and Alexis felt woozy. She wanted to head back to the Palace, but remembered she had to stay for the fireworks display that would soon begin.

Alexis scanned the area, hoping to catch sight of Andreh. She was eager to be close to him, but unfortunately, she knew that was unlikely to happen. Whenever she attempted to leave and head to the bathroom, Armbruster immediately interrogated her. He acted ridiculous, making her want to return to the Palace. Alexis did not appreciate being supervised.

As Queen, she had the privilege to move around as she pleased. Now, it seemed as if her movements were guarded and even forbidden. Rather than make a scene and upset Armbruster more, she obliged, giving him a fake smile and turning her head in the other direction, avoiding further eye contact.

Ten minutes before midnight, Yarlen stood up and clapped his hands loudly, shouting, "Attention, Guests! We are heading to the terrace to watch the fireworks, the night's final event. Please exit the building, and we will see you shortly outside."

The crowd dispersed, heading to the verandah to watch the fireworks display Alexis and Aerianna had arranged. It was not the kind you would watch on Earth.

No, this was a magical fireworks show carried out with the help of Florenzzah Lovecraft and a team of Witches. It would be spectacular. The fireworks looked similar to those on Earth, but this type formed into animated scenes carefully chosen by Alexis. Some of the visual displays represented famous places on Alstromia, the Royal Family, the Command Staff, and more. Music accompanied the show, with the famous Viollah Grackenbone performing on a makeshift stage.

The evening was dark, but the two moons shone brightly in the sky. Viollah Grackenbone stood on an elevated platform, wearing a stunning, bright red, flowing gown. Her curly black hair cascaded down her back. She was a stunningly gorgeous Witch. Her dark skin shimmered like magic under the iridescent glow of the moons. Then, suddenly, the fireworks show began, and Viollah approached the microphone and began singing her famous song, *"Alstromia, Our Home."* Her voice brought chills to many. It was enchanting.

Alexis loved the song, swaying back and forth with her eyes closed, thinking about Andreh, wishing he held her. She felt arms wrap around her waist, desiring it was Andreh, but knowing it was Armbruster. He put on a front for the crowd, wishing to show everyone he and the Queen were deeply in love and, hopefully, dispelling the rumors of her affair. Alexis did not resist his embrace.

Instead, she continued to fantasize about Andreh, allowing Armbruster his glory and fake love connection for all to see as Viollah began belting out a new song, *"We Will Win,"* a song performed at the beginning of the Battle Rounds. It immediately elicited excitement from the high-spirited crowd, now chanting the Battle Rounds' famous words, *"Glory to the Victor, Glory to Alstromia."* The attendees cheered as beautiful scenes flashed across the night sky from the explosive fireworks. It was a successful and fun-filled night that no one would forget.

Twenty minutes later, the show ended with a spectacular finale. Viollah fished her performance by singing, *"We Will Prevail,"* another song performed at the Battle Rounds.

When the night's events were complete, Alexis, Armbruster, and the Command Staff headed toward the carriages to fly back to the Palace. Watching the Royal Family members depart by Torrin-Pulled wagons was part of the annual tradition.

Once the Royal Family departed, the rest of the group disbursed, heading back to the Inn's or Clan members' huts for the night before attending the Battle Rounds in the morning.

Alexis exited the carriage at the Palace entrance and sauntered toward her chamber. She could have more easily transported herself using magic, but wanted the fresh air and mind-clearing time by walking. Armbruster stayed behind, chatting with Yarlen and his wife, Sonia. Pauto and Aerianna happily strolled, hand in hand, toward the Palace.

Back in her chamber, after changing into her nightgown, Alexis covered up with the fluffy blanket, feeling tired and melancholy. She never had the opportunity to see Andreh again that night, which saddened her greatly. She wondered if she could fall asleep because he was heavily on her mind.

At the other end of the Palace, Andreh entered his small room and stripped down to his undergarments. He quickly dressed in his sleeping attire and crawled into bed without showering. He was too tired to care. Plus, he was miserable, missing Alexis. Andreh hated that their time together was over. As he drifted off to sleep, he smiled, reminiscing about Alexis and her beauty. He envisioned kissing her, listening to her laughter, standing by her side in the basement as they worked on potions, and so much more. It was a beautiful dream.

CHAPTER 7

Alexis leaned back in bed, unable to fall asleep. She held a photograph of Andreh in her hand. It was his official picture for the Command Staff Team Roster. She wondered if Andreh had returned to the Palace. Looking outside, she considered heading to the basement dungeon to visit Trixxie.

The week before, Alexis arranged Trixxie's relocation with the help of Andreh, Pauto, and two other commoners. Alexis flew Trixxie to the Palace in the middle of the night, hoping to evade nosy guards.

Pauto had been enlisted to help keep the guards away from the Palace dungeon area. Alexis landed near the eastern part of the Palace by the pond leading to the River of Miccay. She knew Trixxie needed water near her, and the basement had direct access to the water. It was perfect.

Now, Trixxie resided in one of the dungeons at the bottom of the Palace, and Alexis was thrilled. It allowed her more contact with Trixxie, and the beast did not seem to mind her new home. At first, Trixxie was slightly depressed, but she quickly adapted and became accustomed to her new surroundings. With Trixxie living in the Palace, Alexis trained daily with her for the Battle Rounds and Race, mainly in the depths of the night.

Finally tired enough to sleep, Alexis waved her hand, casting magic to close her heavy curtains, blocking the twin moons' bright light. She wanted to summon Karita to add more Trimber logs to the fire, but chose to perform another spell instead. She was too exhausted to deal with the girl this late at night. Alexis lacked patience.

Within minutes, she snored lightly, dreaming of riding Trixxie, flying through the air, her hair whipping in her face as she giggled happily.

Armbruster gazed intently at Yarlen. "We are NOT going to do that. Do you understand? I've done everything in my power to suppress the rumors. I'm finished discussing this. It's settled. Handle whatever needs to be done to ensure everything runs smoothly. Tomorrow, I will be by Alexis's side, playing the role of her devoted husband. You need to locate Andreh and instruct him to come to me first thing in the morning. I want to tell him what will happen next." Armbruster slumped in his chair, feeling exhausted. It was the middle of the night, and he was still awake. Yarlen looked worn out, too. His eyes were bloodshot, and he nodded off to sleep, jumping when he realized it was happening.

"Yes, Armbruster, I understand your command. I will obey. It will be done. Rest assured. May I head to my chamber? I am dreadfully tired and wish to retire."

"Of course. I am so sorry to have kept you. Please, get your rest. Tomorrow will be an early and busy day. We start at 8 a.m. with breakfast. Please attend."

Armbruster watched as Yarlen excused himself, shuffling out of the room. Exhausted, Armbruster leaned back, closing his eyes. He wondered how he would broach the subject with Andreh, asking him to move back to Earth. Armbruster assumed he would not take it well, probably whining and complaining, threatening to speak with Alexis about it.

Nevertheless, Armbruster was aware of the necessary actions and was prepared to go against Alexis. The kingdom required tranquility, and Alexis needed to grasp this. Being a wise Witch, she would come to see that ending her relationship with Andreh right away was essential for the good of both the Clans and Alstromia.

So, Armbruster decided to follow through in the morning, asking Andreh to leave Alstromia. If Andreh chose to fight him, he would be officially banned from the planet, something Armbruster did not want to do.

However, the community's well-being had to take priority, and Andreh would have to make a sacrifice to prove his loyalty to the kingdom. Armbruster headed to his bath chamber to shower and change. He was finally ready to sleep.

Aerianna and Pauto kissed goodnight as they headed to their respective chambers.

Aerianna wished Pauto had accompanied her. She wanted some alone time with him, feeling amorous. Unfortunately, Pauto reminded her of the busyness of the next day and reiterated that he required a good night's rest for work. He hoped Aerianna would be understanding. By the look on her face, he saw she did not agree or understand, but he tried to convince her it was necessary.

After a few minutes of her pouting, Aerianna reluctantly agreed to sleep in separate chambers. Disappointed, she quickly kissed him on the cheek and walked away. Pauto shrugged, feeling bad but knowing it was how it had to be, at least for now.

Angrily, Aerianna slammed her chamber door. She felt hurt that Pauto refused to stay with her for the night. She knew he had much to do in the morning, but wanted him near her.

Aerianna sank onto her bed in frustration, gazing at the ceiling. She couldn't help but wonder what had become of Andreh. The only time she had seen him that night was when he came to pay his respects to the Queen and Armbruster. Additionally, she noticed Shawnatar was missing as well, leaving her curious about his absence.

Aerianna stripped off her clothing and draped them over the chair, deciding to sleep naked under the thick comforter. It did not take long for her to surrender to sleep. The night was quiet, and her chamber was dark, only a dying fire giving off some light. A few hours later, the much-anticipated day finally arrived. It was the beginning of the Battle Rounds.

The Battle Races followed the next day. The morning was hectic. The wait staff placed food on the tables in the large reception hall. The breakfast was the first part of the day, ending with a trip to the top of Tullah Mountain, where the Battle Rounds began.

Alexis' eyes popped open, and she felt excited immediately. She was ready to battle Zandorah. But first, they would watch the lesser-known warriors battle before the advanced group started the main event. The stronger and more elite warriors fought toward the middle of the day.

Therefore, Alexis planned to eat a hearty breakfast and then relax for a while before heading to the Colosseum. Armbruster planned to escort her in her carriage. Aerianna and Pauto would probably arrive at the mountain together. Pauto was scheduled to battle Andreh in the first round of the Elite Battles.

The winner of that battle round would then face Zandorah. The winner of the battle match would then challenge Alexis, since she was still the reigning champion. If Zandorah lost to one of the other opponents, Alexis would still battle Zandorah, as it had been officially announced as the main event. Many Clan members were confused.

Such an event had never happened before. Many speculated it had something to do with their ongoing feud. Nevertheless, the decision was made and announced formally before the event began.

Unfortunately, Zandorah awoke with a debilitating headache, which was not an ideal way to kick off such a significant day. She decided to take a brief shower before having breakfast, hoping to feel better afterward. As minutes ticked by, she found herself gazing at the mirror, getting dressed slowly while her eyes throbbed alongside her head. She wished that Alexis would be understanding and go easy on her during their challenge.

Armbruster and Pauto stood in the Command Chamber, going over the final details of the security measures for the event on Tullah Mountain. Andreh hung back, listening attentively but making sure to stay out of the way. Pauto had explicitly told him to keep his distance from Armbruster, and though Andreh followed the instruction, he felt frustrated that he was sidelined from a job he wanted to be a part of.

The night before, Andreh had erotic dreams about Alexis, but eventually woke up sweaty from having a nightmare. Specifically, it was a nightmare about Armbruster, expelling him from Alstromia. It was absurd. *'Why would he do that?'* Andreh wondered, considering he planned on leaving willingly. However, he had not yet informed anyone of his plans.

Andreh still hoped to share that information with Pauto after the Alexis and Zandorah battle later in the day. The event calendar had the epic battle listed as today or tomorrow, depending on the other smaller challenges and competitions taking place beforehand.

Armbruster left with Yarlen and a few others. Pauto walked to the back of the room to chat with Andreh. "So, what are your plans for the day? We will battle later this afternoon. Are you ready?" Pauto teased, hoping to change the mood in the room. He wondered if Andreh was nervous.

"Yes, I am prepared. Ready to kick your butt," Andreh teased back. He realized how much he would miss Pauto once he left for Earth. They had been close and such great friends. Now, with Alexis between them, it became awkward and downright awful.

Andreh wanted to apologize to Pauto but figured he would wait until later, right before giving him the news about his upcoming plans. The two laughed, and Pauto placed his hand on Andreh's shoulder.

"Listen, Andreh. I know we have been through a lot lately. I want you to know how much I still respect you. You are a great Wizzard, and I know your future is bright. I am so sorry everything has become so skewed. I hope you find happiness. I mean it."

"I believe you, Pauto. You have always been a loyal friend, and I am grateful and forever in your debt. I realized you have been there for me, even with everything that has happened. I am sorry. I understand that the situation has made your job harder. Please know that I am working on resolving it."

Pauto smiled and nodded. He left the room, heading to his chamber to change his attire for the Battle Rounds, eager to start. Andreh followed shortly after Pauto but headed to the stables. He planned to jump on his Torrin and fly for a while, mostly to clear his head and make a concrete plan for his future. One that would not include the one he loved the most.

Alexis turned abruptly at the sight of him, captivated by his striking good looks. She gripped Elannah's reins, poised for takeoff.

Andreh approached, a smile lighting up his face. He had no idea she would be at the stables, but the thought suddenly struck him - it made perfect sense. Flying eased her tension and lifted her spirits.

"Hello, beautiful," he said, leaning against a tall post. He immediately noticed Alexis looked melancholy, which was odd.

"Hey, Andreh. How are you feeling? Are you ready to take on Pauto? He seems pretty sure he's going to win. What's your take on that?" she asked, gently stroking Elannah's head.

"Bets have him winning. But never count out the underdog. I have been training with three of my friends. So, we will see how it ends. How about you? Ready to face your sister? Apparently, you are stressed, or you wouldn't be here ready to fly?"

Alexis contemplated his words. Without a word, she jumped on Elannah's back. "Join me. I am heading to Highgrove Mountain. I want some time to relax away from everyone before the battles. I informed the security team to stay away. But you may join me if you like." Her look implied she wasn't asking.

Instead, she demanded that Andreh join her. He marched toward the stables and asked Essten to retrieve Fangoh, his Torrin. Minutes later, the pair flew off toward Highgrove Mountain.

A smile appeared on Essten's face. He was happy to see Alexis flying. Her life had been chaotic the last few years. First, the kidnapping of her baby, then she was kidnapped by Gardone, her father, in an attempt to take the kingdom away from her. What Alexis had been through was unbelievable, making him wonder how she managed to keep her sanity.

Essten had heard the rumors about Andreh and Alexis and found them absurd. There was no way the Queen would lower her standards and have an affair with him when she was married to Armbruster. Essten laughed at the ridiculousness as he returned to his office at the end of the large stable building.

Alexis beat Andreh and landed on a large open field filled with tall winter Bloomitz. Their yellow and bright-red colors looked beautiful. There were also a few rare orange-colored ones with brown stripes. Alexis allowed Elannah to roam around, eating the grasses and Bloomitz as a snack. Andreh tied Fangoh to a large Trimber, knowing his Torrin would take off if he left him to wander.

Minutes later, Andreh and Alexis sat in the middle of the large field, staring at the sky. The twin moons sparkled, and the sky was a vibrant teal color. Alexis finally broke the silence.

"Why don't you come to me at night? I have not seen you in weeks. I miss you. I desire your touch. It hurts me that you choose to stay away." She stared at him and felt bitter.

Andreh was at a loss. He did not know what to say to Alexis. She knew why he stayed away. *'Why is she torturing me by implying that I do not love her?'* he wondered. Andreh loved her more than she would ever know! That is why he stayed away—to make things easier.

Alexis waited for him to speak, growing increasingly impatient. She chewed on her lip to the point of drawing some blood. Realizing how much it hurt, she winced slightly, wiping away the droplets of blood.

Andreh noticed and immediately handed her a handkerchief. She shook her head, refusing it. He rolled his eyes, displeased.

"What do you want me to say, Alexis? I am here with you now. Is that not good enough? Pauto specifically instructed me to stay away from you and Armbruster. He made it clear that it would be wise to avoid any fallout, and I definitely don't want any trouble. This is simply the best approach. I hope you understand. Please don't be angry with me. I'm truly trying my hardest."

Alexis fumed. *'How dare he act so callously? Does he not care about me at all?'* she pondered.

"I see. You want everything to be easy. Yeah, it gets a bit complicated, and you run—

like a coward! Is that what you want? Let's be clear. I have fought for you. I am doing everything I can to find a solution. I am NOT willing to give you up without a fight." Alexis began crying again.

This time, Andreh scooted beside her and held her as she leaned against him, shaking. He felt awful. This is not how he wanted this important day to go, not at all.

"Alexis, please…" Andreh began. Before finishing his sentence, she kissed him passionately, grabbing and pulling him closer to her. Andreh could smell her, and he became weak; reciprocating the kiss, loving her lips on his. He wished they could stay on the mountain forever, forgetting about how messed up everything had become.

Pauto entered the dimly lit dungeon to ensure Trixxie was fed. He had spoken to Alexis, and she asked him to take care of the beast while she took a quick flight on Elannah to calm down. Pauto knew a lot was happening in Alexis's life and did not wish to complicate things further. So, reluctantly, he agreed to care for the creature.

Pauto wondered how Alexis planned to bring her to the Colosseum. *'Will she fly Trixxie to the top of Tullah Mountain? Or will she simply transport her using magic? Probably the latter since it would be less noticeable. Plus, where does Alexis plan on keeping Trixxie? The rest of the participants will keep their beasts, all Braggli's, in the stable.'* Trixxie was way too large and tall to fit into the stable. *'Well, it is not my worry,'* Pauto thought. *'It is her problem.'* He complied with Alexis's request, taking care of Trixxie and making sure she was all set for the race.

Tullah Mountain was a bustling place of pure energy. Commoners worked feverishly to finish decorating and setting up snack stands. The Manor was ready to receive VIPs as well.

The judges for the Battles and Races had arrived and were seated in the conference room in the Manor, discussing the final details before the events.

Armbruster was at the Manor with Yarlen. Sonia, Yarlen's wife, and their son Garlow were also in attendance. Yarlen's son had been residing on Earth against his wishes.

Garlow, always selfish, decided to stay in New England and spend his life relaxing with fellow Warlocks. He had accomplished very little in his life to date. Garlow was considered lazy and uneducated, which seemed strange given his father's job.

Sonia hoped that Garlow would return to Alstromia and work with his father in time.

But it had not yet happened. He refused to come home to Alstromia, preferring the company of unscrupulous Warlocks tied to Gardone.

These Warlocks lacked ethics and were known to take on jobs, usually involving sinister plots. Yarlen hated that his son was involved with these individuals. Many were banned from Alstromia and Iriss because they were characterized as evil.

Garlow had always followed the wrong crowd, something Yarlen and Sonia despised. Garlow was born on Earth, not wanting to attend formal schooling on Alstromia, such as *Alstromia Magical Learning Academy (AMLA)* or the *Academy for Dark Magic and Spells* on Earth. Garlow acted defiant and headstrong. Some saw him as a rebel. Most felt sorry for Yarlen and Sonia because Garlow was considered a failure and an embarrassment.

Yet, Garlow did not care what others thought. He was determined to make his own way, no matter what it took. He refused the help Yarlen or Sonia offered.

Alexis Snipperdoom had even offered him several jobs in the past, and he adamantly declined her offers, stating he was not interested in manual labor. Highly offended, Alexis informed Yarlen to get his son in check before she ordered him to attend educational courses.

In time, Garlow moved away from Alstromia. He was tired of the harassment from his parents, figuring it was effortless living on Earth, away from the scrutiny and pressure. He wanted to live his life the way he wanted. Garlow became close friends with Bartin and Korbin, both troublemakers. The unfortunate bond he held with the two individuals signaled future problems, which worried Yarlen greatly.

Aerianna was still pouting when Pauto came to her chamber in the morning to speak with her before heading to the Manor. Aerianna was sad that he was not planning to accompany her to the mountain. She despised going alone. So, rather than fly, Aerianna slammed down her Sun Ceptre and transported herself to the Manor. Alexis would arrive shortly, so everything had to be running smoothly.

Pauto noticed Aerianna's approach. He was happy she arrived, but was keenly aware he had little time to spend with her. "Hello!" he said as he kissed her quickly on the cheek.

"I need an update for Alexis. How are things going? Is everything on schedule? Have any unforeseen things popped up that I need to be made aware of before she grills me?" Aerianna was nervous.

Alexis would probably be bitchy and anxious. Aerianna knew it would come down to yelling and threats later. She hoped to avoid that as much as possible. That is why she pleaded with Pauto for updates. Hopefully, he and his team were prepared for the large crowd.

"Well, yes. There is a problem. Let's head to the security room in the back. I don't want others to overhear the conversation." Pauto expeditiously led Aerianna down the long corridor toward the security room. No one was inside, and he closed the door quickly.

"What I am about to tell you, you cannot share with anyone. I just had a conversation with Rammadar. His team received some rather disturbing news. Supposedly, Gardone is here, on Alstromia. No one on my team has sighted him yet. However, it makes me worry. I cannot help but wonder if he is trying to start something again. He is a wanted Warlock. I hoped he would stay away. If we find him, we will lock him up."

Aerianna was shocked. "Are you absolutely sure about the information? Why would Gardone make an appearance here? He will most likely be caught! That makes no sense. Oh boy. Do you plan to inform Armbruster? Will you tell Alexis? What will you do?" screamed Aerianna, now panicked.

Pauto pondered her words. "No. I am not yet planning to sound an alarm. I am still unsure if Gardone is here. Rammadar and I have both our security details searching the area. No one will suspect anything since this event is always at a higher level of security." Pauto leaned against the door. He could hear his pulse pounding in his ears. Swoosh, swoosh, swoosh.... The sound was making him nauseous.

Aerianna noticed Pauto looked ill. "Babe, what can I do? Are you feeling okay?" She stood before him. His eyes were closed, and his head rested on the door.

"No, I am okay. I am stressed. Do not worry. Why don't you get ready for Alexis and guarantee Zandorah is here? The Battle Rounds will begin in less than an hour." He attempted to smile, but his facial expression made it clear he was not okay.

Aerianna nodded and gently moved him away from the door so she could exit. Pauto was not handling the news well, and she needed to step up and take over some of the responsibilities.

Armbruster yelled at Yarlen when Aerianna approached. Yarlen looked angry and shook his head. *'Something has happened,'* Aerianna thought nervously. *'If Alexis sees this, she will lose her mind!'*

"Hey, you two need to calm down. Everyone can hear you. That is not good! What has happened?" Aerianna questioned.

"Yarlen just informed me he heard a rumor that Gardone could be on Alstromia. I want him found. Yarlen suggests we let it go and not even bring it up to Alexis. I'm afraid I have to disagree. We must inform her," barked Armbruster. He had sweat beads on his forehead, and his eyes were watery from yelling and being stressed out.

"Okay. Can we please lower our voices? Yes, I heard that too. I have to side with Yarlen on this one. We shouldn't disturb Alexis unless we have solid proof that Gardone is on the planet. There's no need to make her anxious and uneasy before the Battles. That is totally uncalled for. We will NOT do that." Aerianna asserted, standing her ground. She planned to shield Alexis from the rumors. It would only make her more nervous before the battle.

The other two Wizzards stared at her. They had never seen Aerianna act so forcefully. She was usually quite accommodating, preferring to remain neutral.

"Also, while we are at it, why don't you both get ready for the event and stop gossiping? You are adding fuel to the fire unnecessarily. Please, stop it. I must insist." Aerianna turned around and walked away, leaving the two speechless. Yarlen began laughing because he felt that was the most fantastic thing to happen in a long time.

Aerianna walked away, smiling. She had not been that self-confident in a while. It made her happy. She figured it was time to locate Alexis and see how she was doing. Aerianna was hopeful Alexis had not heard the hearsay about her father. It would make her nervous and ruin the mood for the upcoming battles.

Gardone held a lengthy discussion with Korbin and Bartin in the cabin. They were the only ones inside the building. Gardone figured Alexis would not be staying at the house anytime soon after what had happened there. Gardone reiterated his intent to find Lorthana and speak with her.

Hopefully, Lorthana would not turn him over to the guards or the Security Command Team. He assumed she would listen to what he had to say. Gardone wanted his life back and planned to ask his wife for a Dismissal of the Ceremony to formally dissolve their marriage.

Gardone had moved on from his feelings for Lorthana. His heart had found a new home with someone else —a younger Witch living on Earth who was always mindful of his needs. Sharlottah Zipmound offered him refuge when no one else would. Gardone affectionately referred to her as Shar, and although Shar understood that Gardone was not as pure as he pretended to be, her dislike for Alexis fueled her determination to keep him safe.

The trumpets sounded on the top of Tullah Mountain. It was the official ten-minute warning. The Battle Rounds were about to commence.

"Alexis, we must head back. I wish we had more time together, but it is time."

"I know. I was hoping we could stay a while longer. I have missed you terribly. Okay, let's retrieve our Torrins and return," Alexis agreed reluctantly. They swiftly mounted the beasts and zoomed off.

A few minutes later, Alexis handed her Torrin to a commoner as she walked toward the building. She was ready to battle and planned to kick Zandorah's royal butt. Alexis approached the giant stadium, feeling confident. She wore her famous battle warrior uniform.

The dark-blue sparkly pants were securely tucked into her maroon and salmon-colored, tall boots. The magenta, purple-lined cape was wrapped around her shoulders with a hood covering part of her head. She held the

Wand of Grimleah in her right hand. Her hair was tied in sections into a long braid, secured with tiny red rhinestones. Her waist was cinched with a wide belt, which also helped stabilize her back, and she completed her uniform with thin fur-lined gloves. As always, she wore her signature bright red lipstick and nail polish. Alexis looked battle-ready. She was a Warrior Queen!

CHAPTER 8

The Colosseum's deafening roar was historic. Yarlen removed the structure's glass dome using magic to allow for an open venue. The enthusiastic crowd clapped and chanted. It was an event everyone was excited to witness. The first group was about to begin the battles—they were newly trained, and the less experienced battle group—informally referred to as the warm-up team.

Yet, the group received a warm welcome as they entered the center of the Battle Colosseum. The famous red circle, where two warriors battled, was ready. The judges encircled the area in tall seats to allow them a spectacular view, letting them call the matches as they saw them.

The music blared, and the opening song sung by Viollah Grackenbone was *"Alstromia, Our Home."* The next song followed, eliciting more chanting from the crowd as they listened to Viollah sing *"Glory to the Victor, Glory to Alstromia."* The final third song, *"We Will Win,"* finished, and the group went wild, clapping, stomping their feet, chanting her name. Viollah bowed gracefully, then waved to the attendees as she walked toward her seat on the first row of the Battle Colosseum.

Alexis advanced to the podium and addressed the attendees. "Welcome! Thank you all for coming to witness the battles in person. It will be an exciting few days. Also, please be sure to stick around and watch the Battle Races. I have an exciting surprise to share with everyone! Now, let's welcome the young battle warriors. The first two will begin now!" Alexis walked away, allowing the first two battle warriors to enter the circle. The crowd loudly stomped their feet while chanting, "Go, go, go."

Alexis approached Armbruster and slumped down on the bench next to him to watch the match. He scooted closer and whispered into her ear. "What surprises do you plan to reveal during the Battle Races? You have not told me anything!" He was hurt.

"Well, Armbruster, if I told you, it wouldn't be much of a surprise, would it now? You will have to wait just like everyone else," she snidely responded as she moved away from him and sat closer to Aerianna.

Aerianna had no clue what Alexis planned to reveal, and she did not care either. Her surprises were often not good ones. It usually caused issues or quite a commotion. So, as far as she was concerned, Alexis could keep her secret for a few more days.

In the meantime, Aerianna vowed to focus on Pauto and his upcoming battle with Andreh. She wondered if he planned to take it easy on Andreh or if he wanted to destroy him. She assumed it was the latter. Pauto confided in her that he was agitated with Andreh and planned to teach him a lesson. Aerianna thought that perhaps the battles would be how he would initiate the action. Though she wasn't sure, Pauto was a gentleman, and maybe he would still change his mind.

The two battle warriors faced each other, only equipped with one item. They had the choice of a wand, a Ceptre, or a blade. Though you were not allowed to kill your opponent, you were permitted to inflict harm.

The rules and guidelines for battles outlined the details of how much pain you could enforce. Also, the warrior was not allowed to inflict so much pain that the other warrior passed out unless it was unintentional harm.

A trumpet blared, initiating the first round. The tall, thin warrior aimed his wand at the opponent, expeditiously casting a spell. Before the other opponent could react, he became frozen. He stood straight, looking around, unable to move. The tall warrior then walked up to the husky, shorter warrior and zapped him with his wand, casting a *Lightning Spell* that burned like fire.

Instantly, the husky warrior became unfrozen and shook his head briefly, looking confused. He lunged at the tall warrior, grabbing his wand and snapping it in half. The tall warrior ran in circles, attempting to avoid the short, husky warrior. The crowd started booing. The negative response from the group caused the burly warrior to react violently, slamming himself on top of the tall warrior.

Once the opponent was incapacitated, he aimed his wand at the tall warrior's head, casting his final magic—a *Sleep Spell.* The husky warrior then victoriously chanted, "I am the victor," to which the stadium attendees erupted with applause. The judges agreed and pronounced *"Karl, the Killer,"* the first-round winner.

Yarlen approached the microphone near the judges. "There you have it. Round 1 goes to *Karl, the Killer.* He is a first-year battle warrior. Let's give him a round of applause for that amazing battle show of strength and endurance!"

The stadium became louder again, with W3s chanting Karl's name. After a few minutes, Yarlen spoke again: "Witches, Warlocks, and Wizzards. Let us welcome the second group. *Scorching Sara* from Earth will face off against her opponent from Iriss—*Charming Carrlee.*

Yarlen sat down as the two Witches began their battle. Alexis looked bored, and she scanned the crowd, looking for Andreh. His match against Pauto was scheduled to start after lunch.

It was now almost 11 a.m., and the battle was turning brutal. *Scorching Sara* was covered in blood. *Charming Carrlee* tripped her, and Sara face-planted on the hard stone ground. She split open her forehead and bottom lip. Yet, she continued to cast one spell after another, inflicting equal pain on her adversary. After less than ten minutes, *Scorching Sara* knocked *Charming Carrlee* out, using an old-fashioned move of punching her in the head. Immediately, the judges proclaimed Sara the victor of the round. She would now face off against *Karl, the Killer*, in this session's next and final round. First, she would be allowed a ten-minute break to get cleaned up and have a medical assessment to ensure she was battle-ready to face off against Karl.

Aerianna stood up and walked to one of the vendor's stands to purchase two brews—one for her and one for Alexis. When she returned, Alexis smiled, taking a sip from the tall, Ozar tumbler, realizing it was a concoction from Henrii Snubberly's team. He made the tastiest of all brews.

Minutes later, Yarlen stood before the microphone, making another announcement. "Here we are again, friends. This is the exciting moment when we finally discover which first-year battle warrior will be crowned *Battle Victor YR 1* this year. Please help me welcome *Scorching Sara* and *Karl, the Killer*. Both have chosen only to use wands and spells to keep it fair."

Sara approached the red circle first. Karl entered and bowed to Sara. She reciprocated. The group in the stadium went wild. Some chanted Sara's name while others screamed Karl's. The trumpet blared, and Sara quickly flicked her wrist, releasing a spell to knock

Karl on his butt. Shocked it happened so fast, he attempted to get on his feet.

Unfortunately, Sara was much more limber, jumping over him, turning around, casting more magic, causing him to fall again, this time face down onto the ground. He screamed in pain, dropping his wand.

Sara attempted to grab it, but Karl tricked her, stopping her by groping her leg, causing her to fall on her side, dropping her wand. He swiftly jumped up and stood over her, screaming, *"Incapacitate,"* aiming his wand at her. Sara looked like a frozen statue, unable to move. He then took her wand and broke it into pieces, ensuring she would no longer have the ability to use it.

Before casting another spell to release her, he looked at the judges and yelled, "I am the victor. Declare it so!" The judges agreed, and *Karl, the Killer,* instantly became *Victor YR 1 Battle Warrior.* Worried he had harmed Sara, he walked to her side and helped her stand, handing her the broken wand pieces and giving her a gentle bear hug. The W3s erupted, chanting their names. The two had put on quite a battle for the energetic crowd watching.

Alexis fidgeted with her hair, angry she could not locate Andreh. She wanted the opportunity to speak with him before he faced off against Pauto. Alexis knew a few moves that would help Andreh defeat Pauto, even though he was considered the underdog in the upcoming battle.

However, Andreh would not need her advice or strategy tips as he already had a few ideas up his sleeve, having watched Pauto battle against Alexis during their training sessions in the past. He noticed some of Pauto's weaknesses, which he planned to expose during their match. Andreh sat patiently in one of the Battle Stand-By Rooms in the Manor. He looked at his notes and read the enchanting words he planned to use against Pauto during their battle.

Andreh stayed awake late the night before, researching the best and most powerful spells to use, hopefully incapacitating Pauto. The younger group, the *Victor YR 1 Battle Warriors,* were not privy to the complex chants and magic allowed during battle. Andreh knew of several and was ready to release them upon Pauto without fear of repercussions.

Pauto paced outside the Manor, unable to sit still. He knew his battle against Andreh would be impressive. Pauto hoped Alexis had not coached Andreh in any way. Andreh was very talented, but Pauto was the more experienced and wiser warrior. He had more battles under his belt. His training with Alexis made him realize he had improved his skills and was more prepared than before. Pauto's new physical training exercises helped him become more muscular and able to inflict more pain on his opponent. Andreh was well-built, too, but he was much shorter. He hoped Andreh would become a fierce challenger, if for no other reason than to put on a good show at the event.

★*.★*.★*.★*.★

The Security Command Team encircled the Battle Colosseum on their Torrins. Suddenly, one of the leaders directed his Torrin to dive down quickly to the ground. The other members looked perplexed. One after another, they swiftly followed. The young Warlock pushed his Torrin toward the stables. He saw something that alerted him.

At the stables, Gardone handed the Torrin to Bartin. "Alright. You know where I will be. Please be ready." Gardone strode away. Suddenly, he heard a noise and looked up. He saw a group of Warriors on Torrins approaching the stables. Fearing for his safety, he quickly ran into the nearby woods, hoping they would not notice him.

"Fan out. I know I saw Gardone. He is here. I am heading to the stadium to find Armbruster and let him know. Be careful. Pauto warned us that Gardone is gifted and will use magic to escape and harm anyone getting in his way," announced the young Warlock. He took hold of the Torrin's reins and directed the beast to the other side of the area to find Armbruster.

Gardone made it into a thickly wooded forest area off to the stadium's east. He was sweaty, tired from running, and confused about how someone spotted him so quickly, believing he had been stealthy. Gardone slammed down his Ceptre and transported himself back to the cabin, scared he may have underestimated the number of scouts looking for him.

"Sir, I need a moment of your time. Immediately." The young Warlock insisted, approaching Armbruster. The King frowned but realized it had to be an urgent matter for this scout to show up and be so insistent.

Armbruster led the Warlock to a chamber in the back of the Manor. "What is it? Who are you?" Armbruster grilled him.

"Sir, my name is Charter Casterling. I was assigned to your scout unit. I am from Earth. Rammadar hired me. I believe I saw Gardone by the stables. I have ordered the other scouts to find him. I wanted you to know right away. I worry for the Queen's safety."

"Rightfully so. I am worried as well. Thank you for letting me know. Is he alone? What was he wearing when you saw him last?" Armbruster interrogated.

"Sir, it was definitely him. He was wearing his signature purple and black cloak. I saw the famous ring on his finger. I was close enough to see him. He must have cast a *Spell Block,* as I could not follow him into the woods. Sir, what are your orders?" Charter asked, standing at attention.

"Find Pauto. Give an alert to the security personnel, but try to be discreet. I do not want our visitors to know what is happening. Also, please—no one inform the Queen. She is set to battle shortly, and I do NOT want her distracted. Do you hear me?" Armbruster wanted to find Pauto himself. He also wanted to ask for Andreh's help and hopefully enlist Rammadar.

Charter left swiftly to find Pauto and Rammadar. He assumed Pauto would be near Aerianna at the Colosseum. As he approached the stands, he noticed Pauto chatting with Andreh. Charter walked up to them and leaned close to Pauto, whispering into his ear. Immediately, Pauto pulled back.

"Oh my gosh, are you sure? Who sent you? Follow me. Andreh, please join us." The three strode off toward a chamber by the rear entrance of the Colosseum.

"Okay, this is a secure room. Tell me. Who are you, and how did you acquire this information?" Pauto interrogated sternly.

"My name is Charter Casterling. Armbruster requested that I find you to share the information I came across. Rammadar hired me. We were tasked to patrol the stadium's exterior, looking for anything unusual. We were briefed yesterday that Gardone may be on Alstromia. Rammadar asked us to keep an eye out for him. I saw Gardone's Torrin flying toward the stables. I also noticed he walked quickly into the woods alone. I attempted to catch up with him, but I hit an invisible shield and was pushed away as I approached the wooded area. I assume a *Block Spell* was cast. I immediately returned here, hoping to find you and Rammadar. I await your instructions, Sir," Charter bellowed. He hoped Pauto would be impressed by his forcefulness.

"Calm down, young man. I appreciate your enthusiasm, but we must be quiet. We do not want to panic anyone. So, I would like you to locate Rammadar and bring him here. Can you do that?" Pauto asked.

"Yes, Sir. I will be back shortly. Thank you." Charter left Andreh and Pauto alone in the secure room. Pauto paced around, talking to himself.

After a few minutes, Andreh stood before him. "Pauto, what do you want to do? We cannot wait all day for Rammadar and Charter to return. Let's alert Aerianna and Yarlen.

I do not believe we should involve the Queen yet." Andreh observed Pauto as he stared off into the distance.

"Yes, you are correct. I shall find Armbruster and speak with him. Please stay here and wait for Charter to return. Once I have spoken with Armbruster, I will come back here. Okay?" Pauto clarified. He exited the building and pulled his wand from his waist, casting a spell. Immediately, he stood before Armbruster, who appeared taken aback.

"Pauto, where have you been? Did you hear? Gardone has been sighted. What will we do?" Armbruster grilled him.

"Sir, I just found out. Thank you for sending the scout my way. Yes, we must alert the rest of the Security Command Team and cast a spell to hinder anyone from leaving Alstromia. I will find Florenzzah Lovecraft and request her help." Pauto did not wait for a response from Armbruster. Instead, he vanished using magic.

Within seconds, Pauto stood before Florenzzah's hut. She disliked crowds and sizeable events, and even though she had been invited to the Battle Rounds, she turned down the offer and remained on the mountaintop in her hut. Pauto knocked forcefully on her door, calling out her name. A few seconds later,

Florenzzah opened the door, smiling as if she had predicted his visit.

"Come on in, Pauto. I know why you are here. I saw it this morning in my *Book of Insight*. It directed me to display the reason you are here. Gardone has reappeared. He seeks revenge. You must keep the Queen and the Royal Family safe. Also, Lorthana is at risk. He wants to speak with her. Why, I am not sure. Is that why you are here?"

"Wow, we certainly constantly underestimate you, Florenzzah. Yes, that is precisely why I am here. Armbruster and I feel we need to secure the planet with magic. We hope you can help. Do you have any idea what will work best? We do not want him to be able to escape."

"Pauto, let's sit down and discuss this further. I am old, and my body is weak." She walked to her fluffy chair by the fireplace and plopped down, holding her Ceptre, which she used as a cane for support. Pauto knew she had something up her sleeve, so he planned to wait and see what it was.

Alexis paced around in one of the Battle Stand-By-Rooms in the Manor. She felt restless, like a cat stalking its next victim. Except she knew her opponent well. She contemplated the battle between Andreh and

Pauto. She wanted to watch their battle match but was scared she would be biased, and others would notice. Alexis ultimately decided to forgo watching their game and reluctantly chose to stay in the room, hoping to remain calm.

Andreh heard the trumpets and knew he had to head for the Stand-By-Rooms. It was almost time to fight against Pauto. He assumed Rammadar would be in charge of the search efforts while they battled. As Andreh approached the door to enter the room, he heard sobbing. He gently knocked. A woman's voice, one he recognized, shouted, "Enter."

"What are you doing here, Andreh?" Alexis asked. She was surprised and delighted to see him, but preferred he leave.

"I am here to prepare for my round that will start shortly. Have you seen Pauto? No one has seen him in over an hour."

"No. I have been in this room, attempting to remain calm. I am nervous about battling Zandorah. It will divide us even more, and I do not want that for my mother's sake," Alexis explained while pacing around the room restlessly.

"I see. Well, maybe you should sit down and relax. You will not have any energy to fight if you keep this up. I will leave you to it. I must locate Pauto." Andreh rushed toward the door, ready to exit, when Alexis flung her arms around him. She pulled him toward her, and he turned around. Alexis kissed and grabbed him, breathing heavily into his neck.

"Stay with me. I need you. I always need you, Andreh," she whispered.

"You know damn well I cannot stay. I have to go. I love you, Alexis, but...I did not want to tell you right now, before the battles, but...I am leaving. I am returning to Earth. I have decided to depart Alstromia so you and Armbruster can rebuild your family. Once things are going well between you, I may return. For now, I have to go. Seeing you and not being with you is literally killing me. Please understand."

"Like hell you will. You are NOT leaving. I already told Armbruster you would not be shunned and absolutely will not return to Earth. I will NOT allow it. Andreh, please, do not do this to me. Promise me that you will stay. We will work something out. I cannot survive if you leave," Alexis pleaded, crying.

Andreh did not want to upset her, especially since she would soon battle. He decided to lie to her and tell her he would stay. But something in her eyes told him she did not believe him.

"Andreh, do not lie to me. I know you. You do not need to shield me. I can handle the truth. If you truly wish to depart the planet, then go. Just know, it is not what I want."

Reluctantly, Andreh released her hand and pulled away from her as he walked out the door. He planned to locate Pauto. Continuing to stay around Alexis and seeing the disappointment on her face made him feel awful. Andreh would figure out how to disappear later, after the match, hopefully without much attention.

Pauto thanked Florenzzah as he swiftly transported himself to the Battle Colosseum. He did not want to be late for his battle with Andreh. Florenzzah reassured him the planet would be secure shortly, and Gardone could not counter her magical abilities. She stood by her round cauldron as he left, making a foul-smelling potion to use with a spell. Pauto felt confident she was the right Witch to complete the job.

Pauto approached the building and ran into Andreh. "There you are. I was coming to look for you. It is almost time to begin the battle round. Are you battle-ready?" joked Andreh. He admired Pauto and was eager to engage him in the battle zone.

"Always, my friend. You'd better be prepared. I am not planning on making it easy for you. You will have to fight for victory."

"Pauto, I wouldn't have it any other way." Andreh laughed, and Pauto joined him. It had been a long time since the two had laughed together, and it felt good.

Andreh had no doubt Pauto was serious. He would definitely challenge him. Somehow, it did not matter if he lost to Pauto. Andreh wanted the battle to be over so he could start the rest of his life on Earth.

Yarlen officially announced that the next Battle Round would begin in 10 minutes. Pauto and Andreh walked together, side by side, toward the arena. Andreh felt his hands becoming clammy. He wanted to win, but more than anything, he hoped Alexis would not be there to watch. He hated the idea of her witnessing his loss to Pauto, especially if it was physically horrible. Pauto was known to be quite aggressive. The last time he trained with Alexis, he split open her forehead. Most likely, it had not been intentional. Nonetheless, he was powerful. So, Andreh prayed she would stay away.

Armbruster listened to Rammadar. "So, no sighting? Are you sure? Can we trust Charter? Could he be mistaken? How do we know it was Gardone?" Ambruster interrogated. He wanted to be sure Gardone was on the planet before informing others.

"Sir, I have known Charter for a while. He is an honest Warlock. I have no reason to believe he would lie or sound an alarm unless he was 100% certain. I am confident he is not mistaken. If he stated he saw Gardone, then I believe it to be true," retorted Rammadar.

The two Warlocks spoke a bit longer while formulating a plan on how to proceed. The decision was made to forgo an announcement until after the final Battle Round. Armbruster did not want to upset Alexis or other Clan members and guests.

In the heart of the forest, Gardone gazed at the Trimber stump and chose to take a seat. He felt weary and didn't expect anyone to recognize him. Strangely, he thought he had used a *Disguise Spell,* but he must have overlooked it in his rush. His mind was on other things, and his main objective was to locate Lorthana and chat with her.

Yarlen approached the microphone and announced a one-hour break before the next battle to allow guests and contestants time to eat and relax. Armbruster asked Yarlen to make the last-minute announcement, hoping it would not elicit questions. Yarlen, once again, reluctantly agreed. Yarlen had been briefed on the supposed Gardone sighting and wished Armbruster would cancel the rest of the day's events. However, Armbruster almost lost his mind when he heard Yarlen's suggestion.

"Are you crazy?" Armbruster bellowed. "We are not canceling anything. Gardone's presence is not going to stop all we have planned. Alexis will lose her temper. We are giving Pauto and Andreh a small break to relax before they battle, since both were part of the search. I believe it is fair to them. The event will go on as planned. Are we clear?"

"Yes, Your Majesty," Yarlen meekly replied, feeling stupid for even making the suggestion. He could see Armbruster's nose flaring. His face was bright red, and he clenched his fists. Yarlen opted to excuse himself and return to the bench in the arena to sit and wait for the next round to begin.

Sonia was still sitting on the stone bench as he approached the area, laughing and looking happy as she talked with their son, Garlow. It was the highlight of Yarlen's day.

Florenzzah cast her complex enchantment in her hut. The green fog in the cauldron turned blood-red. A loud, popping noise emanated from it. She chanted as she waved her bony hands over the kettle, swaying back and forth robotically. A minute later, the sky outside flickered a bright green for a second but quickly returned to its usual color.

Florenzzah cackled with delight, happy she was successful. Now, Armbruster would owe her again. She loved that idea. Feeling proud of her recent accomplishment, she slammed down her Ceptre and transported herself to the Colosseum to ask him how he planned to compensate her. This time, she would be clear about what she demanded, and Armbruster would comply, or she would reverse the magic without a second thought. She was tired of being used by the Royal Family.

CHAPTER 9

No one could deny Alexis was capable of hiding her feelings when she tried. Other times, she wore her emotions on her sleeve, allowing others to see every painstaking moment of her hurt. Today, she planned to keep things to herself until after the last battle round and the official announcement of the Ultimate Winner.

There was no need to introduce more drama into the already volatile environment. After the disturbing conversation with Andreh, she felt perplexed. She never thought he would abandon Alstromia or distance himself from her. Alexis wondered if Armbruster or Pauto were responsible for his sudden departure plans. She wanted to confront them both, but figured it was best to wait. Andreh and Pauto's battle match was about to begin shortly, and she had every intention of sitting in the front row, watching.

Once the battle round ended, Alexis planned to ask Pauto about his involvement in Andreh's sudden urge to escape the planet. Alexis doubted Andreh wanted to leave voluntarily. Instead, he was forced to do so by either Armbruster or Pauto. She sought to find out who was directly responsible. Then, she would have a friendly chat, demanding details, and happily hand out punishment for their participation. She was sick and tired of their meddling.

Lorthana sat patiently next to Zandorah. She noticed her daughter acted nervously, tapping her feet and wringing her hands. Zandorah looked around as if she were searching for someone or something in particular. Lorthana assumed it was either

Alexis or Shawnatar. Sadly, Lorthana had not seen Shawnatar at all since the beginning of the Battle rounds, which was unusual. He was never absent when Zandorah needed him, so his lack of presence was worrisome. Lorthana excused herself and took off toward the Manor, hoping to find Alexis and Armbruster. She wanted to verify if either of them had spotted Shawnatar today.

The noise of trumpets filled the stadium. It was the first of the big battles to begin, the Ultimate Battle Rounds. First up, Pauto and Andreh. Yarlen approached the stand on the Ozar platform, facing the Battle Round Judges, and made the grand announcement to the eager crowd.

"Good afternoon, everyone! We are back from the break and will begin the first big battle of the day. Our first match features Pauto Vexxorth and Andreh Darkhill. These two exemplary warriors have matched up in the past. Pauto has defeated Andreh in three out of the four matches in the past. Who will be the victor today? Let us welcome the warriors," Yarlen bellowed as he sat down while the crowd chanted the battle-ready warrior names.

Andreh strutted confidently into the middle of the circle, bowing to the Queen, who sat across from him on the first level of the Battle Colosseum. She reluctantly decided to attend the battle. Alexis forced a smile and nodded approvingly.

Next, Pauto joined Andreh, also bowing his head respectfully before Alexis. The Queen acknowledged by lowering her head. The two warriors shook hands and quickly separated into their respective sides of the circle, awaiting the loud gong noise to begin their match.

Alexis leaned forward, eager to see her lover fight against her friend. Armbruster abruptly sat down next to her. He kissed her on the cheek, surprising her.

"Well, hello, dear. Are you ready to watch your lover get annihilated?" teased Armbruster with a wicked smile on his face. He could not wait for Pauto to destroy the little weasel. In the past, Armbruster held great respect for Andreh. Now, with the blatant infidelity, he wanted him gone.

"You assume Andreh will lose. How do you know that? I have trained with him for months. He is quite capable. I would love to place a wager. What do you say?" Alexis retorted, smirking. She hoped he would take the bait.

"What is your bet? Tell me first, and I will decide if it is worth it." Armbruster crossed his arms, glaring at Alexis.

"Very well, Armbruster. If Andreh wins against Pauto, he will not be forced to leave

Alstromia. In fact, he will be allowed to remain in his current job without any more harassment from you, Pauto, or anyone else. Is that clear?" Alexis stated. She felt it was a fair wager to make and would allow Andreh to stay on Alstromia. She contemplated whether Armbruster would agree. In the pit of her stomach, she worried he would refuse the bet.

"Ha-ha. Okay. And what if Andreh fails to win? Then what, Alexis?" Armbruster asked, feeling amused at the idea of Pauto losing to Andreh.

"Well, I suppose, if Pauto should win, I will allow Andreh's departure without further interference," Alexis reluctantly agreed. She hoped Andreh did not lose, but realized the odds were stacked against him.

"Okay, we have a deal," Armbruster boldly announced. "I just hope you are ready to send your lover to Earth. Once he is there, he will remain there forever!"

"Andreh can return any time he wishes once the rumors have stopped. I disagree with keeping him away from Alstromia indefinitely. That is NOT going to happen, Armbruster," Alexis replied, now facing him, looking sternly at her husband.

"Very well, Alexis. We have a deal. Shall we shake?" Armbruster rolled his eyes, hoping to piss her off.

"Of course," Alexis said as she shook her husband's hand, quickly dropping it to watch Andreh stretching. She worried now more than ever. This match would determine if Andreh stayed or had to depart for Earth. The thought made her feel woozy. The giant gong near the observers made a loud bong-bong-bong noise, and the two warriors jumped into the middle of the circle.

Immediately, the spectators stomped their feet loudly, chanting the names of Andreh and Pauto while wielding their Ceptres and Wands. The head judge, Kristah Villainnow, announced, shouting for all to hear, "Let the round begin!"

Andreh waited for Pauto to make the first move as he held his wand in his right hand. Pauto lowered his head, looking down at his trousers. He hid the other wand in his boots, just in case something happened to the main wand. The two faced off.

Andreh was tired of waiting and flicked his wrist, casting a *Screecher Spell*. Immediately, Pauto jumped, missing the red bolt that flew off Andreh's Wand. Andreh looked confused. *'How did he manage to evade the stream of light and the Screecher Spell?'* Pauto jumped into the air, aimed his wand toward Andreh's head, and screamed, *"Freezer, Teaser."*

Instantaneously, Andreh froze, unable to move. However, within a few seconds,

Andreh moved because he had anticipated Pauto's go-to move. He previously witnessed Pauto using it against Alexis in the first part of their practice battles. As Pauto aimed his wand, Andreh had already counter-spelled his chant by using a *Release Spell*. It worked perfectly. It also gave Andreh the upper hand. Immediately, Andreh limberly jumped into the air and grabbed Pauto by his neck, incapacitating him.

Andreh withdrew his dagger and held it up against Pauto's neck as he nicked it. Trickles of warm blood ran down Pauto's neck, and he panicked. Instinctively, Pauto elbowed Andreh in the groin, hoping to get away from him.

Andreh doubled over in pain. Instantly, he dropped the dagger and fell onto his knees, head lowered. Pauto stood over him, about to take a swing and punch at Andreh. However, Andreh looked up just in time, and before Pauto could do any other harm to him, he used a *Levitation Spell* and jumped behind Pauto again. This time, he also snagged Pauto's dagger from the back of his pants. Perplexed at how quickly it all happened, Pauto looked around, trying to plan his next move.

Before he had a chance, Andreh slammed Pauto to the ground using all his might. Pauto became incapacitated as Andreh straddled him. Andreh swiftly slid his hands around

Pauto's neck, applying pressure, forcefully choking him, hoping he would pass out from lack of oxygen. The crowd cheered.

Pauto tried to pry Andreh's hands away from his neck. Feeling lightheaded, he dropped his wand. Surprised that Andreh had been so quick and clever, Pauto desperately attempted to arch his back to gain strength and push his opponent off him. Andreh lost his grip, and the two rolled around in the middle of the Colosseum's ground, fighting for survival. It was an intense scene.

Seconds later, Pauto managed to stand and shakily held his recovered wand. As he was about to use it, Andreh cast a powerful spell—*The Blind-Sided Spell,* which caused Pauto to drop to the ground, screaming out in pain, unable to see. Pauto rubbed his eyes, hoping to regain sight.

Andreh casually walked up behind Pauto, believing he had won. Feeling victorious, he was about to take Pauto down in a final, swift move. Unexpectedly, Pauto jumped up, aimed his wand, and tried to freeze Andreh again. However, Andreh expected this move, too. He punched Pauto in the stomach, and as he bent over in pain, still blinded by the previous spell, Pauto aimed his Wand directly at Andreh and hollered, *"Crush and Plow,"* hoping he would be *"plowed"* down by the crushing and excruciating pain.

Unfortunately for Pauto, Andreh anticipated he would use the famous *Crush and Plow Spell*. So, Andreh preemptively cast a *Shield Spell*, which surrounded him, causing the *Crush and Plow Spell* cast by Pauto to ricochet. The stream of white light bounced off the shield and hit Pauto in the head.

Swiftly, Pauto tumbled to the ground, unconscious, blood now oozing and dripping from his head. The spectators went wild, chanting Andreh's name, realizing he had just won the spirited match! It was an exhilarating moment.

Alexis jumped out of her seat, clapping, joining the crowd, yelling, "Andreh the Victor, Andreh has won!" The only one not smiling was Armbruster. He honestly did not believe Andreh stood a chance against Pauto.

Aerianna looked shocked and scared, immediately jumping out of her seat, ready to head to her lover's aid. Lorthana remained seated, surprised at how quickly Andreh defeated Pauto.

The Medical Assessment Team (*MAT*) rushed to check on Pauto. Yarlen arrived first, standing over him, casting an *Awaken Spell*. Within a few seconds, Pauto opened his eyes, confused. He did not realize he had been knocked out, though he felt the ground under his back and saw the sky above.

Pauto stared up at Yarlen and reluctantly accepted he had lost the match. Frustrated, he closed his eyes, allowing the medical team to lift him off the ground, transporting him to the Medical Assessment room. Aerianna followed the group and Pauto to ensure he was okay. Her heart was beating out of her chest with fright, worried for the love of her life. It was an unexpected match, to say the least!

Andreh humbly remained in the circle, awaiting the official announcement from the judges. Kristah Villainnow approached and raised his right arm toward the sky, proudly declaring, "Witches, Warlocks, and Wizzards… I am proud to announce the winner of this round. Let us congratulate Andreh Darkhill. He is the Victor!" She dropped his arm and shook it approvingly. Kristah bowed and walked away as the crowd threw Bloomitz and Victor Coins into the arena. Andreh blushed, smiling, still shocked that he defeated Pauto without much effort. He noticed Alexis approaching, wearing her battle uniform.

Finally, standing before Andreh, Alexis shook his hand politely, ensuring everyone saw how official she acted toward him. She wished she could have kissed him, but that would not happen today. Next, she raised her arms into the air, swaying back and forth, chanting Andreh's name with the crowd's approval.

"I am proud of you. You deserve this victory! Congratulations, Andreh," she whispered, moving quickly away from him. A few minutes passed. Andreh remained in the battle circle, letting the moment sink in.

Pauto was sprawled out on a cot in the Medical Assessment room while a Healing Warlock looked him over to confirm he was okay. Aerianna stood nearby, watching with impatience. She wanted to hug and kiss Pauto, but knew he needed prompt medical attention.

The Healing Warlock found a deep laceration on Pauto's chest and a smaller one on the head, probably caused by the ricocheting bolt from the magic cast. Pauto acknowledged a stabbing headache, adding that his back ached, too. Besides that, he seemed in good spirits, though his ego was bruised from the loss to Andreh.

After several minutes, Andreh moved out of the Battle Zone and away from the area. He headed toward the Manor to change out of his battle uniform and relax. He heard Yarlen announcing that the main event—the battle between Alexis and Zandorah would commence in the morning. There would be a break for the rest of the day to allow spectators to eat, mingle, and celebrate.

Alexis managed to evade Armbruster as she headed to the Manor. It was the only place she could think of where Andreh would go after winning his battle.

As Alexis entered the large room in the back, intended as a Warrior Ready-Room, she saw him stripping down to his undergarments. Alexis quickly closed and locked the door as she walked toward him with a naughty smirk. Andreh grinned and stood naked before her, pulling Alexis into his arms and kissing her passionately. She breathed heavily, moaning. Finally, she would feel his body again.

Armbruster searched for Alexis in the crowd, knowing he had to congratulate her. Andreh won, which meant he would be allowed to remain on Alstromia. Though it bothered him, Ambruster planned to find someone to watch Andreh, spying on him. Armbruster did not trust Andreh and figured, eventually, he would seek out Alexis. Hopefully, Armbruster would catch them in the act. Then, he would have the ammunition he needed to use against her, forcing her out of office. He was tired of her charades.

Alexis dressed quickly and stood over Andreh, who lay naked on the carpet. His grin said it all. He knew he had won in more than one way. Alexis shook her head.

"Don't think that this will ever happen again, Andreh. It was the adrenaline that caused my reaction. I was pumped after watching you win. You looked so strong and sexy. I couldn't help myself," she coyly admitted, with flushed cheeks.

"Are you blushing?" Andreh asked, jumping up to hug her. "You are one sexy Witch, darling."

"Stop it, Andreh. I mean it. What just occurred between us was not supposed to happen. It cannot transpire again anytime soon. You know this. Please hurry up and get dressed before someone finds out we are in here. It will look bad," Alexis fiercely demanded, throwing his clothes at him.

Reluctantly, he picked them up and proceeded to get dressed. He loved that Alexis continued to pretend it would never happen again. Andreh knew better. She could not, and would not, keep her hands off his body. She wanted him as badly as he wanted her. It made him happy as hell.

Alexis left the room a few minutes later, heading back to the Colosseum to find Armbruster. Andreh remained in the room for a few more minutes, enjoying his multiple victories in one day. He believed it was the best day in years, and he planned to head to Henrii's Potions and BrewHaus for a few strong celebratory brews.

The official trophy would not be bestowed upon him until the event's final day. So, in the meantime, he planned to relax. Andreh was also excited about the upcoming battle between Alexis and Zandorah. He could not wait to see his woman kick ass. There was no doubt she would beat Zandorah, and he planned to celebrate with her privately afterward. He laughed out loud to himself with delight.

Armbruster waited impatiently in the private box area of the arena. He knew Alexis would return. Finally, he saw her approaching. Alexis looked radiant, which seemed odd to him. Her smile was wide, and her cheeks were rosy. Her lips looked full, pouty, and kissable. Armbruster wondered why she looked the way she did.

Alexis scooted beside Armbruster, gloating. "So, a bet is a bet, correct?" she smugly said, batting her eyes, trying to infuriate him. It worked like a charm. She noticed his disapproving look.

"Enjoy it while you can, love. Just because Andreh is not leaving now does not mean he will remain here forever. So, did you speak with your lover?" Armbruster asked her, rolling his eyes with evident annoyance.

"You saw me congratulate him. I have no idea where he is right now, and frankly, I do not care. I hear the committee wants to wait until tomorrow for the battle against Zandorah. Any idea why? I was prepared to engage her now," Alexis whined.

Armbruster explained that Shawnatar was missing, and Zandorah and Lorthana were looking for him on Iriss. They planned to return in the evening in time for the elaborate dinner event in the Village of Miccay.

"That is odd. Why would Shawnatar be absent? He is always around to support my sister, especially during a special occasion like the Battle Rounds. What is going on?" Alexis asked, bewildered.

"I have no idea. I have asked Yarlen to locate and return them as soon as possible. I also enlisted Rammadar to ask his team to find out what they could do. I believe this has everything to do with Gardone," Armbruster divulged.

"Gardone? Umm, why? Do you suspect he is here on Alstromia? I doubt he would be so bold. I mean, that would be outright stupid. He will be caught," Alexis responded. She folded her arms, looking around, now feeling paranoid. If Gardone were on Alstromia, he might try to kidnap her again. The horrific thought brought chills to her, and she shivered.

"Yes, he may be caught. Hmmm, that is curious, though. Do you believe he wants to be apprehended? That seems ridiculous. He knows that he will be locked up. No, I do not believe he would risk his freedom."

Alexis disagreed. She knew what Gardone was capable of, and thinking about it made her stomach turn. Alexis assumed he would give up and stop trying to destroy her. Gardone was never happy with anything or anyone. She was surprised he was still married to her mother. Alexis assumed Lorthana would have dissolved their marriage when Gardone ran off to hide from the authorities.

Lorthana wanted to remain his mate, which confused Alexis even more. She had no idea why her mother wanted to stay in a relationship with a Warlock who tried to destroy her daughter.

Alexis shrugged her shoulders, thinking about Gardone. There was a time when she loved him. He used to be a good father, supporting her dreams and ambitions. Alexis wondered what had changed. He became distant in the last few months and spent too much time on Earth with other Clan members. Some of those members were wanted by the law or expelled from the Clans. They were genuine troublemakers. Gardone chose these Warlocks as his confidants and friends. *'Not a great idea,'* thought Alexis, almost feeling sorry for him. Alexis remained next to Armbruster for a few more minutes. She noticed he became fidgety, rubbing his beard.

Alexis stood up and excused herself before he could say anything else, heading to the stable to retrieve her Torrin. Alexis planned to fly back to the Palace rather than transport herself using magic.

Armbruster watched her walk toward the stable. He considered following her to continue their conversation, but reluctantly decided against it. He would have a better opportunity tonight at the dinner in the village. Maybe he could get her alone and make a move to see if she still wanted him.

Armbruster was curious if Alexis would kiss him. He missed her lips and wanted her desperately. Somehow, he figured, she would reject any effort he made. It seemed as if their marriage was over. He attempted to flirt with his wife numerous times, hoping to coax her into sex. Sadly, Alexis continually turned him down, citing various flimsy excuses. Armbruster was sick of the reasons she gave him. It was one excuse after another. He demanded action. He needed his wife to make love to him.

Pouting, he stood up and slammed down his Ceptre, instantly transporting himself to his chamber in the Palace. Armbruster planned to nap and stop thinking about Alexis for a bit. It was too physically and emotionally exhausting.

At the stables near the Manor, Alexis mounted Elannah, her Torrin, and pulled back on the reins. The two flew off into the sky. Alexis tilted her head back, allowing the breeze to hit her face. She smiled, feeling relaxed.

Sadly, not everyone was as happy as Alexis. Pauto sat on the cot's edge, staring at Aerianna as she carefully helped him put on his boots. His head hurt, and he felt like crap. Pauto was still shocked that he had lost to Andreh. Now, he assumed it was because of Alexis.

Undoubtedly, Alexis had trained with Andreh, helping him prepare for the battle. Pauto wondered why she would want Andreh to win. But then, he remembered seeing them kiss as they pretended to train. Yeah, those two were definitely having an affair. Pauto wanted to discuss it with Aerianna. He wondered how she would take the news. She believed Alexis was in a platonic relationship with Andreh.

Aerianna wanted to believe Alexis when she denied the affair. Pauto found it strange that Aerianna was so gullible. It was unlike her. Maybe she chose to believe Alexis because it was easier to face Armbruster. Really, it made no difference. Aerianna needed to accept that Alexis was involved with Andreh.

"Can you stand up?" Aerianna asked, attempting to assist Pauto by offering her hand and smiling at him sweetly.

"Of course. I am not an invalid. I can manage on my own," Pauto carelessly swiped away Aerianna's hand, hurting her feelings. She struggled to keep herself from crying.

"I am sorry, Aerianna. You do not deserve my wrath," Pauto tried to make amends, noticing a tear rolling down her right cheek.

Aerianna rushed out of the room, leaving him to his misery. She refused to keep trying to be nice. He was acting like a complete jerk. Aerianna was tired of being his emotional punching bag. *'Yes, he lost the match against Andreh. So what?'*

Pauto watched her storm off in a huff. He also heard her crying, which made him feel worse. It was not his intention to push her away. Irritated with himself, he shook his head and stood up, feeling shaky. Immediately, he felt a sharp pain, like a bolt of lightning, run down his back. He winced in pain, but managed to stand erect, his extremities shaking uncontrollably.

Ready to head back to the Palace, Pauto summoned his Ceptre, leaning against the wall by the window. Once he held it securely in his left hand, he forcefully smashed the Ceptre to the ground and bellowed, *"Home again,"* disappearing into a gray fog.

Seconds later, he appeared in his chamber at the Palace of Snipperdoom. Exhausted and now in excruciating pain, all Pauto wanted was to sleep. He placed his Ceptre in its stand by the bed and swiftly stripped off his clothing, allowing them to drop onto the floor. By some miracle, he managed to crawl into bed naked, his entire body aching. His head throbbed, making him feel sick. He contemplated casting a *Healing Spell,* but fell asleep before mustering up the energy.

At the other end of the Palace, Aerianna paced around her chamber, still fuming. She was curious if Pauto was back from the Manor. Though she was eager to see him, she realized it was best to leave him alone right now. Aerianna felt he had to sort out his emotional hurt on his own. She felt unwilling to be the supportive fiancée he expected. This time, he could come crawling back to her and apologize for his reaction toward her. He acted like a fool, and she refused to help him anymore. Pauto had to learn to communicate as a couple, regardless of the circumstances. Just because he lost the Battle Round to Andreh did not mean he could treat her with such disregard. As her mind wandered, Aerianna thought about Alexis and her upcoming battle with her sister. Zandorah was a worthy opponent, but she would have a challenging time beating Alexis. Feeling exhausted and still upset, Aerianna chose to forget about the battles and focus on rest. She planned to confront Pauto shortly, hoping to clear the tension between them. She refused to allow this rift to make things uncomfortable.

In the City of Miccay, Andreh approached Henrii's Potions & BrewHaus. He could hear a boisterous group inside chatting and laughing. He smiled to himself, ready to enjoy the night. As Andreh entered the BrewHaus, the long bar ahead was lined with bar stools and Clan members. He recognized quite a few.

One of them was Sonia, Yarlen's wife. She looked intoxicated, holding a tall, narrow Ozar mug with a bright green fog swirling on top. He knew what she was drinking. It was one of Henrii's special Brews—*HexinsBrew*. It was a pungent brew and a special-order drink.

Henrii only made the concoction for special occasions because the recipe was time-consuming, and the ingredients were difficult to find on Alstromia. Henrii usually traveled to Iriss to get the main ingredients, which grew in the wild.

Henrii intended to establish a garden behind the BrewHaus to cultivate the ingredients for the future. In the meantime, he maintained a stash in the stockroom located in the basement.

Andreh approached Sonia. She gave him a crooked smile, apparently quite drunk. She swayed side to side, singing a song he did not recognize. Andreh wondered why she was alone. *'Where is Yarlen?'* He sat down beside her and asked Henrii for a *HexinsBrew*.

"Welcome, Andreh. Your drinks are on the house tonight in honor of your victory. I must tell you, I made a bet on you, and I won a huge amount of Victor coins doing so, ha-ha. I am glad you managed to knock out Pauto. Though I must confess, I was surprised. You were not the favorite to win!" Henrii said as he smiled, pushing a tall jug of *HexinsBrew* toward Andreh.

"Why, thank you, Henrii. I appreciate it. Yes, I was surprised as well. I assumed Pauto had something up his sleeve to destroy me, but I was mistaken. Though he was a worthy opponent, I am thrilled to have won," Andreh confessed, now gloating.

Many other Clan members approached, shaking Andreh's hand and congratulating him on a spectacular battle. A few young, beautiful, and available Witches made passes at him, but he chose to ignore them, his heart belonging to Alexis. Sonia watched Andreh. She smiled and grabbed his hand.

"Listen, Andreh. I know you love someone who is not available. Do not let that stand in your way. Fight for your love. I have spent the majority of my life alone. It is not what I had planned. Now, as I get older, I am lonely and sad. I would hate for that to become your future. You are handsome, intelligent, and talented. Love and live, friend." Sonia kissed him on the cheek and jumped off the tall stool, almost falling. She managed to make her way toward the Trimber door. Sonia turned around, waved, and left alone.

Andreh watched her and pondered why she had said what she did. *'What does Sonia know about my relationship with Alexis?'* Andreh decided to focus on fun and not worry about Alexis.

As Andreh celebrated his victory, Alexis made her way to her chamber. She stripped off her battle uniform and left it on the ground for Karita to put away. She strutted toward the shower to clean up for the upcoming dinner event. Alexis wished she could stay at the Palace, but knew it was her responsibility to attend the event. Her husband would be furious if she skipped out and stayed away. Alexis wondered if Andreh would be there. She had not heard from him since leaving him at the Manor. Standing in the shower, with hot water pouring over her body, Alexis leaned against the smooth stone wall. She closed her eyes, wishing to crawl into bed for a little while, relaxing. She heard a strange noise coming from her chamber.

Alexis grabbed a towel off the stool and wrapped it around her as she exited the room. As she opened the door, she saw him sitting on the edge of her bed. Immediately, she became enraged.

"What the hell, Armbruster? Again? Why do you continue to enter my chamber without asking? Do I need to post a guard outside my quarters? You are ridiculous," she yelled, approaching him.

"Well, dear, that is up to you. However, I have every right to be here. You are my loving wife, and I adore you," he teased, knowing she would be furious at his comment.

"Okay, spill it. Why are you here? I was attempting to shower and relax before you so rudely interrupted." Alexis sat down next to him, still scantily clad. She shivered, soaking wet from her shower.

"I wanted to ensure you will accompany me to the dinner tonight in the city. I have made arrangements for us to arrive by carriage. Pauto and Aerianna will accompany us. I hope you will be dressed and ready in an hour." Armbruster stood up and was about to exit the room when Alexis roughly snatched him by the arm.

"Not so fast, Armbruster. I was not planning on arriving at the dinner with you. Why did you make plans without my consent? You are overstepping, Armbruster." She released his arm and glared at him, still seated.

Infuriated, Armbruster looked down at her and shook his head in disgust. "Be ready—no more bullshit, Alexis. I expect you to be on the Landing Deck, ready for take-off in an hour. Got it?"

"Of course, dear. I will be there," Alexis replied snippily as Armbruster walked out, slamming the heavy chamber door.

Alexis giggled to herself. She loved it when he overreacted. It amused her. It was easy to push his buttons and make him angry. Now, she would hurry to ensure she was on the Landing Deck on time so he would have no reason to act like a fool in front of others.

In the BrewHaus, Andreh continued drinking one potion and brew after another. He did not realize how intoxicated he was until he planned to return to the Palace to change his attire for dinner. As he stumbled down the path toward the Palace, he felt an odd sensation in his stomach. Something was wrong. *'Is someone watching me? Or, worse, following me?'* Andreh turned around briefly, and his heart stopped when he saw him. Gardone flashed him a smile. Andreh noticed his two accomplices as well. He realized he was in trouble. They were after him for some reason.

Andreh backed away, hoping they would leave him alone. Korbin approached with his wand aimed directly at Andreh. Though Andreh was intoxicated, he was aware of what was happening. He quickly withdrew his wand and cast a *Freezer Teaser Spell,* incapacitating Korbin. The second he stopped moving, his friend leapt forward, attempting a physical fight with him. Unfortunately, he was about to learn a harsh lesson. Andreh flicked his wrist, casting a spell using his wand.

Instantly, the Warlock disappeared. Gardone panicked, now realizing he was on his own. He felt ill-prepared to face Andreh. Before Andreh could do anything else, Gardone slammed his Ceptre to the ground and disappeared into a fog, leaving Andreh wondering why he tried to harm or kidnap him.

Andreh walked away, leaving Korbin standing in place. The magic would wear off shortly, and Andreh hoped to regain his composure and return to the Palace.

Andreh was rattled. He thought about using magic to reappear inside the Palace, but needed to walk off his intoxicated state. He refused to face the Queen and Armbruster drunk at the dinner.

As Andreh approached the gates of the Palace, he looked around. A few security commoners nodded as he passed. Andreh sprinted toward his chamber, now worried about his safety. As he entered his room, he locked the door and sat on his bed, slightly shaking.

Andreh realized Gardone and his two accomplices were after him for only one reason—to get to Alexis. They probably planned to use him as bait. Luckily, he managed to escape before they could complete their evil plan. Now, he had to change his clothing and quickly head to dinner in the city. It was imperative that he locate Alexis to inform her of what had happened. He also wanted to find Pauto and notify him about the attempted kidnapping.

CHAPTER 10

Alexis dressed and admired herself in the full-length mirror while Karita handed her the sparkly silver and gold high heels. The dinner before the Main Event—the battle between the sisters, was considered the most significant social event for Clan members to mix and mingle. Strangely, it would not be held at the Palace this year.

Yarlen's idea was to conduct it in the Village to show goodwill toward the commoners. Upon hearing of Yarlen's newly formulated plan, Alexis attempted to convince Armbruster and Aerianna to move the feast back to the Palace. Alexis feared for her safety out in public. Until Gardone was caught and imprisoned, she planned to stay away from most major events unless they occurred in the Palace or other places where she felt secure.

The Village was not a safe place. It was open and vast. The Security Command Team would be present, but Alexis doubted they could provide adequate security to keep stragglers away from her.

Commoners loved seeing Alexis in the Village and usually flocked toward her. It was a rare occasion to see the Queen in the Village for more than a few minutes at a time. Most commoners sought the opportunity to be near her and potentially chat a bit, sharing their ideas, gripes, and praises.

Unfortunately, Alexis was not a fan of mingling with commoners. She felt it was beneath her to spend time listening to their whining. She preferred to keep her distance, insisting Aerianna speak with them instead. Now that Gardone was supposedly sighted on Alstromia, Alexis feared what he might be planning. There was no way she wanted to become a kidnapping victim again.

Alexis also wondered if he intended to kill her this time. It seemed odd that he would be audacious enough to show himself publicly, knowing he would be arrested on the spot.

No one understood Gardone's motives, not even Alexis. She used to have a great relationship with her father. At times, she wondered how it all went so wrong. She contemplated his actions and could not help but wonder what triggered the evil within him.

Alexis decided not to worry too much about Gardone for the night and would try to enjoy the evening in the Village. She also hoped Andreh would be around so she could speak with him. She wanted to share the good news that he did not have to move to Earth. Hopefully, he would agree and stay on Alstromia.

A few doors down, Armbruster dressed in his royal attire in his chamber. He looked regal in his black pants tucked into his tall charcoal-colored boots. He also wore a long gold and black tunic—embroidered with the royal insignia displaying a purple Draghoon and twin bedazzled flaming swords. He added a red wrap belt and a long black cloak. Lastly, he planned to bring his commanding Ceptre to the dinner as protection.

Armbruster did not intend to wear his crown, which remained displayed in a case in his chamber by the fireplace. It was rarely worn. Armbruster would probably wear it on the event's last day if Alexis chose to wear hers. He closed his chamber door, heading toward the Landing Deck, wondering if Alexis would be on time. He hoped she would not play games or be late. They needed to arrive in a timely manner.

Aerianna wanted to stick to the schedule, and the Security Command Team was ready to protect the Royal Family. Princess Lilah would not be in attendance. She would remain in the Palace with her caretaker, Carmin, and a security officer.

Alexis left the chamber with Karita on her heels. She held the Queen's Ceptre for her. They walked onto the Landing Deck and were immediately greeted by Pauto and Aerianna. Karita handed Alexis her Ceptre and walked back into the Palace, planning to clean the Queen's chamber before her return.

"Alexis, you look stunning! I have never seen that gown on you before! WOW," professed Aerianna, feeling envious. The gown was an icy blue with an attached long cape, with silvery grey and gold pearl accents. The dress cinched in at her waist, accentuating her flawless figure. Alexis also wore sparkly silver and gold high heels, making her look extremely tall. Her black hair was pulled up, showcasing a circlet around her head, which sparkled with tiny diamonds imported from Earth, with a few stray and unruly strands of hair dangling down the sides of her face. Alexis knew how to make an entrance. She smiled as she took Armbruster's hand as he helped her into the white carriage. Armbruster thoughtfully placed a fluffy white blanket over Alexis' legs for added warmth.

The night was brisk, and the wind was picking up. He scooted next to her to keep her warm. She did not resist.

Aerianna sat across from Alexis, wearing a red gown, a dark purple cape, and a faux fur-lined hood. The hood covered her hair and part of her face to keep her warm. Pauto sat next to Aerianna, wearing his formal attire—black pants and boots, dark navy tunic, black wrap belt, and short dark grey cape. He opted to use his wand for the night, which was tucked into the belt on the right side of his hip. He held Aerianna's hand as the carriage driver steered the coach toward the field for takeoff.

Within a minute, the carriage was airborne with the four Palace members on board. The driver directed the Torrins, pulling the carriage, toward the Village below.

In the City of Miccay, a growing crowd eagerly awaited the arrival of the Queen's carriage in the open field near the Vizzork Community Center. Over 200 Warlocks, Wizzards, and Witches attended the night's event. A band was set up to play music, and Viollah Grackenbone was slated to entertain the crowd. The Security Command Team flew overhead on Torrins, ensuring the area was secure for the Queen's imminent arrival, staying vigilant and on the lookout for the fugitive, Gardone.

On the ground, another team led by Rammadar conducted security sweeps of buildings, looking for anything unusual, hoping to avoid catastrophe. A smaller group, including Steffen Starleight and Sheillah Hexxon, patrolled the inside of the Vizzork Community Center, where the event was about to commence.

Inside the Vizzork Community Center, the large ballroom opened up to an expansive rectangular deck facing the River of Miccay. One of the stages inside the ballroom held two long tables covered in black tablecloths. The first table was reserved for Armbruster, Alexis, Pauto, and Aerianna. The other table was intended for Yarlen, Sonia, Sheillah, and Steffen, just a few feet apart from the first.

On the ballroom's main floor, there were over forty tables assigned to guests. Each table held up to six guests. The tables were grouped in sets of four across and ten rows long. The double doors leading to the enormous deck stood ajar, permitting guests to mingle outside.

The terrace was covered in tiny lights, glistening in the darkening sky. It looked enchanting. The band would be moved inside to the other stage opposite the other end of the room, allowing Viollah to belt out songs during the night and entertain the group.

The carriage circled overhead, and Alexis waved to the crowd below. Within a few minutes, the carriage landed safely on the right side of the Vizzork Community Center.

Armbruster exited first. He held out his hand, eager to assist Alexis so she could safely step down from the tall carriage. Even if it was fake, she smiled sweetly at Armbruster as she held his hand. Alexis looked down at the ground, ensuring her footing was stable. She liked that Armbruster was so attentive and realized it had been quite a while since she had been intimate with him. She missed his muscular body and wondered if there was a way to save their marriage.

Feeling sidetracked by her thoughts, Alexis shook her head briefly and stood next to Armbruster, waiting for Aerianna and Pauto to join them before approaching the double doors to the Center.

The Community Center was lively. Alexis entered the building and was escorted by security to the Grand Ballroom, where she had a seat at the head of the table on stage. Armbruster walked behind Alexis as any royal husband would. However, he was tired of standing beside her, pretending to be in love.

Earlier in the day, Armbruster and Yarlen formulated a plan to force Alexis to either step down as Queen and admit her affair with Andreh, or Armbruster would ask for a recall and remove her as head of Alstromia. Now, he had gained more supporters to do so and was ready to challenge her.

After his secret meeting on Earth, Armbruster knew it was the only thing he could do to appease most W3s. Armbruster aided Alexis as she finally managed to sit in the wide, white chair facing the ballroom. She nodded to Armbruster, acknowledging his assistance, wishing she could find Andreh. Reluctantly, Armbruster sat beside Alexis.

Peering around the room, Armbruster noticed it was filling up quickly and becoming quite noisy. Armbruster also saw an increase in security, which reassured him. The last thing he wanted was any kind of issue with trespassers attempting to ruin this elaborately planned night.

The ballroom filled to capacity, and W3s finally seated themselves, ready to eat and celebrate. Most were also eager to hear the Queen's speech, an annual tradition at the dinner. Every year, she unveiled a surprise. Sometimes, it was an announcement. Other times, it was a drastic change she planned to implement.

The time arrived, and the Queen stood, immediately causing the room to quiet down. All eyes were on Alexis. "Welcome, friends and family. Alstromia welcomes you! Armbruster and I are thrilled you are here. It has been a challenging year, but we have arrived at a place where we can now celebrate and enjoy the year's end. First, we will continue celebrating the Harvest Festival and all it offers. We will also wrap up the Battle Rounds, Battle of Ceptres and Wands, Battle Flight—Fight or Flight, and end with the Battle Races. Once we have completed the competitions, we will finish with the monumental Victory Celebration Day, to which everyone is invited. As you know, I usually make a grand announcement every year. However, that proclamation will not be made this year until the end of the Victory Celebration Day. Please, enjoy the night!" Alexis sat down.

Many W3s were shocked that the Queen would not share the message as usual. However, within a few seconds, most were ready to have fun, and the room became active again. W3s clapped as wait staff brought food into the room on large Trillays.

Yarlen stood up and approached Armbruster, bending down to whisper into his ear. Armbruster quickly jumped out of his seat and followed him out of the room. Alexis wondered what had happened. Instead of following them, she remained seated, allowing the staff to serve her food. She observed Aerianna, who watched Yarlen and Armbruster standing by the main doors, animatedly chatting.

Alarmingly, a few seconds later, Aerianna arose and walked toward Armbruster and Yarlen. Alexis knew instinctively that something was wrong. Two security members stood protectively next to Armbruster, looking around the room. Suddenly, two other security members approached Alexis and stood behind her chair.

Alexis turned around, and one of the Security Command Team members bent down to speak with her, whispering into her ear.

"Your Majesty, there is a problem. We have received a verifiable threat against you and the Royal Family. It would be best to take you back to the Palace for your protection."

Alexis became infuriated, grabbing the security member by the shirt and pulling him closer to her. "No. We will not be doing that. I am not planning on ruining this event. You may stay and ensure our safety, but do so in the background. You are drawing attention, and I must insist you stop that immediately!" Alexis glared at the young commoner, and he backed away swiftly, nodding and acknowledging her request, now fearing for his job.

Alexis regained her composure and smiled as she looked out at the crowd. Everyone was watching her. Alexis knew she had to do something. "Hello again!" she began as she stood up. "I just wanted to let you know there was a small hiccup at the Palace, and I have been informed about it. There is nothing to worry about at this moment, I promise. Please enjoy the rest of the evening, drink, eat, and mingle." Alexis sat down and stared at Aerianna, furious at the interruption from the Security Commoner.

Aerianna knew what that look meant and shook her head, mad that Alexis would hold her liable for whatever was happening.

"What is transpiring? The Queen is already furious, and I will not be held responsible for a fiasco," Aerianna insisted.

Armbruster roughly grabbed Aerianna by the arm and pulled her out of the room, Yarlen following. The three stood outside the ballroom. "Yes, a threat has been made against Alexis and our family. I asked security to remove her and bring her to the Palace to ensure her safety. She blatantly refused. So, our only choice is to increase our security forces and keep an eye out for anything or anyone suspicious," Armbruster explained, looking worried.

Aerianna took a deep breath and exhaled, feeling sick to her stomach. She considered why every major event had to entail some drama. Recognizing the need for discretion, she nodded and walked back into the room, heading toward Alexis.

Armbruster and Yarlen followed, avoiding Alexis and opting to sit at the other end of the table. She was busy talking to Aerianna, drinking a potion, laughing, and looking content. Armbruster hated ruining her seemingly good mood, but realized it was imperative he spoke with her and found a way to convince her to head back to the Palace.

"What is it now, Armbruster? You and your goons can leave. I am staying. Do not even begin by saying I need to be kept safe. I am well aware of what is happening. Just stop," Alexis demanded. She looked around the room and saw it filled with happy W3s.

There was no need to panic, or so she believed. Alexis would remain at the function, and there was nothing Armbruster, Aerianna, or Yarlen could say or do to convince her to leave. This night was a monumental part of the event, and it was not going to be destroyed by their drama. Alexis sat back in her seat, sipping her potion and admiring the crowd. She was pleased with the turnout and grateful to Aerianna for making it successful. Alexis reminisced about Andreh. She thought about his kiss and how extraordinary their lovemaking had been earlier. She closed her eyes, remembering his touch, and her body tingled, making her feel giddy.

In the Palace, Andreh felt much better after a shower and dressing in his battle uniform. He slammed down his Ceptre and instantly entered the ballroom. Andreh's wand was attached to his belt as extra protection. The minute Andreh saw Alexis, his heart raced, and he felt his hands become clammy. She had that effect on him every time. *'Is it love or lust?'* Andreh wondered. She looked stunning. Andreh wished he could be near her, but realized all eyes were on him as he advanced the table.

Alexis tried to keep herself from smiling as she saw him. He looked handsome and downright hunky. She bit her bottom lip nervously, wringing her hands, hoping no one noticed her edginess. Andreh was someone she adored, and her emotions were all over the place, and she had to force herself to disguise them. So, she remained seated, allowing him to stand in front of her, acting like any other warrior.

Andreh bowed before Alexis respectfully and looked up, a smirk on his face. She immediately noticed it and blushed, feeling the warmth rush to her cheeks. She wished she could have stopped the reaction, but it was too late. She looked down quickly, hoping to hide it. But others noticed.

"My Queen, thank you so much for hosting this event. It is my pleasure to attend. Thank you for the invitation," Andreh gushed, staring at Alexis. "I look forward to witnessing your battle against Zandorah in the morning. Also, it is imperative I speak with you later about an important matter if you have the time."

"Hello, Andreh. Thank you for attending the dinner. Yes, I will find you later to discuss the matter."

Andreh bowed again before turning around and leaving to find a seat at the other end of the room. He planned to stay away from Alexis until later in the evening.

Armbruster's blood boiled after witnessing the silent interaction between the two, and he felt the desire to punch Andreh. But Armbruster forced himself to remain focused on his plan and stay calm. He was ready to remove Alexis from her position as Queen.

Armbruster clutched her hand, smiling. "Your lover sure makes you blush, doesn't he? Well, I have a surprise for you, dear. We will discuss it in private, later, in the Palace." Armbruster released her hand, noticing she was about to speak. Surprisingly, though, she said nothing to him. Alexis looked perplexed and angry. It took everything out of her to stay composed.

Alexis faked a smile, pretending not to care, quickly turning her head to stare at Aerianna, seeking support. Alexis speculated what Armbruster meant by that vague statement. *'What can he do to me?'* His nasty, condescending smirk meant he had something planned. Alexis felt a wave of panic hit. She stood up lightning-fast and snatched Aerianna's hand. Alexis managed to pull her out of her seat.

Aerianna followed Alexis out of the ballroom, realizing something was very wrong! Aerianna yanked herself away from Alexis' firm grip. Her arm ached. "What is your problem, Alexis?" Aerianna hissed, utterly confused by her actions, her arm aching.

"My problem is Armbruster. He is up to something. He said something cryptic. He stated he had a surprise and would discuss it privately with me later. I am sure he and Yarlen have something plotted against me again! What are we going to do about it?" Alexis stared at Aerianna, demanding help.

"I have no clue what they are conspiring against you. How do we even know they are plotting anything? Are you sure you are not overreacting? I will speak with Pauto. I am sure he has heard something. He is keenly aware of what is happening in Alstromia. I will let you know. In the meantime, can we get back inside the ballroom to enjoy the rest of the evening?"

The two Witches returned to the ballroom a few minutes later. Aerianna walked behind Alexis, allowing her to take the lead. As usual, Alexis took the opportunity to speak with a few friends, ensuring everyone could see her.

The dinner was spectacular. The meals were delicious, and the talk was boisterous. Alexis beamed with pride, knowing the night was a success. She considered why Andreh stayed away, remaining on the other side of the room and talking with others. Alexis hoped to have the opportunity to speak with him, missing him more than she believed she would.

All of a sudden, he appeared. Andreh walked up behind her and whispered into her ear. "We have to talk now, Alexis. It is important. Please meet me in the hallway, outside the ballroom." He left a few seconds later, hoping she would follow.

Alexis joined him in the empty hallway. She spotted Andreh leaning up against the wall. He wasn't smiling as she approached, and Alexis immediately wondered why.

"I am here. What is it? Why do we have to talk out here?" Alexis interrogated.

"I have something important to share with you." He took her hand into his and looked deeply into her eyes. "Gardone and his accomplices tried to kidnap me earlier today. I assume they planned to use me as bait to get to you!"

Alexis pulled her hand away and stepped back, a puzzled expression on her face. "What? Are you certain? How do you know Gardone was part of this?" she cried out.

"Lower your voice, Alexis. I know he was involved because he was there! I saw him. Using a spell, I transported one of his devious Warlock cronies to Earth and physically fought off the other one. As soon as Gardone realized he was on his own, he fled," Andreh explained.

"Are you kidding me? What the hell? What is Gardone trying to do now? What can we do? Did you inform Pauto?" Alexis asked.

"No. I have not told Pauto yet. I wanted you to know first. Do you want me to tell him, or do you want to inform him? Or should we talk to Aerianna first?" Andreh was not sure what Alexis wanted to do about the news. So, he figured it was best to allow her to decide.

"I will speak with Aerianna, Pauto, and Armbruster. I am so sorry that happened to you. Are you okay?" Alexis became worried for his safety. She figured if Gardone attempted to kidnap Andreh to use him to get to her, Gardone probably knew about her affair. This could become a huge problem for her.

"Yes, I am fine. I just wanted you to be aware of what transpired. You are out in public, and I do not know how many other collaborators he has here. Hopefully, he will not return," Andreh pointed out. He was about to exit the building when she took two steps toward him. They now stood inches apart. She leaned forward and kissed him unexpectedly. He remained in his position, shocked at the public display of affection, something risky for her.

Andreh pushed her away. "Alexis, no. This is not the place. There are W3s everywhere. Your security team could appear at any moment. We do not want to give anyone anything else to say about us."

Alexis contemplated his words for a second. "I suppose you are right. Please, just promise me that you will be more careful. I do not want anything happening to you." Andreh nodded, walking briskly toward the main doors, leaving her alone in the hallway.

Gardone figured he had to take a chance and locate Lorthana. She needed to know he wanted to dissolve their marriage. He also planned to find out more about the affair between Alexis and Andreh. Lorthana would have information to share. In the past, she kept up to date on everything her daughters were involved in, making a point of telling Gardone about it. Since he had been in hiding, the conversations with Lorthana stopped.

Luckily, Gardone ran into her on Iriss and confronted her earlier in the day. Lorthana was angry with him for many reasons. The primary reason was that he dared to ask her for a Dismissal of the Ceremony to dissolve their marriage formally. She felt a twinge of horror when she thought about all that had happened in their marriage. At least her name would no longer be associated with a wanted Warlock!

Lorthana sat quietly on the bench at the Castle of Zandor, listening to Gardone speak. She wanted to puke, feeling disgusted with him. It had taken her a long time to realize their marriage was falling apart. Though she desperately hung on to it, only because of convenience.

After listening to Gardone ramble on about the plethora of illegal activities he was involved with, she knew she was ready to sign the Dismissal of the Ceremony paperwork to be filed with the Royal Courts. The love was gone.

Lastly, Gardone admitted to seeing someone else. A young Witch named Sharlottah Zipmound from Earth. He wanted to be released from his marriage to Lorthana so he could plan a future with Sharlottah. The thought made Lorthana want to throw up. Eager to rid herself of Gardone, she signed the paperwork and handed it to him. He grinned and left without saying anything else. He got what he wanted from her.

Lorthana remained seated for a while, contemplating her long marriage to Gardone. It seemed absurd to her that it came down to numerous lies and infidelities in their relationship. Lorthana decided to head back to Alstromia to join Alexis and the rest of the family for the planned dinner in the city. She would share the news with her family about the end of her marriage and seeing Gardone.

Alexis walked back into the ballroom, eager to find Aerianna, Pauto, and Armbruster. She wanted them to know about Gardone. However, she wasn't sure how to explain the way she gained the information. As Alexis walked toward the head table, she noticed Aerianna and Pauto looked blissfully happy. She envied their relationship and was even more jealous of the fact that they were not required to hide their love and affection. It made Alexis sad that her own relationships were so dysfunctional. Alexis continued to observe Pauto and Aerianna. They lovingly touched each other and smiled.

Alexis noticed several times that Pauto brushed Aerianna's long hair away from her face. He was thoughtful and very attentive. She wished she had someone in her life who paid attention to her in such a way. Alexis felt lonely and abandoned. Armbruster was furious with Alexis and wanted nothing to do with her. Andreh wanted to be with her, but could not be near her as it drew negative attention.

So, Alexis was alone, feeling like complete crap. She wished things were different. Suddenly, Alexis had a brilliant idea. Maybe she could take a vacation and enjoy time away by herself to get her head straight. She thought about her good friend, Shell, and planned a vacation, heading to Earth. Shell would be delighted to host her, and Alexis wanted to be around someone non-judgmental. In Alexis's opinion, the most remarkable thing about Shell was that she never judged her. She supported Alexis unconditionally. That is why they had been friends for so long. Alexis had a few good friends, and Shell was one of them.

"Hello, you two. I need to have a word with you. Do you know where Armbruster is hiding? He needs to hear this as well?" Alexis looked around the room, hoping to find her husband.

"I believe he is outside speaking with Rammadar and his group. Do you want me to retrieve him?" offered Pauto.

Alexis declined his offer, opting to sit down by them. "Listen, I have to be quiet. I do not want others to hear. I have received information that Gardone tried to kidnap Andreh earlier. Two other Warlocks accompanied him. The assumption is they wanted to kidnap him to get to me. I need you, Pauto, to inform the Security Command Team and tell Armbruster. I will stay here and play the hostess to keep things running smoothly, agreed?" Alexis stated. She surveyed the room. It was active—everyone was having a great time.

"Absolutely. I will take care of it. Aerianna, please join me," he insisted as Pauto helped her out of her chair. The two expeditiously left the large room, looking to find Armbruster.

The evening finally came to an end. Alexis was tired and wanted to retire, eager to get her rest. She would finally face off against

Zandorah the next day and could not wait. Earlier in the evening, she noticed her sister leaving before the event finished, probably to get a good night's rest. She seemed restless and on edge most of the evening. Alexis saw it right away.

Zandorah sat in her seat, fidgeting with the cloth napkin on her lap. When she was not fiddling with it, she twirled her hair, mindlessly gazing into the crowd.

Alexis wondered what was going through Zandorah's head. It seemed like she was in her own world, not really paying attention to anything or anyone.

Previously, when Lorthana approached, both sisters were excited to see her until she dropped the bomb on them, informing them about her meeting with Gardone, including his request to dissolve their marriage. Alexis was furious the second she heard what had happened to her mother. She felt her father was a coward. Not only had he stayed away, not accepting legal punishment for his actions, but now he was also breaking up the family. Though Alexis hated him for all he had done to her and the family, she still felt awful. After all, Gardone was her father, a fact she could not change.

Lorthana acted nonchalantly as she explained their brief and strained encounter. She almost seemed okay with it. She even joked about the ability to date again. It was an awkward moment for the sisters to listen to Lorthana. Obviously, she was hurting, but she attempted to hide the fact. Neither of the Witches believed her. They could see the devastation on her face as she spoke to them. Ever the caring and loving mother, Lorthana tried her best to shield her girls from the pain, though inside, she felt like hiding and dying.

Lorthana ended the conversation by reassuring her daughters she would be okay and that after the festivities concluded in a few days, she planned to return to Earth to visit with some of her friends. She needed to take an extended vacation to find herself and figure out what she wanted to do next. Alexis and Zandorah agreed with her plans, hugging their mother tightly as Lorthana desperately held back the tears, not wanting to draw attention.

Alexis felt it was a shitty way to end the day. But she knew there was nothing she could have done to prevent it. She wanted to find Gardone and wring his neck for putting her mother through so much misery, as well as the attempted kidnapping of Andreh. Gardone constantly hurt Lorthana and everyone she cared about, and she was sick of it.

However, she figured he would be caught and face legal charges for all his actions in time. It would be a great day of justice! Alexis refused to allow more Gardone drama into her life. She planned to forget about it for now and focus on tomorrow and the ultimate battle.

CHAPTER 11

Alexis and Armbruster sat next to each other like strangers. The night was cold, but Armbruster scooted away from her, opting to lean on the side of the carriage, ignoring his wife. He did not care that she shivered. Pauto and Aerianna had departed the dinner early, probably heading back to the Palace for some intimate alone time. Armbruster was furious with Alexis.

He knew exactly how she came upon the information about Gardone attempting to kidnap Andreh. It made him want to scream! Though Armbruster did not witness Andreh divulging the story to Alexis, he could imagine it in his head. It pissed him off the more he thought about it. *'Oh well, too bad,'* he thought, almost laughing. *'Too bad Gardone failed. I would love to see Andreh at Gardone's mercy,'* Ambruster said to himself.

Alexis stayed quiet, rubbing her numb hands, wishing she had used magic to transport herself back to the Palace. She reluctantly agreed to take the carriage back with Armbruster. He insisted, stating it would look strange if they did not depart together. After contemplating his words, Alexis half-heartedly agreed. She wanted to keep up the facade. Others needed to believe things were okay between the Royals. Hopefully, it would put all other rumors to rest.

The flight seemed abnormally long to Alexis. Armbruster looked away from her, resting on the side of the carriage. At this point, she wondered why he didn't just move to the other side. They were away from the crowd, and no one would see what was happening inside the vehicle.

"So, are you not going to discuss any of this information with me? How long do you plan to ignore me, Armbruster? You are overreacting. Stop the nonsense," Alexis announced, upset at his childish behavior.

"What do you want me to say? Oh, wait…how about…how did you manage to get that information about Andreh? Oh, let me guess…he told you directly?" Ambruster now looked straight at her, his eyebrows furrowed, anger on his face.

"Well, yes. Andreh approached me at the dinner and asked to speak with me. Later, he informed me about the situation when we were in the hallway outside the ballroom. I looked for you to share the information, but could not locate you. I tried. So, I informed Pauto and Aerianna." Alexis let out a sigh of frustration, tired of the constant belittling by Armbruster.

"Oh, and now, you are scared for the safety of your lover and want our Security Command Team to protect him? Am I correct?" Armbruster asked with sarcasm.

"Hardly. I informed you that Gardone was here on Alstromia, and he is a threat to our family and safety. Believe what you will. I really don't give a shit either way. Oh, look! We are back at the Palace. Screw you, Armbruster. I am heading back to my chamber to get rest for tomorrow."

Alexis removed her high heels and opened the carriage door, jumping down in a very unladylike manner. She ran away barefoot from the carriage, tired of Armbruster and his inquisition.

Armbruster watched her as she scurried down the path in her fancy gown, holding her Ceptre in one hand and the high-heeled shoes in another. It made him laugh. Alexis was feisty and determined, and he still deeply loved her, no matter what. Perhaps that was why it bothered him so much that she continued the affair. If Andreh would just go away, maybe he could have a chance to mend the volatile relationship with his wife.

Alexis cried the entire way to her chamber. Yes, she could have used magic to transport herself to the room, but she had to release the energy, which was making her feel like she was about to explode. One thing was for sure—Armbruster knew precisely how to get to her. He knew every trigger point and was not shy about using them. He probably loved watching her suffer. But then again, maybe not. Maybe he still loved her in his strange way?

Entering the Palace, Alexis received strange stares from the Security Command Team. They wondered why she was barefoot. Embarrassed, she looked away, pretending not to notice. Alexis dropped the shoes and placed her Ceptre into its stand as she entered her chamber. Exhausted and angry, she plopped down in the chair, screaming for

Karita to help her get out of her gown. It was already after midnight, and she was tired beyond anything she had felt in a long time. She wanted to rest, hoping to wake up refreshed for the scheduled breakfast with the family at seven in the morning. Minutes later, the Queen jumped into the shower to warm up before sleeping. She could not wait to slip into bed and close her eyes.

Armbruster jumped down from the carriage, thanking the driver. He acknowledged the King by nodding. As soon as Armbruster left, the carriage driver steered the wagon and Torrins toward the Royal Stables so that Essten could tend to the exhausted beasts.

Armbruster thought about the night and was extremely grateful it had gone as smoothly as it did. In his opinion, it could have ended up worse. He wondered why Gardone showed up on Alstromia during the Harvest Festival. *'What does Lorthana know?'* He planned to speak with her in the morning. *'Why did Gardone risk apprehension?'* It had to be something vital, and Armbruster intended to find out.

★*.★*.★*.★*.★

Pauto and Aerianna undressed in her chamber, the fire roaring, keeping them warm on the cold fall night. It was wonderful to be alone. Aerianna looked beautiful, and Pauto could not wait to make love to her, feeling her sensual body. She jumped into bed playfully, waiting for him to join her, casting a spell to close the velvety curtains for privacy. Neither wasted a moment as they embraced in bed.

Down the hallway, Carmin heard Alexis returning from the city and the dinner engagement, slamming her chamber door. Carmin felt upset that Alexis chose to return to her room rather than stop by to see her child. It was a selfish act, or so she believed.

Carmin closed Lilah's bedroom door and headed to her room. Lilah was asleep in her bed. She was a beautiful, young, and precocious Witch. Every day, Lilah displayed signs that she had magical gifts. She could move things at the age of two and demand that items disappear at her request. Lilah could also make things appear at her will or request. Lilah called it her *Wish* or *Wishing*. Carmin could not wait to see what Lilah would accomplish after she was old enough to attend formal schooling.

Unfortunately, Lilah's parents, Armbruster and Alexis, were very busy and had little time for her. Most of Lilah's days were spent with Carmin. On occasion, Lorthana popped in to visit her granddaughter. Other times, Zandorah would come to see her niece. Other than that, Lilah led an extremely sheltered life. Thank goodness for Carmin. She encouraged the child's magical curiosities and fostered them, though she would not inform Alexis about them yet.

There was no way the Queen would approve of her child practicing magic at such a young age. Carmin felt she had only one choice. She would keep training Lilah in secret until she thought the Queen was ready to acknowledge her child's advanced magical abilities.

★ *. ★ *. ★ *. ★ *. ★

The morning finally arrived, and Alexis woke up to Lorthana sitting on her bed, which promptly annoyed her. "Mother, really? What are you doing?" she asked, removing the heavy blanket from her body and sitting up.

"I need to speak with you before breakfast. It is imperative we have this discussion now," Lorthana explained in an urgent tone of voice.

Alexis's interest was piqued. "Okay, what do we need to discuss?"

"Please, do not be mad," Lorthana began apologetically.

"And why would I be mad, Mother?" Alexis asked, getting angry.

"I need you to lose the battle against Zandorah. Please, allow her to win," Lorthana pleaded. Alexis began laughing hysterically. She could barely catch her breath. After a minute of roaring with laughter, she stopped abruptly.

"I know you are NOT being serious. Why the hell would I lose on purpose? You must think I am stupid. That will NEVER happen, Mother," insisted Alexis. She jumped out of bed, grabbing her long, black cloak. Furious with Lorthana, Alexis walked toward the fireplace. She turned around to face her mother.

"I am quite serious, dear. You have to throw the battle round. If you win, there will be war. As a family and Clan, we cannot afford for that to happen. The only way it will not happen is if you lose to your sister. I am sorry, dear, but I must INSIST you throw the match and lose." Lorthana rose and approached Alexis.

"I know you are upset, but listen. I already discussed this with Armbruster. We agree. Both of us have met separately with Clan leaders, and they are convinced that your victory against Zandorah will elicit a war between the planets. She will be furious and ready her army. You already want war so that it will end badly for all of us. You cannot do this, Alexis, please. Be reasonable," Lorthana pleaded one last time. Alexis looked away in silence.

Lorthana awaited her response. Minutes later, Alexis had not moved and remained standing. Her back was turned to Lorthana.

"Do you plan on saying anything else?" Lorthana asked, perplexed.

"Oh, I have plenty to say. Listen up!" Alexis started as she turned around to face her mother. "One – I am NOT willing to throw the match. Not now, not ever! Two – you and Armbruster can kiss my royal butt – I owe you nothing! I do not know why you would believe I would give up. I informed everyone that if Zandorah did not give up and I won the match, I planned to declare war on her and all of Iriss. I am tired of being bullied by everyone, and I am shocked you are now attempting to do the same. What the hell has gotten into you, Mom?"

Lorthana shook her head in disgust. It was inconceivable that her daughters were both so stubborn. They were willing to destroy their homes and harm Clan members just to make a point. It was irresponsible and downright evil.

"You are mistaken, Alexis. This has NOTHING to do with you or your sister. It has everything to do with two planets and the innocent residents that your recklessness will harm. It makes me sick. I cannot and will not support either of you!" Lorthana walked out of the chamber, done with the ridiculous conversation.

Alexis fumed, standing by the fireplace. *'How dare she?'* contemplated Alexis. She could not understand why her mother remained adamant, insisting she lose on purpose. Alexis had no issues standing up against Zandorah, who lied and spread false rumors about what happened between her and Gardone. It was no surprise, really, considering that Zandorah had always been Gardone's favorite child. Zandorah never challenged anyone or anything, remaining neutral.

Alexis was eager to get the day started on a positive note. Though her mother's unexpected visit irritated her, she ignored the negativity and looked forward to the day, especially the battle against Zandorah. She dressed quickly and headed down the long corridor, ready to face the family at breakfast.

On the other side of the Palace, Armbruster leaned against the wall in the Security Command Chamber, his arms crossed, listening to Rammadar's briefing. Andreh was present and sat in the back of the room, trying to avoid Armbruster. He kept his head low and said nothing.

The only one still absent was Pauto. Seconds later, he finally appeared and apologized for his tardiness, sitting near

Andreh. The briefing lasted less than half an hour, and Rammadar and his team left the room to give orders to the rest of the group. Today, security needed to be at its highest. The battle between the sisters would draw the largest crowd to date. The Queen's safety was everyone's top priority.

Aerianna met Alexis in the large room where the breakfast service was about to begin. The servers were already busy placing food and potions on the table. Alexis looked extraordinary in her battle uniform, radiating strength and confidence. Her hair was braided and draped down the right side of her shoulder. Aerianna thought Alexis looked refreshed and ready to battle, which made her happy. It appeared as if the Queen was in a decent mood for once.

"Good morning, Aerianna. How was the rest of your night?" Alexis asked, noticing she looked beautiful, acting cheerful. There was no doubt in her mind that Pauto and Aerianna had spent the night making love, enjoying each other's company.

"I must confess, it was very romantic and wonderful. I am so in love with Pauto. He is the best thing that ever happened to me," Aerianna responded joyfully.

"Yes, you two lovebirds certainly had a difficult time last night keeping your hands off each other," Alexis said as she looked away.

She felt a hint of jealousy but did not want Aerianna to see the look on her face.

"I hope you feel that kind of love again, Alexis. You deserve it," Aerianna replied, feeling guilty about gloating. They sat down and waited for the others to join them. The food smelled delicious, and Alexis heard her stomach growling.

Unexpectedly, Alexis felt a wave of nausea. She assumed it had everything to do with the potential outcome of the battle. Many things could change depending on who was declared the victor. Alexis was still upset with Lorthana and Armbruster, suggesting she throw the match to Zandorah for the sake of the Clans. It disturbed her greatly. Alexis was tired of the unequal treatment.

Within a few minutes, Zandorah appeared with Lorthana. The two were laughing as they approached the table. Armbruster entered the room next, accompanied by Yarlen.

The last two to make an appearance were Andreh and Pauto. They left the meeting together and chatted as they entered the chamber, ready to eat. The group sat around the round table. All eyes were on Alexis. She was about to stand up and make an announcement when she saw him coming through the door. She immediately lost her train of thought. He looked dreadful. He had a long and jagged gash across his forehead and a bandage on his left arm. He hobbled as he fought to move closer to the table.

"Someone, please, help Shawnatar," Alexis urgently insisted. She worried about her friend and ex-lover. Zandorah turned around and saw her husband. She flew out of the chair and ran toward him. He flung his good arm around her shoulders as she helped him sit down.

Alexis stared at Armbruster and Aerianna. Both looked perplexed. No one knew what had happened. Finally, Alexis spoke, primarily out of curiosity.

"Shawnatar, what happened to you? Do you need the services of a Healing Warlock? You look absolutely awful." She questioned, assuming he was in pain.

Zandorah turned her head. She could not bear to look at his injury. Shawnatar held Zandorah's hand for support.

"Alexis, do you believe we should postpone our battle today? Perhaps tomorrow would be better?" she begged her sister.

Alexis contemplated Zandorah's words. Instantly, she felt guilty. She would appear heartless to others if she said *'no'* to her sister's request. If she said *'yes,'* then she would be forced to wait another day to battle. Luckily, Armbruster intervened.

"I believe we should postpone the battle until tomorrow. Instead, we could begin the

Battle of Ceptres and Wands. We could allow the Beginners Group to start. What do you think, Aerianna? You are in charge of events." Armbruster suggested. Aerianna concurred. She planned to meet with the judges of the Battle Rounds and inform them of the urgent and immediate change.

"May I speak?" Shawnatar asked, doing his best to stand without falling over.

"Of course. Say what you must," retorted Alexis, nodding.

"Your Majesties—I have some horrible news to share. I tried to stop Gardone from another evil act. I met with some of his accomplices on Earth. I found out about some horrible things. As I was leaving my meeting, I was attacked, beaten, and left for dead by the side of a hut. I believe Gardone has gone off the deep end. He is after you, My Queen. We must ensure your safety. He is here, on Alstromia!" Shawnatar collapsed into his seat, exhausted. Everyone glanced around the room with anxiety. The news was startling.

Armbruster summoned his security detail and demanded increased protection. Pauto left the room to find Rammadar and inform him of the new developments. Andreh followed Pauto, assuming it was best to help as much as possible. Alexis and Aerianna remained in the room. Zandorah excused herself and escorted Shawnatar to her chamber, planning to summon the Healing Warlock to assess Shawnatar's injuries.

Minutes passed, and Alexis continued to pace around the room. "Aerianna, please speak to the judges and inform them of the changes for the day. Please do it now! I will be in my chamber if you need me."

Alexis swiftly exited the room. Seeing Shawnatar's extensive injuries ruined her entire day. It elicited many different emotions, some of which she tried to suppress for years. The uncomfortable feeling in her gut only grew worse. She wished to lie down, but realized she was still hungry. Perhaps she would eat something once she returned to her chamber.

As she marched down the long corridor toward her room, she recalled a time when Shawnatar was the love of her life. He made her happy beyond anything she had ever felt. Then, tragically, one day, he fell in love with her sister, Zandorah. It almost broke Alexis' heart. For months, she stayed away from Zandorah and Shawnatar. Eventually, she agreed to attend their Ceremonial Exchange, mainly because her mother begged her to do so. Lorthana claimed it was best for the family to show support and cohesion.

Alexis sat in the chair, restless, watching them exchange their vows. Her stomach flip-flopped the entire time. It made her realize that true love was something precious, not to be taken for granted. Perhaps that was why she refused to give up Andreh. She loved him, and losing him would destroy her.

★*.★*.★*.★*.★

Aerianna approached Kristah Villainnow in the Manor on Tullah Mountain. Kristah was reading the posted schedule as Aerianna asked to speak with her.

"Hello, Aerianna. What may I do for you today?" Kristah asked, curious why Aerianna looked upset. The expression on Aerianna's face made Kristah apprehensive. She knew bad news was about to be announced.

"Alexis wants me to inform you about some pressing changes we must make to the battle schedule for the day. Due to a family emergency, the battle between Alexis and Zandorah must be postponed until tomorrow morning. Instead, we would like to begin the Battle of the Ceptres and Wands, followed by the Battle Flight. Both can take place today. Then, tomorrow, we will end with the Battle Races and Alexis and Zandorah's match. Does that work for you and the others? Yarlen will announce the updated events schedule in a while if you agree," Aerianna said forcefully. She refused to take no for an answer.

"Of course. Whatever the Queen wants," Kristah responded snippily. Obviously, she was not happy about the unexpected changes. She would have to meet with the others and make arrangements to alter the schedule, something she despised.

Aerianna expressed her gratitude and intended to return to the Palace to request that Yarlen handle the necessary announcements. Although he wouldn't be particularly happy about it, he would do as asked. Public speaking was something he truly dreaded. While Yarlen liked going to events, he preferred not to participate in them. He'd rather have Armbruster step in, as he was a natural at public speaking and enjoyed the spotlight, in contrast to Yarlen.

Alexis threw herself onto her fluffy bed in the chamber, pouting and feeling restless. She wanted to see Shawnatar to ensure he was okay, but knew Zandorah would not appreciate her presence. So, she chose to stay away, hoping all was well.

It was not long before Aerianna knocked on the Queen's Chamber door. She entered the room and found Alexis still on the bed, staring at the ceiling. She seemed to be daydreaming or at least uninterested in having company. She looked tired and fiddled with a pillow beside her.

"My Queen. I have made the arrangements you requested. Kristah Villainnow will comply and reschedule the battle. Your match against Zandorah will begin in the morning. We will wrap up the day tomorrow with the Battle Races. Hopefully, you will not be too tired from the match to participate?" Aerianna cautiously asked. She worried the Queen would potentially want another change in the schedule, which could be challenged by some.

"Nothing will stop me from racing. You know this. Elannah is ready to race, too. I have trained with her and know we will excel in the competition. I am so excited about the Battle Flight today. I have a secret and cannot wait to see everyone's reaction!" Alexis teased.

"Secret? What secret? Please fill me in. I cannot stand anything else happening today," Aerianna complained. She hated surprises, especially when they came from Alexis. None of her surprises ended up being anything that did not cause a commotion or issue. Aerianna was not thrilled with the idea that Alexis was about to do something without first informing her about it. Plus, Aerianna felt that as her Second-in-Command, she should be informed of all changes to events. Now, she realized that would not happen and had to brace for the worst. She knew Alexis would make her wait. Aerianna would hear the secret at the same time as everyone else.

Alexis rolled her eyes, shrugged her shoulders, and jumped off the bed. She sauntered toward the window to gaze at the scenery, blatantly ignoring Aerianna. She was not about to tell her about her secret plans.

Unfortunately for Alexis, Aerianna was persistent. "Alexis, please, no more secrets. What do you have planned? You know I will not tell anyone." She stared at Alexis, furious that she refused to divulge the new secret.

Alexis did not care. She would not disclose her secret nor reveal Trixxie before it was time. Two individuals knew about Trixxie—Pauto and Andreh. Neither would say anything. They knew better than to betray Alexis. She planned to surprise everyone with Trixxie at the Battle Flight portion of the competition. She knew it would be better than any announcement she could have made this year! For now, she would sit back and enjoy the stares, and ultimately, she hoped to beat the competition.

Gardone arrived on Earth. Alstromia's security teams were hot on his trail. He knew it was best to leave the planet for now. Luckily, his chant worked, and he was able to bypass whatever worthless spell had been placed over the planet. Though he wanted to confront Alexis, he knew the timing had to be just right. Gardone had a false sense of security because he believed himself to be safe in the large crowds on Alstromia. He also figured he would blend in perfectly, away from spying eyes.

Once he made his way through the streets, he noticed a few commoners staring at him. Panicked, Gardone quickly dashed behind one of the huts and chanted, immediately changing his appearance.

Unfortunately, the only spell he knew to perform such a task was limited in time. He could not stay incognito for long. The enchantment would wear off, and Gardone could not risk that happening while out in public.

Gardone entered the small hut on Earth and smelled something delicious. Sharlottah greeted him with a tall jug of steaming potion. He offered up a grin as he walked toward her, taking it from her long, thin hands. He kissed her cheek quickly, then walked toward the old, comfortable chair by the fireplace.

Sharlottah left him alone to relax while she finished preparing dinner. She knew it was best to leave him alone when he first came home. He looked exhausted and preferred to unwind in solitude.

Gardone sipped the delicious potion, approving of the taste. It was a recipe Sharlottah invented. She was extraordinarily creative with her potions and brew concoctions. This particular potion was a bit twangy with a hint of sweetness. It was also warm and comforting.

Gardone slouched in the squishy chair, allowing his body to sink into it. It felt safe and secure. He wondered how many commoners had recognized him before changing his appearance on Alstromia. He noticed several security commoners following him, probably analyzing his moves and motives before attempting to arrest him.

However, Gardone evaded them by expeditiously smashing down his heavy Ceptre, transporting himself back to Earth before anyone could capture him. He knew attending the festival was risky, but he hoped to see Alexis. Sadly, that never happened, and now he was forced to formulate a new plan. Gardone was not going to give up so easily. He was determined to speak with his daughter and set the record straight about what had happened in the past. He also planned to demand that she withdraw the orders for his arrest. After all, he was her father and deserved a few favors from his daughter, the Queen. He felt it was more than appropriate, given her power and abilities.

Gardone wanted to live out the rest of his life on Earth, not having to worry about the law or any repercussions. Deep in his heart, he knew he would never be able to replace Alexis as head of Alstromia. So, he implemented another plan that would involve someone less challenging. He felt prepared to make a move soon. His future would be bright if all went as smoothly as he expected. A snide grin sprang across his face. He closed his eyes, feeling content.

Alexis contemplated Aerianna's words and felt ready to start the Battle of Ceptres and Wands against Zandorah. Needless to say, she assumed she would beat her. The first group of young W3s would begin the first rounds shortly. Most spectators did not attend these rounds as they were quick and rather boring since the inexperienced, younger group rarely made a show out of it.

Alexis, however, felt ready, equipped with new spells. She was eager to use them against Zandorah. Time permitting, she was also scheduled to face off against Pauto and Andreh. Happy at the idea of seeing Andreh, Alexis displayed a sly grin. Aerianna watched Alexis as she daydreamed. Feeling bored, she interrupted her.

"Alexis, do you need anything else from me? I wish to find Pauto and ensure everything is ready for the Battle of the Ceptres and Wands," Aerianna conveyed, hoping to get out of the chamber quickly. Alexis was acting odd, and she was done with all of it.

"Sure, do what you must. I will stay here for a while and change for the upcoming events for the day. See you later, Aerianna," Alexis said as she closed her eyes, trying to relax and meditate. She had every intention of preparing herself to win.

Alexis refused to divulge any more information to her, and at this point, Aerianna surmised she could spend her time in more productive ways. She planned to head to the Security Command Chamber to find Pauto and Armbruster.

Aerianna wondered if there was an update about Gardone's presence on Alstromia. She worried for the safety of the Royals and hoped he would choose to stay away. No one wanted to fight Gardone and his group. Right now, the time belonged to warriors and the Harvest Festival, not Gardone and his crazy followers. The last thing anyone wanted was for him to spoil the day. It would upset Alexis and cause issues with other Clan members, something Aerianna wished to avoid.

Shawnatar perched himself on the edge of the bed in Zandorah's chamber. His breathing was labored, and he hurt severely all over.

The Healing Warlock, Edwinn Shivvers, waved his wand and sealed the deep gash on Shawnatar's forehead. Almost immediately, Shawnatar experienced an intense tingling sensation, followed by a warmth that flushed through him. While conducting his examination, Edwinn assessed Shawnatar's arm and determined it was broken.

With a flick of his wand, he cast another spell to mend the fractured bone. Shawnatar felt an improvement and managed a smile, although he still dealt with a pounding headache that strained his eyes. He squinted, hoping to regain his focus.

"Shawnatar, again, how exactly did you acquire these injuries?" Edwinn asked.

"A group of Warlocks on Earth beat me up. I recognized a few of them, but I had no chance to fight back. It happened rather quickly. They managed to snag my wand from me before I could escape." Shawnatar clarified, though his thoughts were fuzzy, as his head pounded, making him want to puke.

"They surely pummeled you, young one," replied Edwinn, noticing the bruise on Shawnatar's neck. Edwinn was a grey-haired, older Warlock. He was extremely tall and chubby, but a very gifted Healer. He had been Chief Healer on Earth but opted to move to Alstromia to serve the Queen and her kingdom. Currently, he resided in the Palace two doors down from Yarlen, and they were good friends, having grown in their magic together from a young age.

Wrapping up his exam of Shawnatar and noting nothing else was medically wrong with him, Edwinn departed the chamber ten minutes later. He returned to the Manor on Tullah Mountain, preparing for the day's battles, eager to aid the competitors if they sustained injuries.

Shawnatar half-heartedly curled up on the bed. Zandorah removed his boots, planning to crawl into bed with him to take a nap. Shawnatar closed his eyes, hopeful the headache would subside. He was glad his wife was beside him.

Zandorah wondered if Alexis was upset that their match had been postponed, though she did not care. She knew it was the right thing to do. Zandorah would not be able to battle against Alexis, worrying about Shawnatar. She was grateful that Armbruster suggested changing the battle schedule. It was a huge relief. She would have been forced to do it if he had not suggested it. Zandorah feared Alexis would not have been so accommodating if the request came from her.

Alexis stopped fiddling with her wand and placed it into the loop on her waist. She looked at herself in the mirror. Her eyes looked puffy, and she had dark circles under them. It was abnormal for her to look this awful. Most of the time, she looked refreshed. Alexis reasoned her current appearance had everything to do with the stress of worrying about Gardone and his wicked new plot. *'What is his plan?'* Alexis pondered. She placed her hands on the back of her neck and massaged it, feeling achy.

Lastly, Alexis summoned Karita to bring her some food. She needed sustenance before heading to the mountain for the Battle of the Ceptres and Wands. *'Hopefully, everyone will be in attendance.'* She wished for Shawnatar to appear, too. Andreh was scheduled to battle against Pauto for a second round. The Battle of Ceptres and Wands was a well-attended event. It was action-packed, and new spells were introduced.

In the Security Command Chamber, Armbruster agreed with Yarlen and Pauto. Increased security was a significant step to ensuring safety, but something else needed to be done. Rammadar suggested using magic. Yarlen felt that was drastic and difficult given the circumstances, with the large crowds, probably impossible.

Not much later, the decision was made to increase security and keep things as they were. It was best for all involved. Yarlen worried that if Clan members figured out there was a spell in place, they would fret about why it was there in the first place. So, to keep things at an even keel, security measures were all that was agreed upon by those in the chamber.

Yarlen and Armbruster left first, heading to their rooms to change clothing for the afternoon events. Rammadar ordered his teams to be on standby, heading out to locate Zandorah to update her on all that was happening on Alstromia. Pauto and Andreh left the meeting shortly after Yarlen and Armbruster, eager to don the battle uniform for the competition about to take place on Tullah Mountain.

Alexis snagged her Ceptre on the way out of her room. She planned to head to the stables to retrieve her Torrin, Elannah. From there, she would fly Elannah to the event and later introduce Trixxie. Andreh grudgingly agreed to ensure Trixxie's safety, coordinating the covert plans with Pauto, hopeful of keeping the beast a secret until the last moment, before her startling reveal.

Trixxie had been carefully moved from the Palace dungeon the night before and placed in the cave by Lake Blayden, near the Manor. Only three individuals knew of her presence at the lake. Alexis was ecstatic about showing off Trixxie and her extraordinary abilities. Undoubtedly, it would cause a stir. No one had ever entered a Draghoon!

Andreh would have preferred not to be tasked with handling Trixxie. It was just one more thing to connect him to Alexis.

CHAPTER 12

The day was glorious, and it was warming up, considering it was Fall, which was a welcome change. The excitement of the event was felt by most. Enthusiastic spectators mingled happily, drinking potions and brews, eager to witness the Battle of the Ceptres and Wands. It was no secret that the majority of the W3s were excited to observe the long-awaited battle between Alexis and Zandorah.

A few wanted to see if Pauto and Andreh would face off against each other again, especially after witnessing the previous match between them. The Manor was lively. The stadium would be, too, shortly. The crowds made their way to the Colosseum to watch the upcoming events.

Alexis mounted her Torrin and flew off toward the Manor on Tullah Mountain, followed by three security team members. She felt ready to face Zandorah. Looking down at the valley below, Alexis grinned to herself. She was thrilled to see so many visitors on Alstromia.

The crowds in the valley finally disbursed, making their way to the Manor, ready to watch the Battles. Zandorah arrived first at the Manor, followed by her mother and husband. She chose to wait in one of the holding rooms in the building, attempting to calm down. Her stomach flip-flopped, and she felt anxious.

Zandorah felt inadequately prepared to face Alexis and secretly wished she had not agreed to battle against her in the Ceptres and Wands competition. Instead, she should have only agreed on the Battle Rounds. Now, it was too late. The announcements had been made, and the spectators were seated, anxiously awaiting the start of the match.

Alexis landed and handed her Torrin to one of the stable keepers near the Manor. She strode confidently toward the large doors to enter the building. Her security detail followed closely behind, looking around to ensure no harm would come to the Queen.

As Alexis entered the Manor, she was greeted by judges, fans, and her mother. She smiled sweetly, adoring the attention. It did not take long for Alexis to make her way to the holding room, which was reserved for her. She sat on the stiff sofa, fidgeting with her boots, when Andreh appeared. She sat up, delighted to see him.

"Hello, My Queen. How are you today? Are you ready to destroy your sister?" Andreh joked as he plopped down next to her.

"Funny, Andreh. I am. Though I must confess, I have contemplated throwing this match against her." Immediately, Andreh jumped off the sofa and faced her.

"Alexis, you cannot be serious. Why would you do that? That is not like you. What is wrong? Are you ill?" Andreh asked her, feeling concerned.

"No! I have had plenty of time to contemplate things and thought that perhaps, if I threw this match, Zandorah would gain confidence. Maybe she would be over-confident, and then I could destroy her when we face each other at the Battle Rounds and Races. I know she cannot ride or fly the way I can. I will outmaneuver her and win!"

Andreh was not thrilled at the prospect of her voluntarily giving up anything. He frowned, wanting her to fight for it and do her best, no matter the outcome. He felt she was giving in, and that was not like her.

Alexis continued to stare at him, waiting for his approval, something he would not provide her. He shook his head, sitting down, furious with Alexis.

Andreh sat silently for a few minutes, pondering how he would broach the subject with her. He informed her that he could not support her idea. It was not fair to throw any match. It was also dumb to outright give Zandorah false hope. Andreh continued to explain why it was unethical and a waste of her time. He hoped she would want to excel and beat Zandorah fairly.

As he sat next to her, he noticed her crying. He felt awful for making her feel guilty, but it had to be said. It was imperative she knew why he felt the way he did. She should compete and let her abilities decide the match's outcome against her sister.

Alexis wiped away her tears in anger. She pushed Andreh away, jumped up, and walked toward the door. "I completely understand what you are saying. What you don't know is that Mom has already asked me to throw the Battle Rounds to appease Clan members. I informed her I would not do so. Instead, I will let Zandorah win this match. It will boost her confidence, allowing me to destroy her in the only confrontation that matters…the Battle Rounds. Zandorah has no chance against me in the Battle Races, so that is a moot point."

Alexis opened the door and left the room, allowing Andreh to stew in his misery. He felt like crap about bringing up the subject but still believed she needed to hear it. He was highly irritated with his lover over her obstinacy. In his opinion, she was making a grave mistake, and he hoped she could pull it off so it would not be evident to the judges.

As Alexis slammed the door, she faced Lorthana, who looked at her, perplexed. It was apparent she was confused as to why Alexis seemed so angry. Instead of prying, she chose to follow her daughter as she walked toward the Colosseum, ready to begin the match.

Zandorah sat meditating on the hard, cold floor in the holding room. She hoped it would eliminate her nervousness. Zandorah craved alone time, especially before such a significant event. Clearing her mind of negativity and focusing only on positivity was the goal. For once in her life, she wanted to beat Alexis, fair and square. Zandorah had carefully prepared a few spells she hoped would grant her victory.

The spells were courtesy of Florenzzah Lovecraft, a known enemy of Alexis. When approached by Zandorah about helping with unique spells, Florenzzah was more than happy to oblige, providing her with her favorites. It would become an epic battle of Wands and Ceptres, as far as Zandorah was concerned.

The referees were seated and chatted as they waited for the competitors to arrive at the Colosseum. The spectators were boisterous and ready as well. Commoners walked up and down the narrow aisles, handing out potions and brews to those wishing to purchase some. At the same time, another group of commoners held large bags overflowing with snacks, hoping to earn some extra income from the events at the Colosseum.

Armbruster sat on the first row, facing the battle circle, opposite the judges. Yarlen and Sonia joined him. Aerianna sat next to Sonia, looking around the area and hoping to spot Pauto.

Shawnatar approached, still limping, looking tired. He sat a few seats away, allowing room for Lorthana and others. Though they were his relatives, he preferred a distance between himself and the rest of the family. He despised their dramatic ways. It always led to fights, disruptions, and hurt feelings.

Pauto entered the Colosseum with other security forces. They surveyed the territory, ensuring the Queen's safety. Alexis was ordered to stand by while they secured the area. Pauto refused to allow Gardone or his thugs to interfere with this event. After a few minutes, Pauto deemed the area safe and ordered a security commoner to retrieve the Queen.

Alexis entered the arena, and the crowd went wild. They quickly jumped to their feet, yelling and clapping with excitement. As she strutted toward the battle area, Alexis waved to her fans and fellow Clan members, eager to begin the match.

A few seconds later, her opponent, Zandorah, walked out, and she received a similar welcome. Clan members shouted both their names, taking sides, ready to witness the battle between the sisters, the most anticipated event of the year!

As Alexis made her way to the middle of the circle, she stared at Armbruster, who looked pissed off, his arms crossed, seated by Yarlen. Aerianna waved to her enthusiastically.

Shawnatar was nearby, staring off into the sky, unaware of her presence or blatantly ignoring her. However, when Zandorah entered the arena, Shawnatar quickly rose from his seat, applauding his wife and yelling her name in excitement, displaying his love and pride for Zandorah.

Kristah Villainnow approached the sisters and gave them battle instructions. The sisters nodded in acknowledgment, waiting for Kristah to return to her seat. A few minutes passed, and the two stood in the middle of the circle, listening to the spectators, chatting, yelling, and clapping. Zandorah sighed, worried and feeling unprepared to face off against her sister.

A loud gong noise gave the one-minute warning that the event was about to begin. The crowd hushed and sat down. Zandorah graciously shook Alexis's hand before heading to her part of the circle. Alexis nodded to her sister and stood steadfast, ready to begin. Her heart raced as she wondered if she could throw the match against Zandorah. It would not be easy for her to do so. She wanted badly to win. However, her mother's words kept playing through her head, begging her to let Zandorah win for the Clan's sake.

So, reluctantly, Alexis decided she would allow her sister to win. Andreh entered the Colosseum and headed toward an area where he would have an unobstructed view of Alexis and Zandorah. He chose to sit next to

Shawnatar, avoiding the rest of the group. His heart raced as she saw Alexis in her battle uniform, holding her wand. Zandorah had chosen to use her Ceptre, which seemed odd, considering it was heavy and awkward. However, Zandorah held it firmly as she stood erect, looking regal and ready.

Alexis noticed Andreh and had to force herself to ignore his presence. She did not want the guilt weighing heavily on her mind as she was about to battle. Andreh was right. She should fight fairly against Zandorah, allowing fate and skill to determine the winner. But that was not going to happen.

The gong noise reverberated around the arena. Kristah Villainnow yelled loudly for all to hear, "Let the battle begin!"

Alexis expeditiously jumped into the air, casting her first spell, which caught Zandorah totally off guard. She fell backward on the hard, stone ground, dropping her Ceptre. Alexis smiled, realizing this was going to be quick and easy!

Torrins flew over the Colosseum with Security Command Team members surveying the area, ensuring the Queen's and spectators' safety. Rammadar watched from the sidelines as Alexis and Zandorah began the second round.

Zandorah managed to jump up and retrieve her Ceptre quickly. Alexis cast a *Levitation*

Spell, allowing her to hover over Zandorah and confusing her. Before Alexis cast her next spell, Zandorah unleashed the first spell she hoped would win her the battle. It was the *Shield and Freeze Spell* from Florenzzah.

Before Alexis could avoid the bright purple stream of light that emanated from Zandorah's Ceptre, she fell to the ground, frozen in place. The beam of light also shielded Zandorah simultaneously as it froze Alexis. The Queen turned a light blue color as she lost consciousness. The crowd erupted with applause, realizing Zandorah had beaten Alexis, winning the battle in less than a few minutes.

Kristah Villainnow appeared and held up Zandorah's hand, declaring her the victor. She then ordered the Medical Assessment Team to rush to the Queen's aid to ensure she was okay.

The second Andreh witnessed the Queen collapse onto the ground, he swiftly jumped out of his seat, heading to be by her side. Armbruster wanted to kill Andreh.

It infuriated him greatly that the boy decided to run to his wife. However, Armbruster chose to leave it alone and smiled to himself with the satisfaction that Alexis had lost. He quietly gloated, happy she would have to live with the loss until the next event, the Battle Flight, assuming she was physically ready to participate.

Andreh arrived at the same time as the Medical Assessment Team. The Healing Warlock, Edwinn Shivvers, tended to her. She was still frozen and unconscious. Edwinn decided it was best to remove her from the center of the arena and examine her in one of the rooms so he could privately attend to her needs. His team lifted and carried her off on a stretcher, Andreh on their heels.

Zandorah enjoyed her victory in the battle circle, waving to the crowd and eagerly picking up Victor Coins, grinning.

Shawnatar stood nearby, waiting to congratulate his wife in private. Kristah Villainnow spoke with Zandorah briefly and then announced that the Battle Races and Battle Round between Alexis and Zandorah were postponed until the morning. The Queen's health and safety took priority. No one knew yet if the Queen was okay.

Instantly, Zandorah worried about Alexis. She never thought about the actions of the spell. She had also never bothered to ask Florenzzah if the chant was temporary. Now, fear crushed her, causing her to drop to the ground, gasping for air.

"What if I killed my sister?" Zandorah screamed face-to-face with her husband. Shawnatar lifted his wife off the ground, placing his uninjured arm around her.

"Alexis will be fine. You know this. Your spell was quite unforeseen by her! She froze instantly. Did you know that would happen?" Shawnatar inquired.

"I knew it would freeze her in place. I had no idea she would collapse and turn blue! Oh, my God, what if I killed her? Can you imagine? It goes against all Battle Guidelines! The consequences will be severe! It will surely start a war! What have I done??!" Zandorah hysterically screamed for all to hear. She shook with fear, wishing she could undo the catastrophic event.

Shawnatar tried desperately to shut Zandorah up. He noticed Clan members were starting to stare and listened to their conversation. Even Kristah Villainnow squinted her eyes, whispering to one of the other judges.

Shawnatar knew it was in Zandorah's best interest to remove her from the Colosseum and secure her in one of the rooms in the Manor. He would ask for security personnel to ensure no one would bother them. He planned to learn more about the enchanting spell and see how he could calm down his panic-stricken wife.

In the spacious room at the back of the Manor, Alexis lay on a table, rigid and still blue, completely frozen. Edwinn tried to rouse her with different magical spells, but none were effective. Just as he was casting his third spell, Armbruster showed up.

Immediately, Armbruster realized the situation was dire. Andreh sobbed, holding her right hand, which was ice cold. When Andreh spotted Armbruster, he dropped her hand and ran from the room, not wanting to confront her husband. Armbruster cautiously approached his wife, his heart pounding out of his chest, feeling nauseous. *'What if Alexis is dead?'* He wanted to puke. They argued and had issues, but he did not want her dead. Never!

Edwinn shook his head, realizing he could not unfreeze her. Instantly, he panicked, wondering how they would save the Queen. He had no idea what to say to Armbruster or what to do. He had done all he could to revive her.

Yarlen entered the room a minute later, holding the Ceptre of Argin, ready to aid Edwinn if need be. Edwinn massaged his aching temple, then asked Yarlen to meet him in the hallway outside the room.

"Yarlen, I am afraid I am not familiar with the magic used against Alexis. I am unable to release the Queen from the spell, nor can I get her to regain consciousness. Can you locate Zandorah and ask her what kind of magic she used? Time is of the essence. We must work quickly before it is too late!! I am worried the Queen could die!" Edwinn stated in a loud, panicked voice.

Yarlen's eyes became wide as he realized the Queen's fate. He left the hallway and ran toward the Colosseum to locate Zandorah. He knew she was the Queen's only hope!

Zandorah and Yarlen literally plowed into each other while Shawnatar attempted to hold her up. She was physically weak and shaky. Yarlen viciously yanked her away from Shawnatar. "You better tell me what magic you unleashed on the Queen. If she dies, you will be charged with her murder. I will personally see to it! Do you hear me, Zandorah?" Yarlen was still gripping her arm, now hurting her.

"Stop it, Yarlen. You are hurting me," Zandorah screamed, trying to break away from him.

"No, tell me now!" Yarlen insisted, furious with Zandorah.

Shawnatar attempted to push Yarlen away from Zandorah, but Pauto appeared and ripped Shawnatar away, protecting Yarlen.

"Tell Yarlen what he needs to know, or I will take you into custody for the attempted murder of Alexis Snipperdoom," warned

Pauto, tired of her stalling. Andreh approached, now aiding Pauto.

"I used the *Shield and Freeze Spell* provided to me by Florenzzah Lovecraft. She guaranteed it would incapacitate the Queen."

"It apparently worked. Did Florenzzah also inform you about how long the effects would last?" Andreh yelled frantically.

"No, I never bothered to ask. I assumed it was temporary. Honestly, I never contemplated the long-term consequences. It was not my intention to hurt Alexis. It was just part of the battle. Please, you have to believe me!" Zandorah insisted, crying.

Pauto gruffly took her hands, placing them behind her back, loudly announcing, "I hereby arrest you for the attempted murder of your sister, the Queen of Alstromia, Her Majesty Alexis Snipperdoom." He harshly placed black ties on her hands and cast a spell to remove all her powers, rendering any resistance futile.

Zandorah stood on the pathway between the Colosseum and Manor, accepting the charges and arrest. She did not resist, with her head down. Zandorah figured this would happen.

Shawnatar became furious, trying to punch Andreh and Pauto for what they were doing. But Andreh managed to subdue him and placed him under arrest for attempting to harm the head of Security, Pauto, a crime punishable with jail time in the High Tower.

By now, a large crowd surrounded them. Lorthana watched, motionless, unable to speak. Aerianna stood next to her, holding her hand. She worried about what had just happened to the Queen, Zandorah, and Shawnatar. Aerianna was left speechless.

The head Judge, Kristah Villainnow, walked up to Zandorah and spat in her face. "You are a disgrace! You are hereby stripped of the victory against the Queen. You have gone against the Battle Guidelines and will be charged accordingly. May the Justice System prevail." She stomped off with the other two judges, having said her peace.

Zandorah closed her eyes, unable to say anything. She wanted to die. It was her ignorance that caused the tragic event. She should have known better than to trust Florenzzah Lovecraft! Her belief that the spell would not seriously harm Alexis was stupid. Zandorah fully planned to accept responsibility for the spell she cast and the tragic results. She hoped someone would visit Florenzzah and ask for a *Reversal Spell* before Alexis would fade into the *Eternal World of Guidance,* never to be seen again!

Armbruster requested that Alexis be moved to the Palace in her chamber. He also insisted Edwinn Shivvers stay with her until a cure or *Reversal Spell* was found. In the meantime, Armbruster planned to head to Florenzzah's hut with Pauto and a few Security Command Team members. He would not leave until he had a way to revive his wife!

Pauto turned Zandorah over to Andreh. "Please, take her to the High Tower and secure her. I will notify Head Legal Counsel Jamessihn Shorttar of Zandorah's and Shawnatar's arrests. I plan to head to Florenzzah's hut and will ask Armbruster if he wishes to accompany me. Can you handle this on your own?"

"I will take care of it, Pauto. You can trust me," responded Andreh, taking custody of Zandorah and Shawnatar. Andreh immediately ordered two of his Security Command Team commoners to remove the two prisoners and escort them to the High Tower, where they would be retained until their law representative could advise them of their rights.

Alexis looked beautiful despite her critical condition. She glowed a light blue color as she lay on her bed. Armbruster covered up her body with a thick blanket. He realized it was a silly gesture, given she was blue, frozen, and ice cold to the touch from a spell. Nothing attempted so far had made a difference or revived her. After kissing his wife gently on the forehead and speaking to Edwinn, he left the chamber to locate Pauto. Armbruster was eager and ready to confront Florenzzah.

Florenzzah Lovecraft cackled as she heard the news. It made her happy that the dark spell turned out just as planned. Now, she would be able to negotiate for something she really wanted. She had previously been promised a position on the Royal Staff. However, that job was mundane and not what she had hoped it would be, and she had something else in mind. Without a doubt, Armbruster would give it to her without blinking an eye to save the Queen.

Pauto managed to locate Armbruster as he entered the Palace. He stood in the Security Command Chamber, waiting for Pauto. The two formulated a plan to confront Florenzzah. Pauto assumed she had intentionally given the spell to Zandorah to ensure it backfired, causing Alexis to become a victim.

If that turned out to be true, then Zandorah would not be held responsible for Alexis' tragic accident stemming from magic gone awry.

"So, we agree? We will head to Florenzzah's hut and confront her. We are not leaving without a cure. We must get it no matter what it takes," Armbruster confirmed.

"Agreed. I will have our team ready in ten minutes. We will meet you by the Palace's main gate," added Pauto confidently. He knew Armbruster meant business. He was firm in his stance and looked angrier than he had ever seen before. He wondered what had changed.

★*.★*.★*.★*.★

Edwinn stared at Alexis. She was positioned on the bed, motionless. He touched her right arm and quickly withdrew it. She was ice-cold to the touch. He had never seen anything like it. The magic had lasting effects, which was unusual. Most spells lasted a few minutes, hardly ever more than that. On rare occasions, a spell was used to last days, but those were complex spells and took time to complete.

At first, Edwinn believed it was a *Ghosting Spell*, but just the way Alexis looked told him it was not. Later, Pauto informed him that Zandorah divulged it was a *Shield and Freeze Spell*. Edwinn was unaware of a *Reversal Spell* for the *Shield and Freeze Spell*. He hoped someone could concoct a potion or cast a new magic to save Alexis before it was too late. Lastly, Edwinn wondered how Zandorah could cast the spell so quickly and effectively. Edwinn sat on the edge of the bed, observing Alexis. She was not breathing, so by most definitions, she was dead. But he knew in the magical realm, there were different levels of death. Some were impermanent. This was one of those.

Alexis was basically in a deep-frozen sleep, unable to move, speak, or breathe. What worried Edwinn was the fact that most spells like this one had a limited time for a reversal. Since he did not know precisely how this enchantment was formulated, he had no clue how much time was left to save the Queen.

Edwinn let out a long sigh, stood up, and walked to the window to stare at the valley below, hoping Armbruster could convince Florenzzah to help. Edwinn personally knew the Witch and was well aware of her devious ways. She had the unfortunate reputation of being a self-serving Witch.

Suddenly, Edwinn was startled as the chamber door flew open, and Lorthana and Aerianna entered the room. Lorthana hurried to her daughter's side, looking down at the seemingly lifeless body.

"Edwinn, will my daughter be okay? Please do not spare me. I need to know the truth," Lorthana begged, tears running down her cheeks. She held her daughter's cold hand, weeping.

"As I told Armbruster, there is no way to know for sure until we know more about the enchantment used against her. I have tried everything I know. I summoned other Healers, and they, too, have no method to save her. I am so very sorry, Lorthana. I can only imagine how you must feel," Edwinn replied, wishing he could say or do something to change the situation.

Aerianna joined Lorthana and stared at her friend. It was strange to see Alexis in this position. Only one other time had she seen something similar. It was when Yarlen used a *Ghosting Spell* on Alexis. That situation almost ended tragically. Aerianna hoped this spell was reversible. But, as she noticed, Alexis was not breathing. This seemed like a much more complex and challenging spell to reverse. Alexis was still alive during the *Ghosting Spell,* floating around as a ghostly figure. Aerianna wondered how this spell was so powerful. *'What did Florenzzah do?'*

Pauto, Andreh, Armbruster, and five security team members met at the large arch of the Palace. The group huddled in a circle as Yarlen chanted loudly. Two seconds later, the entire group disappeared into a grey fog, quickly reappearing outside Florenzzah's hut.

Yarlen was ready. He was armed with his precious potion.

CHAPTER 13

Yarlen was a resourceful Wizzard. When he realized who was behind the magic, he headed to speak to the one Witch who could help. She was not surprised to see him as he knocked on her door. She opened the creaking door with a smirk, showing him that she had been expecting his visit.

At that precise moment, Yarlen knew he had found the one who would provide him with a helpful spell to use against Florenzzah.

Farla Summerstahr guided Yarlen into the tiny room. The fire roared in the small fireplace, which was warm and cozy. She sat on the worn-out chair, pulling a patched blanket over her legs. She stared at him, waiting to hear what he had to say.

"I assume you know why I am here, Farla," Yarlen began. "Alexis is in trouble, and I need your help. Your nemesis, Florenzzah, gave a spell to Zandorah to use at the Battle of the Ceptres and Wands to destroy the Queen. Alexis is frozen and unable to breathe or communicate. I am afraid we are running out of time to help her."

Farla considered his words. She closed her eyes, rubbing the blanket between her old, thin fingers. She remained quiet for a few minutes. Yarlen grew impatient but realized it was best to say nothing. Doing so would only aggravate her. He wanted her to be helpful, and thus, he waited for her response.

"What did she use? Do you know? There are a few spells that will have similar outcomes."

"Supposedly, it was a *Shield and Freeze Spell*. That is what Zandorah claims."

"Well, I have bad news. If it is a *Shield and Freeze Spell*, only the person who invented it can reverse it. You will need to confront Florenzzah. I can provide you with a spell that will force her to divulge the information. It is a potent spell, but sadly, I do not have the necessary ingredients to concoct the potion. You must mix up a tonic and splash it on Florenzzah while chanting specific words. Can you do that, Yarlen?" Farla asked.

Yarlen agreed to return to the Tower at the Palace of Snipperdoom to retrieve the necessary items. He would then come back and, with her help, concoct the potion. He did not bother to ask her what she wanted in return. He assumed she would make her demands known soon enough!

Before too long, the two stood before her glowing cauldron, adding one ingredient at a time. Occasionally, a crackling or snapping noise emanated from the pot. The potion was complete within a few minutes, and the cauldron glowed a strange orange color. Farla filled a #3 Potion Bottle and handed it to Yarlen.

"We will discuss my payment in the future. Now, go save your Queen. Here are the words you must speak." She handed him a piece of brown, woven cloth, similar to a burlap bag, with words written in bright red.

Yarlen assumed it was ink but wondered if it was blood. He shrugged and thanked Farla, quickly departed, refusing to waste any more time. He knew the Queen's life hung in limbo.

Yarlen met Armbruster in his chamber. He was eager to head to the hut to confront Florenzzah. Armbruster listened to Yarlen explain how they would deploy the potion and spell. It would require swift action. He felt immensely grateful to Yarlen for his preemptive help. He was an ingenious Wizzard, and Armbruster knew he owed him big time.

A short time later, the group stood in front of Florenzzah's doorway. Yarlen carefully held the potion bottle, ready to throw it at Florenzzah when she opened the door. He did not want to wait for an invitation into her hut. She would most likely stall. Alexis was almost out of time. According to Farla, the *Shield and Freeze Spells* usually had a reversal window of less than a day before becoming permanent.

Florenzzah opened the door the minute she heard voices. Just as she was about to invite the group into her hut, she felt something cold hitting her face. Suddenly, she felt the urge to cry, feeling a peculiar sensation in her stomach. She looked at Yarlen, feeling perplexed.

"What have you done?" she shrieked.

"Tell me how to reverse the *Shield and Freeze Spell*! We need to know right now." Yarlen demanded.

Florenzzah heard his words and felt compelled to tell him the order of the spell reversal. She became frustrated, realizing she was divulging exactly how to perform the counterspell. It was never her intention to give Yarlen anything.

Within minutes, the group departed, leaving Florenzzah stunned and confused. *'How did Yarlen manage to force me to give him the information? I had no control over my thoughts or words!'* She became exasperated, slamming the hut door closed and heading back into the home to think about what had happened. Florenzzah realized her plan had failed. Yarlen successfully used magic against her, and it greatly irritated her that he was so darn clever to beat her at her own game!

Armbruster, Pauto, and Andreh entered the chamber feeling optimistic. Yarlen stopped quickly to visit the Tower to retrieve a few more ingredients. He wanted to ensure he had everything this time to save Alexis.

Andreh forced himself to stay in the background, leaning against the wall and watching Armbruster speak to Alexis. He wondered if she could hear him or if she was genuinely dead, unaware of what was happening.

Lorthana sat on the other side of the bed, sobbing. Aerianna stood by the fireplace. Her back was turned to everyone in the room. Aerianna stared at the fire, wondering if she would ever see her friend alive again.

Suddenly, Yarlen burst through the door, carrying an overflowing bag. He dumped the ingredients on the ground, carefully picking out several and mixing them up quickly in a small, round pot. He placed the pot onto the fire in the fireplace, counting down from 200, as instructed. As soon as the loud booming noise startled him, he knew the brew was ready. He returned to the ingredients pile and picked up a Potion #5 bottle.

Quickly, he poured the steaming mixture into the bottle. Then, he returned to the pile and picked up a feather. He walked to the bed and placed the feather on the Queen's forehead. He roughly pushed Armbruster out of the way to have room to work. Surprisingly, Armbruster did not get angry. Instead, he moved to the end of the bed to observe Yarlen's actions.

"Now, I will need one of you to pour the potion onto Alexis at the correct time. I will let you know when. You cannot hesitate. You must do it at the exact moment for the magic to work. Who will do it?" Yarlen asked.

A minute passed, and no one volunteered, obviously too frightened at messing up the exact timing, potentially causing the Queen's permanent death. Andreh knew it was time to speak up. "I will do it. I have nothing to lose. If I mess it up, you can punish me or do what you must. I am happy to do it, to save the Queen." Andreh took the bottle from Yarlen and sat near Alexis.

"Very well. I will begin the chant. When I say NOW, you must quickly pour it over her head, ensuring some of it touches her lips. Can you do that, Andreh?" Yarlen asked, noticing he was getting nervous, his hand shaking.

"Yes, I can," Andreh responded, feeling apprehensive. He knew he had to do it correctly to save her, and everyone watching him made him more fearful than he had anticipated.

Yarlen stood at the end of the bed. "Here we go. Get ready, Andreh. The Queen depends on you!"

Armbruster joined Lorthana on the other side of the bed to witness the ritual. He played nervously with his sleeve. Lorthana was still crying, wiping away her tears, worried that this could end her child's life.

Yarlen began the chant. He swayed back and forth, his hand over the Queen's feet. He looked down at the cloth, reading the words in a specific order. Then he loudly yelled, "Now!"

Andreh did not hesitate. He had already uncorked the bottle. Quickly but carefully, he poured the orange goo over Alexis. It oozed down her forehead, dripping off her nose, finally touching her lips. Yarlen continued chanting.

Strangely, the room became hushed. Yarlen finished the words and placed his hand on the Queen's feet. She was lifeless, still as can be. He worried the spell was not performed correctly and tried desperately to hide his nervousness.

Andreh watched the Queen's face, hoping she would awaken. It seemed like an eternity. Everyone's eyes were on Alexis. Unexpectedly, the room became extremely hot. Everyone felt sweaty and odd. Then Alexis started to regain color. Her plump lips turned a bright pink color. Her skin returned to normal. Her chest inflated, and she took a deep breath, exhaling while her eyes remained closed.

Armbruster rushed to her side, grabbing her hand and squeezing it. Her eyes fluttered open, and she looked around the room, feeling drowsy. Lorthana stared down at her daughter, thrilled she was alive. Lorthana continued to sob, but this time, it was tears of joy.

"You had us scared," began Armbruster, still holding his wife's hand. "How do you feel?" he asked with mixed feelings. She appeared to be okay.

Alexis looked around. She spotted Aerianna standing by the fireplace. Next to her was Andreh. Armbruster smiled at her as she looked at him. Yarlen released her feet, turning to leave the room, allowing them privacy. His job was done.

Andreh wanted to stay, but realized it was best to leave the room as well. So, reluctantly, he followed Yarlen out of the chamber.

Aerianna stayed for a few more minutes to ensure Alexis was okay. Once she felt confident her friend would recover fully, she excused herself to allow Lorthana and Armbruster time alone with Alexis. Aerianna also wanted to find Pauto and ask him to release Shawnatar and Zandorah. They did not need to be charged with anything, considering Alexis would be fine, and the spell's adverse reaction was Florenzzah's fault. She would be the one to potentially face a trial for what she had plotted against the Queen.

Florenzzah cleverly used Zandorah to carry out her revenge against Alexis. But she would be held accountable. That was for sure. Aerianna planned to pursue actions to have Florenzzah stripped of her magic. Sadly, she was about to learn a tragically harsh lesson!

Aerianna located Pauto rather quickly, figuring he would be in the Security Command Chamber. Sure enough, he greeted her as she entered. Pauto was the only one in the room, seated at the long, oblong conference table, reading over some notes. He smiled when he saw her approach, standing up to kiss her. She felt safe in his arms, glad the day had turned out well.

"So, what news do you bring me, Luv?" he teased.

"Alexis is awake!" Aerianna gleefully responded. "She will be fine. Yarlen and Andreh worked together to make the chant and *Reversal Spell* work. But you already knew that, didn't you?" Aerianna asked, feeling a huge sigh of relief.

"Once we returned from the hut, I knew Yarlen and Armbruster had it handled. I had no idea Andreh would help, but that is great. There was no need for me to get in the way. How is Alexis? Did you have the opportunity to speak with her?"

"No. I left. I felt as if I was intruding. Lorthana and Armbruster stayed behind in the chamber with Alexis. Yarlen, Andreh, and I left. I have to ask you a favor."

Aerianna spent a few minutes pleading her case. She explained that Armbruster demanded that Zandorah and Shawnatar be released immediately. Armbruster also insisted they stay at the Palace for the night so he could meet with them later. He still had a few questions for Zandorah.

Pauto informed Aerianna that he had already spoken with Jamessihn Shorttar, letting him know all charges would be dropped against his clients. He also requested that new charges be brought against Florenzzah Lovecraft for the intentional harm she had planned to inflict on the Queen, using Zandorah as her weapon of choice. Pauto knew the charges against Zandorah and Shawnatar would not stick, especially after hearing Florenzzah admit she had everything to do with the misused magic against Alexis.

"That is why I love you so. You are clever, kind, and the best of the best," Aerianna gushed, kissing him all over. He grinned happily.

"Well, then…perhaps you would want to thank me in person. I mean, we could head to your chamber now?" Pauto teased. But in reality, he wanted her badly. He loved and adored her. Watching Alexis almost die made him realize more than ever how much he loved Aerianna. He saw the look on Armbruster's face as he felt helpless, watching his wife fade away, dying. Not able to do anything to stop her death from happening.

"Okay. Why not? I really think I must show you my utmost thankfulness in person." Aerianna joked as she grabbed his hand. Pauto ran down the hallway, holding her hand. He was eager to make love to her.

★*.★*.★*.★*.★

Alexis managed to sit up. Her head hurt, and she felt nauseous. Her eyes throbbed and felt itchy. Still confused, she grabbed her mother's hand. "Mom, what happened to me? The last thing I remember was facing off against Zandorah?"

"Well, dear, that is a long story. Do you want the quick version?" Lorthana joked. She noticed her daughter looked drained and did not want to keep her up much longer.

"Yes, the short version, please, Mother!" Alexis insisted.

Lorthana sat on the edge of the bed, recounting details of what happened in the middle of the battle circle in the Colosseum. She left out a few parts to expedite the conversation. Alexis yawned, and her eyes fluttered shut a few times, noticeably tired.

"So, as you see, it all worked out. You are okay. Everything will be fine. We were fortunate. You are lucky to have Yarlen in your corner. He worked feverishly to find a way to force Florenzzah to divulge the *Reversal Spell*. He managed to speak with Farla, and she aided him, providing him with a useful spell."

Lorthana kissed Alexis on the cheek, excusing herself. She emphasized feeling tired, and she was ready to retire for the night, promising to check in on her daughter in the morning.

Alexis remained in bed with the blanket pulled up to her face. She shivered, feeling cold. Armbruster decided to do something he knew Alexis would not like, but frankly, he did not care. He stripped down to nothing and crawled naked into bed with her, pulling her into his arms. She warmed up quickly.

It did not take long for Alexis to fall asleep, resting her head against his burly chest, feeling him breathe, lulling her to sleep. His muscular arm was wrapped around her, making her feel secure. It reminded her of the old days when they were happy and in love. The two drifted off to sleep.

Zandorah and Shawnatar were released from the High Tower and escorted by Pauto and two other Security Commoners. They brought the couple back to the main Palace, where Zandorah stayed in a guest room.

Once inside her chamber, she sat on the bed crying. Shawnatar did not know how to handle what was happening. Instead, he sat across from her on the chair, letting her release the pain. She sobbed for a while. Feeling tired and emotionally spent, she jumped off the tall bed and removed her clothing. She walked to the bath chamber to take a hot shower.

Shawnatar decided to leave her alone. He was hungry and wanted to eat. He also needed time to think, furious with the mishandling of the entire situation. Getting arrested and being treated like a criminal rubbed him the wrong way.

Shawnatar planned to address it with Armbruster the next day. He wanted a public apology for his wife. Zandorah had been embarrassed unnecessarily, and he knew her reputation had been tarnished in the process.

Lorthana entered the guest chamber and collapsed onto the bed. She curled up into a ball, rocking back and forth, crying. The day had been one of the worst ones of her life. She witnessed one daughter almost die, and another was arrested and taken away, locked up in prison. Her heart ached for both.

She also felt awful for Shawnatar. He was a reserved Warlock, never saying too much. Lorthana knew it was difficult for him to see his wife suffer. He was probably already trying to figure out a way to reestablish Zandorah's credibility with the Clan and her security team. It would take some serious conversations and patience. Lorthana did not doubt that Shawnatar would be able to help her. He had always been steadfast and by her side. There was no way he would leave Zandorah now that she needed him the most. After all, he was known to be loyal and caring.

Before the evening ended, Kristah Villainnow received a nasty message from Armbruster. He ordered her to apologize publicly to Zandorah in the morning. Armbruster explained how another party was responsible for the spell's misfiring and that Zandorah was not to be held accountable for what occurred. Armbruster also reminded Kristah that her handling of the situation was completely unacceptable, and she could face repercussions after the Battle Rounds were complete.

Armbruster made it clear that he was not happy. Kristah had let her personal feelings interfere, and creating a scene in front of the Clan members was unprofessional, to say the least.

Kristah realized she had made a grave mistake when she walked away from Zandorah after spitting in her face. She allowed her emotions to get the best of her. Now, she wished she could undo her actions.

The only thing she could do now was apologize to the Supreme Ruler and beg for forgiveness. Kristah also planned to resign as head Judge, hopefully still keeping some of her dignity and respect.

Andreh entered his small chamber alone. The room was dark and cold. He missed Alexis and wished he could have stayed to speak with her. Seeing Armbruster there made his stomach turn. Yes, he knew Armbruster was still her husband and the King of Alstromia.

However, Alexis made it clear that she and Armbruster were no longer intimate. Their love had faded. Andreh planned to discuss it with Alexis once she felt better. He wanted to know how he fit into her life. If she were unwilling to commit to a relationship with him, he would still depart Alstromia and head to Earth to begin a new life without her.

Andreh felt unwilling to waste his life waiting on someone who would never be available. He was not bad-looking, and other Witches always threw themselves at him. He chose to reject them as his heart belonged to Alexis. Nonetheless, now he wondered if he should explore other relationships. He was lonely and wanted to live a life full of love. Andreh always hoped Alexis would eventually declare her unconditional love for him and leave Armbruster.

However, after his conversation with Alexx, he knew that would never happen. The best he could hope for was to stay her lover but never receive any public acknowledgment, as it would destroy her public persona.

He was deeply hurt because she seemed unwilling to make any compromises for their relationship. However, he could not help loving her as his heart had its own desires, and he felt powerless to alter them.

Gardone was restless, unable to sleep. He knew there was no way he would be able to do anything to remove Alexis from power. He gave up. Hoping to stay a free Warlock, he hid on Earth and Iriss, often changing his locations. He was weary of fleeing. He contemplated the idea of surrendering to the authorities and facing the repercussions of his choices. But selfishly, he decided against it. He could not imagine living out the rest of his life in prison. The thought made him cringe.

As Gardone tossed and turned in bed, he stared at Sharlottah and wondered what kind of life they would have if he constantly had to evade the law. Maybe it would be kinder if he let her go, giving her a life of freedom where she could be happy. He doubted she enjoyed their constant moves. It was getting old. She seemed much less willing to relocate and started complaining regularly. She was beginning to remind him of Lorthana, and that was making him feel sick to his stomach.

Florenzzah finally made her way to her small but fluffy bed, hoping for sleep, though she was restless. She drew the cover over her old, achy body, feeling unwell. Ever since the run-in with Yarlen and his group, she felt strange.

Her stomach ached, and she wondered if she would be held accountable for the spell she gave to Zandorah. Suddenly, Florenzzah felt an odd sensation rush through her body as she noticed sleep taking over. She opened her eyes briefly. Apprehensively, she stared up at the ceiling, realizing what was happening. She closed her tired eyes one final time with a slight smirk, fading away alone.

The morning arrived, and Alexis woke up feeling warm and sweaty. She rolled over and saw Armbruster still asleep. Feeling amorous, she decided to wake him up. She jumped on top of him, slowly but passionately kissing and caressing him.

Armbruster momentarily opened his eyes, needing to confirm that her actions were real and not just a dream. He smiled when he looked up at her, surrendering to her touch.

The Manor was already bustling. Vendors were restocking potions and snacks for the day's events. The judges arrived at the venue. Kristah asked the other two judges to join her as she wanted to personally apologize to them for her actions and share her desire to step down as Head Judge. She preferred someone else to take on the role of Head Judge and finish out the event.

After discussing all the details, it was decided that Steffani Vonderfill would replace her as Head Judge. She was known to be fair and recognized as a gifted athlete, having previously participated in the Battle Rounds. She was also familiar with the Battle Rules and Guidelines.

Pauto, Andreh, and Armbruster were already stationed outside the Manor discussing security measures. Armbruster was laughing and joking, which was unusual for him. He seemed very happy.

Andreh wondered why. Pauto gave Andreh a strange look, contemplating the same thing. Though Armbruster was not always grouchy, lately, he seemed more irritable than usual. Perhaps that is why it seemed odd to see him so jovial.

Armbruster pulled Andreh aside. "Listen, I know we have not always been on the best of terms. I just wanted you to know everything is water under the bridge. Please, let us start fresh. The Queen is safe, and we worked together to make that happen. I am thankful she has you as a friend." Armbruster walked away after his quick chat, leaving Andreh stunned.

Pauto overheard the conversation and quickly commented on Armbruster's words, still confused about why he would act so kindly toward Andreh. "You know, it took a lot for him to say that. If I were you, I would be grateful and accept his offer of peace. It is not like him to forgive and forget so quickly. I am not sure what caused that, but…take it!" Pauto chuckled while rushing off into the Manor, making sure that Rammadar and his team were ready for the upcoming events.

Alexis dressed and waited for Edwinn Shivvers to appear. He was scheduled to complete a medical exam to ensure the Queen could physically compete in future events. As Alexis waited, she reminisced about the previous night and the morning. She was stunned to realize how much she still cared for

Armbruster. He had made her feel things she had tried to forget. Feeling conflicted, Alexis was overcome by guilt about loving Andreh. She planned to see him later to speak with him. Alexis knew he was upset when he left the night before, unable to spend private time with her. She was appreciative that Andreh chose to leave without making a scene.

There was a loud knock on the door, followed by the door opening. Edwinn entered, bowing quickly. "My Queen. How was your night? I hope you are feeling well?" he inquired as he approached.

"Yes, it was a quiet and restful night. I am ready to battle. Please permit me to enter the rest of the events. I feel fabulous." Alexis still had a headache but refused to let it get in the way. She was upset that some of the Battle of the Ceptres and Wands competitions were postponed. Zandorah's and Alexis' match was over. The judges ruled it a draw, and neither would receive a trophy or face off against others.

Usually, there were two final matches. In the first one, two competitors faced off with Ceptres, thus determining the winner of the Ceptres match. That W3 would be crowned at the end of the Harvest Festival on day 7—the Celebration Events Day. The second match featured the remaining two competitors using Wands.

The winner of that match would also be crowned on the Celebration Events Day. Since Alexis and Zandorah had been disqualified, Pauto and Andreh were left. Both chose to use their Wands. The only trophy this year to be awarded would be the Battle of the Wands Winner.

Alexis only cared about the Races and Flight potions of the competitions. She felt prepared to participate. The Ceptres and Wands competition was fun, but not her priority. She could not wait to introduce Trixxie and fly like no other!

After completing Alexis's medical examination, Edwinn determined she was fit to finish the events. He wanted to inform the judges immediately that she could proceed as planned. Alexis was ecstatic as Edwinn swiftly left to locate the judges at the Manor. Alexis changed into her Battle uniform to prepare for the next round. This one was the Battle Flight—Fight or Flight.

Alexis hoped Andreh had prepared Trixxie and brought her food, ensuring her energy level was up and she would be competition-ready. Alexis assumed he had fed Trixxie since they had discussed it days before. Trixxie would be flown directly to the Colosseum by Alexis right before the start of the contest.

Not far away, Trixxie was restless in the cave. She was unaccustomed to being confined to one area. She walked back and forth in the cave, her long tail swishing around. She blinked her huge eyes, staring at the cave's entrance, wondering when she would be released.

Finally, after a few minutes, she gave up and plopped down onto the sandy ground in the cavern, curling up. Andreh watched her, feeling awful. He could sense her eagerness to leave the surroundings. Nevertheless, he promised Alexis to watch after Trixxie and was determined to follow through.

Alexis felt greatly relieved that she had been cleared to participate in the last events. Shortly, she would head to the cavern to fly Trixxie to the Colosseum. It would be her shining moment of the event and the year!

Armbruster, Pauto, and Yarlen discussed the upcoming events. Ambruster felt apprehensive about the latest news about Gardone. He could not help but wonder if he was still hiding out on Alstromia, ready to start more trouble. Plus, Armbruster worried for his mother-in-law, Lorthana.

With the upcoming termination of her Ceremonial Exchange and marriage to Gardone, Armbruster assumed there would be ill will toward Lorthana, and he vowed to keep her safe. Lorthana did not deserve the pain and suffering Gardone put her through. Lorthana was taking it in stride, but he noticed her quiet demeanor. She was less lively than before, more reserved. Lorthana appeared dressed in all black and, reluctantly, removed her Cape of Dismay as she realized too much attention was being paid to her. She did not enjoy it and preferred to grieve silently.

Not far away, Zandorah stretched on the cold floor in her room. Her back ached. She wanted to limber up before she competed against her sister. Shawnatar was not around, and she assumed he was with Armbruster and Pauto, though maybe not.

At times, Shawnatar liked to stay away from others and meditate on things. He was still shaken up from the prior incident and felt uneasy. He informed Zandorah that he planned to take a few days and head to Earth to visit friends, though he was not specific on the timeframe. Alstromia was not a friendly place, in his opinion. Shawnatar also did not want to return to Iriss, worrying that his father-in-law, Gardone, could be around.

Shawnatar had never been a fan of Gardone's. He felt he was too secretive and less than forthright. In his opinion, he was sneaky and unethical. He heard the rumors about his dealings and stayed away from

Gardone, so his name was not associated with him. Zandorah encouraged Shawnatar to get closer to Gardone, hoping they would bond. She felt they should get along since they were family. Both Warlocks meant so much to her.

Unfortunately, she noticed neither was too fond of the other. So, she chose to leave them alone to work it out. Now, it seemed like they preferred to stay away from each other. Rather than fight the issue, she backed off. With the Harvest Festival and Battle Rounds, she hoped Shawnatar would attend and support her participation. Though she wondered if he would stay away, fearing Gardone could show up and start some trouble.

Zandorah stood up and leaned against the stone wall. It was cold and felt amazing on her back. She rested her head on it, closing her eyes, wondering how much time she had left to relax. Zandorah was not ready to face Alexis.

She was convinced it was an uneven match between them. Alexis was far more skilled and a highly-rated warrior. It scared Zandorah. She wanted to back out of the competition, but knew it would upset her Clan and mother. Feeling the pressure, she decided to face her sister, regardless of the consequences, and hopefully, she would not be injured in the process. It was something she feared greatly. In the past, Alexis hurt her badly, and even though there were rules in place about how much a warrior could do to the opponent, it was at the judges' discretion.

Most judges admired Alexis and gave her excessive amounts of leeway, not calling out some of the unfair moves they noticed during matches. Instead, they gave Alexis points for her genius way of handling herself in the battles. In Zandorah's opinion, it only added to Alexis' self-inflated ego, allowing her to get away with too much.

Still feeling guilty about the magic she cast against Alexis and its unexpected repercussions, Zandorah reluctantly decided to let it go. She would face her sister and do her best to defend herself.

Alexis realized greatness required more than just training. She planned to make history today with Trixxie. Alexis was eager to show off the majestic beast. However, at the end of the day, she knew someone would lose, and there would be consequences. She hoped to beat Zandorah, and then she, Alexis, would decide whether or not to start a war, though she was unwilling to hurt her Clan.

War was never taken lightly. In many ways, it would hurt relationships and destroy two planets in the process. Instead, she planned to be gracious and forgive Zandorah, proudly showing others what it meant to be a leader.

Alexis used magic to transport herself to the cave. From there, she and Trixxie planned to fly toward the Colosseum to begin the races. Seconds later, Alexis appeared in the illuminated cavern. Andreh stood near Trixxie, talking to her. He petted her head, and she nodded as if she understood him. He jumped when he heard a noise.

"Alexis! Is it time?" Andreh asked.

"Almost. I cannot believe this is about to happen. Did Trixxie eat?" Alexis questioned, not seeing any food.

"Of course. A while ago. I did not want the beast to fly with a full stomach. I worried it would upset and make her tired. She enjoyed the food I provided. Trixxie took a short swim in the lake, though I had to rush her as I did not want anyone seeing her."

"Yes, I would not have been happy if my surprise had been given away early. Thank goodness no one saw her. Well, I will take her from here," she remarked, approaching Trixxie.

It was evident that Trixxie was happy to see Alexis. Her tail swished around, much like a dog wagging its tail. Alexis laughed, amused at the beast. Andreh smiled, realizing their strong bond.

Within minutes, Alexis mounted Trixxie. The two walked casually out of the cave and headed toward the open field for take-off. Andreh remained behind to ensure all went well. Once the two soared high in the sky, Andreh cast a spell to transport himself to the Colosseum. He could not wait to witness her landing with the beast, shocking the crowd.

Shawnatar handed the reins to Zandorah, who looked frightened. He knew she was ill-prepared for this day. Flying was not something she performed well, and frankly, she disliked it immensely. The Braggli was restless, jerking and prancing like a wild Torrin, adding to Zandorah's nervousness.

"Zandi, it will be okay. You must relax, or you will not be able to compete," insisted Shawnatar.

It was evident that Zandorah was not ready. She shook her head and kept playing with the reins, wrapping them tightly around her hands to the point where it was causing pain, cutting off her circulation.

"I know, Shawnatar. You do not need to remind me. I am well aware of my apprehensiveness. I want to finish this day. Has anyone spotted Alexis?"

Shawnatar informed Zandorah that the judges were still waiting for Alexis to arrive.

Though she still had plenty of time, it was strange that she was not early. Alexis disliked tardiness from others and was always punctual.

Armbruster, Aerianna, Pauto, and Lorthana sat in the assigned seating area to watch the next event. Armbruster searched the stadium for any sign of Alexis.

Aerianna felt quite disturbed that Alexis was still absent. As she was about to get out of her seat to speak with the judges, the crowd began clapping and yelling. Aerianna's eyes darted to the sky, and she could not believe what she saw. *'Is Alexis on the back of a Draghoon? What the heck?'* she wondered. The crowd went wild. No one had ever seen such a thing. It was the most surprising event of the year.

Alexis circled high in the sky with Trixxie, waving to the crowd below. She heard the roar of the group and their loud clapping. Alexis smirked. Trixxie seemed to enjoy the attention as well. She flicked her tail and dove down quickly, then accelerated back into the air, putting on a show for the spectators.

Armbruster shook his head. *'What is Alexis thinking? No one has ever entered a Draghoon into any competition.'*

Zandorah entered the arena and saw Alexis. Her heart stopped. *'Alexis entered a Draghoon? Why?'* Zandorah trotted into the area with her Braggli, which was pretty slow. Zandorah realized she was in trouble. Her Braggli would not be able to keep up with the Draghoon.

Zandorah contemplated the statistics of the Braggli. They are a much smaller beast than the mighty Draghoon. They tend to stand under 7 feet tall. Bragglis can be fast, but their smaller and more delicate wings cannot keep up with the Draghoon. Zandorah shook her head, fearing she had already lost.

The Braggli is described as a mix of a dragon (sizable, pointy head) and a snake with a long, scaly tail. They also have two large feet with long claws. The most unusual aspect of this species is its three arms. One arm is on the right side of its body, one on the left side, and one on the lower tail, which is convenient for grabbing items or enemies from a distance.

These creatures are sky blue, pitch black, mint green, grey, or off-white in color. However, the most distinctive color is mint-green. Most Bragglis do not live long, with a life expectancy of around five years. They tend to become lazy as they age, sleeping their lives away. Regardless, many W3s keep them as pets or use them as battle dome challengers.

Alexis finally forced Trixxie to land in the open area of the Colosseum. She dismounted the creature and ordered Trixxie to sit. Ever the well-trained Draghoon, she obeyed, bowing her head to the Queen and plopping down onto the hard ground.

Spectators were in awe of the Draghoon and its good manners. Some believed it was quite unusual for a large creature to act so demurely.

Alexis approached Zandorah. "Hello, Zandi! Are you ready to race?" She teased, seeing the look of panic on her sister's face.

"If we must," she responded, wishing she could drop out of the event.

"Well, let us head to the starting line on the race track, shall we?" Alexis announced, loving the fact that her sister was hesitant.

All ten participants stood before the starting line of the race track, ready to begin. The Battle Flight competition had always been fierce. Only ten participants were allowed to enter the Fight or Flight portion.

This year's participants were listed on the active roster: *Alexis Snipperdoom, Andreh Darkhill, Arlow Zwitting, Carhlston Hillstrom, Juannah Ogarstan, Pauto Vexxorth, Rammadar Ximberton, Sheillah Hexxon, Steffen Starleight, and Zandorah Snipperdoom.*

Part I - of the competition mandates that every participant arrive with a Torrin or another type of flying creature. The goal is to outmaneuver and outperform the other competitors in flight. Each warrior is evaluated based on their flying difficulty, aerial tricks with their beast, speed, and ability to reach the goalpost at the end of the race track without losing control. Participants are required to execute a minimum of four tricks, each varying in difficulty from levels 1 to 5. All contestants must successfully pass a rigorous tryout and demonstrate proficiency across all skill levels.

Part II– The Battle Flight consists of the Fight or Flight Portion featuring the two remaining champions from Part I. In this segment, the finalists attempt to knock each other off their beasts while making at least five laps around the Colosseum. Contestants are permitted to use magic and their wands, but Ceptres are not allowed. The second part of the contest concludes when the first W3 finishes all tasks and reaches the goalpost. It is a heated event that may lead to harm or even death. The victor is crowned at the Victory Celebration on the last day of the events. To date, only one Wizzard died in the previous ten years. It should also be noted that this event is separate from the Battle Races, usually held the next day.

The crowd watched enthusiastically, anticipating the beginning of the competition. Alexis smiled as she stared ahead, concentrating on the task of winning. She had practiced a variety of tricks at different difficulty levels but planned to use a few new moves taught to her by a friend on Earth. She was prepared and eager to get started.

Zandorah, on the other hand, was less prepared. She only perfected a few skilled moves and realized they were nothing spectacular or eye-catching to the judges. At this point, she did not care. She planned to complete the round without getting hurt or killed, falling off her Braggli.

Pauto was positioned next to Alexis on his Torrin. He smiled at her, but she was not paying attention. She seemed to concentrate on the gong noise, which would start the flying competition part of the event. Pauto preferred the race portion. It was more physically demanding, and he loved watching the competitors display their skills.

Andreh chose to drop out of the match, though he had been named on the roster. He did not inform Alexis of his last-minute decision. He figured he stood very little chance against Pauto and Alexis. Rammadar was also a strong opponent. He had won numerous other events last year.

Sheillah and Steffen were side by side. Both chose to fly on Torrins. They were strong warriors, but neither was a gifted flyer. At the very end of the long line, Arlow Zwitting, Carhlston Hillstrom, and Juannah Ogarstan waited for the event to commence. Juannah was not a great flyer and barely made the cut.

Carhlston and Arlow were also mediocre competitors. Neither had ever won any awards or trophies. It was Carhlston's second year entering the event, and he did not plan to join another if he did not place this year.

The King remained quiet while seated beside Lorthana, waiting for the competitors to begin. He watched Aerianna as she shifted in her seat nervously, probably worried about Pauto. It made Armbruster smile. He envied their relationship.

Armbruster would give anything to start over with Alexis. To let bygones be bygones. He wanted his wife back and wished to begin fresh. Alexis was still the fiery and sexy Witch he had fallen in love with so long ago. Sadly, he felt she would never want to resume their relationship.

It seemed she was deeply in love with Andreh, though she still denied it and tried to hide her feelings. Unfortunately, she was not successful. Most noticed how she looked at Andreh and how he responded to her attention.

Armbruster shook his head, feeling deep sorrow. He hoped to speak with Alexis once the Battle Rounds were complete and ask her if she wanted to end their marriage. He no longer wanted to be with someone who did not love him. Though it hurt him to think about separating from Alexis, in a way, it was a relief. He would be free to find love and grow old with someone else.

The judges were seated and ready to begin the first part of the event. The gong rang, the noise echoing throughout the arena.

Without hesitating, Alexis took off with Trixxie. They soared into the air, and Alexis pulled back on the reins, loudly shouting commands at Trixxie. The energetic Draghoon flipped in the air, completing a double somersault, diving down to the ground, buzzing the crowd. The audience went wild with applause. What a show!

Alexis grinned, hearing the roar. She gently kicked her heels into Trixxie's side. Immediately, Trixxie zoomed straight into the sky, swirling like billowing smoke. She was swift and limber, even though she was a giant creature. The crowd loved her, clapping and chanting, "Draghoon, run, win, fight…"

Alexis believed she could win. She completed a few less intense tricks to appease the audience and the judges, then quickly landed, allowing Trixxie to rest.

Zandorah was performing poorly. She almost fell off after her second trick on the Braggli. Her Braggli was tiring quickly, slowing down and panting hard. Zandorah feared the beast would land and quit cooperating.

But her Braggli continued to follow the commands she received. Within a few minutes, Zandorah landed, knowing she had not performed her best but was elated to have finished this portion of the event.

Pauto observed Alexis and Trixxie. He knew he had to do something spectacular to catch up to her. She would definitely outscore him. He pulled back on the Torrin's reins and attempted a tricky move. Maizzeh, his Torrin, seemed confused, hesitating.

Pauto kicked her hard on the side of her belly with his boot, causing her to flinch. However, she got the message. Immediately, Maizzeh soared into the sky, repeatedly flipping as Pauto desperately held on, trying not to fall off. His hands were getting sore, and he fought to keep from dropping the reins.

Suddenly, Maizzeh corrected herself and zoomed down toward the ground, surprising everyone as she made one last flip before gracefully landing in the center of the arena.

The audience erupted with clapping and yelling. Pauto and Maizzeh had completed a spectacular and challenging performance. The judges agreed. They, too, stood, bowing their heads in approval.

Alexis frowned, jealous of the attention Pauto gained from his routine. The other participants finished their tricks and landed safely. The results would be announced quickly, as the next part of the competition was the one that most were eager to witness.

Alexis approached Pauto, leaving Trixxie alone to sit in the middle of the Colosseum. Trixxie gazed around the arena, bored, and finally lay down, resting on the dirt. She closed her eyes.

"Wow, Pauto. I had no idea your Torrin could fly like that. Where have you been training?" Alexis inquired. She was pissed off at the spectacular performance he displayed with Maizzeh.

"Well, Alexis, we all have secrets, don't we?" Pauto responded snippily. He walked away, guiding Maizzeh toward the crowd, searching for Aerianna. He was uninterested in listening to Alexis and her demeaning comments.

Alexis fumed. "Okay, Pauto. See you in a bit," she yelled, hoping to elicit a response. Yet, he seemed more concerned about finding Aerianna, ignoring her.

Aerianna stood in the front row, watching Pauto approach. She clapped loudly. He flung his arms around, whispering in her ears. "I love you, gorgeous."

"I am so proud of you and Maizzeh. That was spectacular. I worried you would fall off Maizzeh during the third or fourth twirl in the air! How did you manage to stay on her back?"

"We have trained for a long time. In the past, I fell off numerous times. It wasn't easy to stay on her back. However, I figured out that if we moved fast enough, by some miracle and force, I would not fall. So, the trick is to move super-fast!" Pauto announced, feeling proud of Maizzeh. Though the Torrin looked exhausted, she looked around attentively, allowing spectators to pet her.

The gong in the area made a bong, bong, bong noise, and the crowd hushed. The judges entered the arena. The new Head Judge—Steffani Vonderfill, approached the microphone.

"Witches, Warlocks, and Wizzards…we are ready to announce the winners and those who will advance to the next round. In First Place, Pauto Vexxorth! In Second Place, Alexis Snipperdoom! The Third Place goes to Rammadar Ximberton. Fourth Place belongs to Zandorah Snipperdoom. Finally, Fifth Place is awarded to Sheillah Hexxon. We wish to thank all participants. Unfortunately, only two can compete in the next round. When the Harvest Festival and Battle Rounds Competition end, we will crown the top five winners at the awards ceremony. In the meantime, we will watch the epic battle between Pauto and our Queen commencing after lunch! Also, we will have a special battle event in the morning between the two sisters,

Zandorah and Alexis Snipperdoom! Be sure to attend the event if you have time." The judges left the arena and headed to the Manor for lunch.

Alexis was fuming. She could not believe that the judges chose Pauto over her. She should have been given bonus points for entering a Draghoon. In the end, it did not matter. She would face off against her friend and beat him. He would not be able to match her witchcraft and spells. Alexis felt confident she would win.

Aerianna and Pauto followed the crowd toward the Manor. Maizzeh was in the stable, and Essten personally watched over her. Trixxie slept outside the stables, tied up under a large weeping Trimber, providing her shade.

Armbruster escorted Lorthana to the Manor for lunch. They chatted during the walk about the upcoming event. Both believed Alexis would win. Armbruster hoped Pauto would defeat Alexis, but doubted he had enough experience.

Alexis plowed through the front doors of the Manor. She was hungry and tired. She felt a tap on her right shoulder as she headed to the bathroom. She spun around and faced Andreh. He beamed with pride.

"I knew you would excel! I am so proud of you. See, all those lessons at the lake helped. Are you ready to destroy Pauto?" he teased.

What he really wanted was to kiss and take her into his arms. He knew that could not happen in such a public space.

"Umm, he received first place. I was only awarded second! I have no idea why. It seems ridiculous. I entered a Draghoon. It was epic. The judges are foolish not to give extra points for that. I want to determine what we scored and why I did not win. Yes, I feel confident I will be victorious. However, I am tired. Let's eat. I will meet you inside." She strutted toward the restroom, finished with their conversation. Alexis was frustrated, still shocked that Pauto managed to place first.

Inside, the dining room was packed. The staff worked feverishly to fill plates with wonderful-smelling dishes. Tall jugs of potions and brews lined the middle of the tables. Some of the concoctions provided by Henrii Snubberly and his BrewHaus were quite potent. The crowd was joyous, appreciating the warm fall afternoon and the feast inside the building after the races ended.

On Iriss, Gardone sat back in the oversized black chair. He closed his eyes. The woman stared at him. "Well, what do you think? Your daughter did not make it to first place. She only received second! Victory, ha-ha. Obviously, Alexis is not that great."

"Silence! You will not criticize my child! Do you hear me? Get out!" he shouted, pointing to the door.

Shocked, Sharlottah Zipmound sprinted from the room. She knew Gardone was disappointed he could not attend the Battle Rounds, but she was tired of his abusive ways. Sharlottah decided it was time to head back to her house on Earth. He could rot on Iriss as far as she was concerned. Outside the door, she flicked her wand and disappeared.

Steaming with anger, Gardone jumped out of the chair. He bolted toward the door to speak with Sharlottah. It was not his intention to yell at her. He knew she meant well. She was ever so supportive, and he had misbehaved. He regretted acting like a fool. Now, he planned to correct the error.

"Sharlottah, where are you, honey? I am sorry, come back inside. I am upset at Alexis, not you!" He looked around and realized she was gone. "Figures!" he yelled.

Gardone felt abandoned. "Why do these Witches always leave? None of them understands me!" He complained as he sank down in the chair. "Well, I will wait and see if she returns." Gardone was not used to others doing what they wanted. He was the one in charge. Sharlottah had to learn that!

Gardone wondered why she believed that she could scurry off without informing him where she planned to go. He planned to cast a spell to locate her. Then, he would retrieve Sharlottah, and she would stay! He would see to it. After all, she owed him, and he needed her. It was just that simple!

Lorthana fiddled with her eating utensils. She gazed around the room, wishing she were back on Iriss. She hated Alstromia. It was not her favorite place. Though she loved spending time with Princess Lilah and Alexis, she wanted to return home. She was getting old and tired. The last year had been hell, and she tried to find something to give her joy.

Secretly, Lorthana had met with a group of Witches on Earth and planned a trip to the New England coast. They arranged to stay at an old Bed and Breakfast high on a bluff overlooking the ocean. It sounded like an enchanting time to her. She yearned for relaxation.

"Hello, Mother," Alexis announced as she sat beside Lorthana. "What is good to eat today? I am starving. What did you think about the competition? Were you surprised to see Trixxie? Wasn't she just majestic?" Alexis beamed.

"Yes, dear. It was quite a performance. I am so sorry you did not win first place. You must be disappointed. I hear you still plan to battle against Zandorah no matter what! Why? You cannot just let things go, can you?" Lorthana asked, feeling perturbed.

"Oh, Mother, really! You knew we would battle regardless of the outcome. I ensured this would happen. I created the event. Zandorah knows this, too! I do not care if you are upset. It has to happen. You know this. We must close this chapter and end the drama. Only one of us can win. I will be the victor, and then I will decide if I want war."

"Alexis, you have nothing to prove. Everyone knows you are a much stronger warrior than your sister. Why put on this grand show? You are gloating and making Zandorah look bad. Is that what this is all about? Be honest. I believe you two need to work it out privately, not for all the Clans to witness. I am very disappointed in you!" Lorthana rose, throwing down her fork. She stormed off, leaving Alexis to stew in her misery.

'How dare she?' Alexis wondered. *'Mom is constantly defending her favorite daughter! I wish Amberrah were still alive. Then it would be different.'* Alexis ate a few bites of the food on the dish before her. Exasperated with Lorthana, she lost her appetite.

Alexis shoved the plate away, standing up and exiting the room. She planned to head to her chamber to rest until the next competition began. Alexis needed time to figure out a way to confront her mother later to impress upon her how much she hated the preferential treatment toward Zandorah. It was hurtful, and Alexis was sick of it all.

No matter the outcome of their conversation, she figured it was best to confront the demon between them. Lorthana would probably reject the implication, but in her heart, she knew it was true. Zandorah was her favorite—for no reason other than the fact that she was easier to have around. She never challenged anyone or anything.

Alexis frowned, realizing that Zandorah would probably remain her mother's favorite. Unfortunately, she had become accustomed to it, and it felt awful. On this day, Alexis vowed never to treat her child in such a hurtful manner. She now understood it had scarred her and made her unsympathetic toward Zandorah. Their relationship was ruined.

CHAPTER 14

The group of Warlocks stood outside the gate. They knew the time had arrived. Most attendees were inside the Manor, eating and oblivious to what would happen. Gardone's friend and confidant, Cheeve Illton, summoned the group to the mountain. He placed the map with the plan on the ground for all to read. The ***GRAW-*** *Gardone's Righteous Army and Warriors,* were ready. Cheeve created a secret organization to help Gardone overthrow Alexis and Alstromia.

"We should wait, Cheeve. It is still too early. It would be better to postpone the attack until tonight's final battle. Alexis will be weak, and her magic will not be fully restored from the battles. It will be the best time to attempt to take over Alstromia," suggested Bartin.

"Perhaps. Let us vote. Who wishes to begin our invasion now? Who wishes to wait?" asked Cheeves. The group voted. The majority agreed to wait until nightfall. *'The rest of the GRAW from Earth and Iriss should arrive by then, too,'* thought Bartin.

"Fine. We wait. Let us retreat to the cave on the mountain until we know all our Warriors are present. Will we have at least 500? I do not believe we can win with less. Alexis has a powerful and capable Army that she will deploy once she realizes what is happening," added Garlow.

"If you did your job, Garlow, we will be able to impose much damage before the Army arrives. Are you sure the Security Command Team will be useless?" asked Cheeves.

"Yes, Garrett has everything in place. They will not know what hit them."

"Plus, it will look as if Iriss is waging war! It is perfect," beamed Cheeves.

"Let us not forget. We begin with spells. No actual battles will begin until later. First, there will be fire, lots of pain, and suffering," announced Gardone, feeling powerful.

Alexis dropped her filthy uniform on the ground by the fireplace as she made her way to her bed. She was exhausted. Trixxie was challenging to maneuver. It required much strength. Alexis hurt all over, feeling weak. Knowing the next round would begin within an hour and a half, she decided to nap to regain strength. She quickly pulled the heavy blanket over her, partially covering her head. It did not take long for her to fall asleep.

Andreh searched the Manor for Alexis. He wanted to speak with her and discuss the next battle. It occurred to him that some techniques she had previously used would not work in the next round. He wondered if she had something up her sleeve to help or if she planned to wing it. Pauto was a hell of a warrior, and he could fly. It would not be an easy feat to beat him.

Andreh worried that if Alexis lost, she would lose confidence. Since she was due to face her sister in the morning in the critical battle determining if there would be war between their planets, he speculated what he could do to help her. Now, if only he could locate her.

Armbruster finished lunch and escorted Lorthana out of the Manor. He stopped and asked her, "I am headed back to the Palace for a while. Do you wish to accompany me, or do you plan to stay here?"

"No, I will remain here. I will relax in the back by the waterfall. I am tired. Thank you for your company, Armbruster. See you later!" Lorthana replied. He nodded, slamming down his Ceptre and disappearing into a fog.

Lorthana returned to the Manor. She walked down the long path toward the field. The waterfall sounded soothing. A few other W3s sat on blankets, relaxing. It was a glorious fall day. Lorthana flicked her wand, and a red and white checkered blanket appeared. She plopped onto it, interlaced her fingers behind her head, and stared at the sky. Within minutes, the waterfall noise lulled her to sleep.

The judges made their way back to the Colosseum. They were ready for the final battle to take place soon. It had been over an hour, and a few spectators filled the arena, prepared to witness the epic event.

Alexis woke up feeling refreshed. She dressed swiftly and washed her face, eager to retrieve Trixxie from the stable. Essten advanced when he heard her by the building.

"My Queen. Are you here for the beast? I just finished walking it in the pasture. It was restless, and I did not feed it. Andreh said she would become lazy and tired if she ate right before the race. So, I only let her walk a bit, allowing her some freedom. She seems more relaxed now! I hope that is okay?" He wanted her to know he followed the instructions given.

"Thank you, Essten. Yes, that is perfect. Where is she?" Alexis asked, eager to guide her to the Colosseum.

"She is behind the stable, under the weeping Trimber. Do you want me to get her for you?" Essten asked.

The Queen declined his offer. She strolled toward the back of the structure to locate Trixxie. Approaching the back of the building, Alexis saw him, and he winked at her.

"Hello, beautiful," Andreh said, handing her the reins. His eyes sparkled as he gazed into hers. She looked away, blushing.

"I should have known you would be here, Andreh. How are you? Also, why did you not compete today? I thought we agreed you would attempt to defeat Pauto?" Alexis hoped to change the subject. She noticed feeling giddy around him. It was a strange feeling.

"No, today is your day. I only trained with you to help you beat him. I have no desire to battle."

"I see. Well, I am disappointed. I hoped to see you compete. Maybe next year?!" Alexis took the reins from his hand and mounted Trixxie. Once she straddled the beast, she looked down at him. "See you in the Colosseum!" Alexis said with burgeoning excitement as she led Trixxie toward the arena. She did not want to fly her, hoping to preserve the beast's energy. Andreh remained behind, watching Alexis, wishing he could have had more time with her. *'Maybe later,'* he muttered under his breath, remaining hopeful.

The arena became extraordinarily noisy. The crowd grew, becoming boisterous. The vendors, primarily commoners from the village, walked up and down the wide aisles, handing out snacks and potions. It was an excellent opportunity to make money. Henrii and his renowned brews always made any occasion better. His elixirs and potions were famous and not intended for lightweight drinkers. Henrii only used pure and potent products to produce his concoctions, and they were well-known for knocking you to the ground if you had too many! Some of the attendees were already much too intoxicated, singing and swaying side to side. Others remained in their seats, chugging down the tall, filled Ozar jugs.

Back in the Palace of Snipperdoom, Zandorah dressed as Shawnatar watched her. "Are you ready to defeat Alexis?" he knew the answer, but still wanted to ask. His wife was many things, but brave and optimistic, she was not.

"What makes you believe I can accomplish such a feat?" Zandorah inquired. She realized she had a slim chance of winning. The epic battle against Alexis would not happen until after the second round of the Battle Rounds, the Fight or Flight portion, was completed.

First, Alexis would face off against Pauto. After that, she would be granted a slight respite, allowing her to relax and recharge before facing Zandorah for the last and epic battle of the event.

"I am ready! Well, I should say as ready as I can be. I hope she will be, too. I am not sure she will be physically able to battle after completing her battle against Pauto. What do you think about that?" Zandorah asked her husband.

Shawnatar ran his right hand through his hair. He leaned against the large fireplace, still hurting quite badly from his extensive injuries. He was reluctant to consume a healing potion, worrying it would make him feel woozy or tired. Shawnatar wanted to remain focused on supporting his wife. He would worry about relieving the pain later.

"Alexis is a champion. She will be a challenge to defeat, but you can do so. You need to believe in yourself and remember that you two battled before. You know her techniques and can destroy her!" Shawnatar wanted to remind Zandorah of her incredible techniques and capability to win. Sometimes, Zandorah lacked self-esteem. It made Shawnatar glum. He wished she could see herself as he saw her—strong and resilient.

Zandorah appreciated the confidence Shawnatar showed her, but she was not naïve. She knew Alexis had always been a much stronger battle warrior.

Armbruster paced restlessly around the Manor, wondering where his beloved wife was hiding. He had summoned her, wishing to hold a conversation before the final battles. At Armbruster's request, Pauto reluctantly sent Andreh to locate Alexis and inform her that Armbruster demanded her presence. Pauto figured Andreh would have better luck finding her. Plus, he wanted Armbruster off his back. He was attempting to prepare himself mentally for his battle against Alexis, and the constant interruptions made it difficult.

Aerianna was nervous, insisting that Pauto drop out of the dangerous event. She knew

Alexis would not take it easy on him and probably did not care if Pauto became a casualty. The thought made Aerianna ill.

Alexis strolled into the Manor and was immediately surrounded by adoring fans. She was there to register for the battle with the judges. Her protection team quickly secured the Queen and kept the fans away.

Armbruster made his way through the large group, looking irritated. He pulled Alexis away by her left arm, dragging her toward the empty hallway.

"Where have you been? I sent everyone out looking for you! The battle between you and Pauto is going to start shortly."

"You can release my arm, Armbruster. You are hurting me," Alexis burst out in anger as she yanked herself away from him. "What do you need? Can we do this later? I must head to the Colosseum to warm up with Trixxie."

"No, it cannot wait, Alexis. Listen, please, do not hurt Pauto. I know you want to win, but he is a good guy and a wonderful friend. I beg you to be kind."

"You are begging for his life? I have no intention of harming him beyond normal battle damage and consequences. I respect Pauto. But this is a battle, and I plan to win."

Before Armbruster could say anything else to her, she stormed off. Alexis arrived at the holding area near the Colosseum. She firmly held Trixxie by the reins when suddenly, Andreh reappeared.

"Alexis, hold on a minute," Andreh shouted.

Alexis faced him. "What is it, Andreh? I need to prepare Trixxie. She is getting spooked by the noise, and I must calm her down."

"Pauto wanted me to tell you that Armbruster wishes to speak with you immediately. I should have mentioned it when we spoke before. Please forgive me," he pleaded, feeling awful, he got sidetracked and neglected to inform her of his request.

"I have already spoken to Armbruster. He demands I take it easy on Pauto. He is worried I will inflict too much harm," Alexis disclosed.

"I assume you will, too! Be kind. Pauto is a wonderful Warlock and Wizzard. We need him," Andreh agreed, laughing. He liked Pauto regardless of their recent tiffs. Andreh hated the thought that Alexis could harm him.

"Well, let's escort Trixxie inside the Colosseum, shall we? I want to be Battle-Ready," Alexis insisted. She was tired of everyone attempting to control her. Battles were meant to be won, and she planned to destroy Pauto and become the victor of this round. Andreh nodded, following Alexis, eager to watch her win.

The time had finally arrived. The head judge picked up the Trimber mallet to strike the gong. The loud noise immediately caused the crowd to stop what they were doing. The herd of spectators eagerly filed into their seats, ready to witness the battle of the day!

Alexis made her appearance and stood in the middle of the Colosseum. Trixxie was calm and sitting on her butt. She glared at the crowd with her ginormous, round eyes, surveying the territory.

Pauto entered the arena, and the crowd cheered. He raised his hands, waving, grateful for the warm welcome. He marched toward Alexis as Maizzeh, his Torrin, followed.

Once both competitors stood side-by-side, they proceeded to mount their beasts simultaneously. The head judge made the monumental announcement.

"Witches, Wizzards, and Warlocks…may I please have your undivided attention? The final event of the day will begin shortly. We ask everyone to pay attention to their surroundings. At times, the two contestants may fly close to the stands…it can become a dangerous situation! Be aware!! If you wish to move seats, please do so before the event begins! Now, without any more hesitation, let me introduce your two warriors. On her Draghoon, the Queen of Alstromia, Alexis Snipperdoom!!!! On his Torrin, the head of

Security for all of Alstromia, Pauto Vexxorth!"

The arena became thunderous. The roar of the crowd was insane. Luckily, Trixxie remained still as Alexis petted her head reassuringly.

The judge continued, "Now, please, allow the warriors to greet each other. When I strike the gong again, the battle will commence!"

Alexis and Trixxie faced Pauto and Maizzeh. Alexis and Pauto respectfully nodded to each other, acknowledging the round was about to begin. Even though the Colosseum was noisy, Pauto heard his heart beating in his ears. His hands shook, and he felt damp from sweat. He was scared to death, suddenly not ready to face Alexis. Strangely, she appeared unaffected. She smiled, rubbing her lips together, holding the reins tightly in her hands, prepared to battle.

The Wand of Grimleah was securely tucked into her battle uniform for easy access. Alexis planned to use at least four different spells against Pauto. She knew he would use several as well. She planned to use the first one against herself, a *Shielding Spell* that would make all of Pauto's magic obsolete, or so she hoped.

The two warriors waited. The loud gong noise finally reverberated throughout the arena. Alexis did not hesitate. She cast her spell quickly and flew into the sky, avoiding

Pauto. Alexis guided Trixxie around the track to begin the first of five laps required to complete the competition. Pauto quickly caught up to her, trying to hit her from behind.

Instantly, his Torrin bounced off the back of Trixxie and dove down, almost smacking into the hard ground. Luckily, Pauto recovered and had Maizzeh back in the air within seconds. It amused Alexis, and she cackled with delight, almost done with her first lap. Pauto was far behind. With a scowl on his face, Pauto aimed his wand quickly, casting a *Shield Destroy Spell*, which worked. He saw the flickering light around Alexis dissipate.

Immediately, he rushed to catch up to her, pushing his Torrin hard. As he managed to fly next to her, Pauto viciously bumped his Torrin into the Draghoon. Trixxie felt the sharp pain in her side. Instinctively, she tucked her wings behind her and dove like a bullet to the ground, buzzing the arena's track. Pauto was disappointed, shaking his head. He hoped Alexis would have plummeted to the ground, crashing with the beast.

By now, Alexis had almost completed the second lap around the track, but Pauto was on her heels. Determined, Pauto raised his wand and expeditiously cast a *Lightning Spell*, hoping to spook Trixxie. He knew Draghoons were frightened by lightning. Unfortunately for Pauto, Trixxie was an intelligent beast. She put on the brakes when she saw the lightning bolt, causing Pauto to fly past her and Alexis.

Trixxie followed, shooting flames from her mouth, a spell Alexis had conveniently cast halfway through the second round on the track. By now, the crowd booed Pauto, reacting to his non-aggressive stance against the Queen. It seemed as if the Queen was running her laps with the beast, minding her own business, while Pauto tried desperately to stop her without much success.

Alexis turned around laughing, with a grin on her face, quickly casting more powerful magic. The beam, looking much like a lightning bolt, collided with Pauto's spell, causing a thunderous booming noise, followed by sparks falling and violently hitting both warriors.

Alexis felt wetness and brushed it away with her hand. She saw it was blood. Angrily, she turned around to cast another spell, but Pauto was already beside her. He managed to push her hard with his Torrin. She almost fell off Trixxie. At the last second, she regained her composure. Pauto felt the bolt hit him hard in his shoulder, courtesy of Alexis and the Wand of Grimleah. He screamed, feeling a burning sensation of flames rush over his body. Almost instantaneously, Pauto felt the blood running down his arm. He looked around, hoping to avoid Alexis and her magic. The crowd heckled Pauto, wanting him to engage and not run away from Alexis.

The Queen was now completing her fourth lap around the track, avoiding the beams of light coming off Pauto's wand. She managed to spin around on Trixxie, facing Pauto. She chanted while holding onto the reins, attempting to stabilize herself.

Pauto felt the throbbing pain in his torso. He grabbed his chest and gazed down briefly in disbelief before almost falling off the Torrin.

Though Pauto had already tried to shield himself using a *Ricochet Spell*, it worked only partially. The spell cast by Alexis hit him in the chest and bounced off him, walloping Alexis.

The Queen fell off Trixxie, tumbling toward the ground. Instantly, Trixxie felt Alexis was no longer on her back and rushed to fly under her, allowing her to drop onto her back. Within seconds, Alexis grabbed the reins and was back in control of the beast, though now she was bleeding from her head and arm.

Pauto grimaced as they were now on the end of the fourth lap, and he had not yet stopped Alexis.

As they began the fifth and final lap, Alexis decided it was time. She whispered into Trixxie's ear. The beast nodded. Trixxie slowed down, allowing Pauto to approach, believing he was finally gaining on her.

Once he was beside her, Alexis withdrew her wand and aimed it directly at him, chanting. Pauto never knew what hit him. He lost consciousness and fell off Maizzeh. The Torrin attempted to catch Pauto by allowing him to fall on her. Sadly, Pauto fell unconscious, smacking hard onto the sandy surface of the arena.

Alexis completed her fifth and final lap! The crowd screamed her name, declaring her the victor. Some shouted for Pauto to get up and get back on the Torrin. The Medical Assessment Team (*MAT*) stood by, awaiting orders from the judges.

Trixxie dove down, landing on the rough track surface, slowing to a trot. She was exhausted. Alexis remained on her back, waving to the crowd, not caring about Pauto. She figured he was okay. The spell was not something that should have killed him. It was a simple *Incapacitate Spell.*

The judges noticed Pauto was not moving and immediately dispatched the Medical Assessment Team to aid him. Alexis and Trixxie stopped in front of the judges. The Queen dismounted and ordered Trixxie to stay and lie down. Alexis stood next to Trixxie, waiting to find out if Pauto was okay. She did not have a clear view. The middle of the field was obscured by medical teams and two supervising judges. It seemed like an eternity to Alexis before the head judge approached.

"Alexis, what magic did you cast at the end? The Healing Warlock needs to know."

"It was an *Incapacitate Spell*—nothing special. Why? Is Pauto okay?" Alexis asked, now nervous that something had gone wrong.

The Witch shook her head. "No, he is not. I must insist you remain here and stay away from him." She ran off in a hurry.

Alexis knew something was very wrong. It should not have taken this long for Pauto to regain consciousness. Alexis wondered why the *Incapacitate Spell* caused him to faint and pass out. That had never happened before. Instantly, she began to question her chant. Had she used the wrong one by accident?

Armbruster approached, rushing to her side. "Alexis, you are bleeding from your head and arm. Let's get you to medical," he insisted.

Alexis pushed him away. "No, I want to know first if Pauto is okay! I will be fine. Please inquire about his health! I was ordered to stay here. I am not allowed to check on Pauto," Alexis whined.

"I doubt they will allow me near him. I will get you help. Wait here. I will be right back," he reassured Alexis.

Andreh was running toward her, and he saw Aerianna in the distance, pushing her way through the crowd to find out what had happened to her future husband. She was crying, looking furious, as she glared at Alexis, swinging her fists angrily.

Andreh finally made it to Alexis and stood beside her. "I brought a Medical Team member, a medic, with me. Please, Alexis, allow her to examine your injuries," Andreh pleaded.

Alexis reluctantly gave in. She sat on the ground while the medic carefully inspected her wounds. "My Queen, you require a *Healing Spell* to stop the bleeding. Do you wish me to do it, or do you want to cast it yourself?"

After a second of contemplating the medics' words, she replied snippily, "Don't worry about it. I am fine. You did your job. Go away." The medic bowed before the Queen and ran off quickly as ordered.

Andreh was furious with Alexis. He noticed the blood gushing from her skull. The side of her face was stained bright red. She had blood dripping down her nose. Her hair was drenched in blood, and she looked as if she was about to faint from the blood loss. She swayed back and forth, unable to remain steady.

"Alexis…stop the stubbornness. Please, let us stop the bleeding. The wound on your head is deep. I implore you to listen to me now!" Andreh screamed into her face. He wanted her to know it was a dire situation. Before too long, she could lose consciousness from the continued blood loss. He did not want that to happen.

"Fine, you do it," Alexis responded, giving in, feeling her head throbbing and making her feel dizzy.

Andreh raised his wand and chanted. The dark purple haze enveloped Alexis. Within a second or two, she felt a warmth surround her, followed by an icy cold stabbing pain in her head. Then she passed out. Andreh caught her. She was still in his arms. It did not take long, and she opened her eyes, staring at Andreh.

"What happened? Am I okay?" she asked Andreh.

"Yes, it is normal. It happens quite a bit of the time. The spell I cast is an *Instant Stop Spell*. It freezes the blood flow and causes you to lose consciousness temporarily. You are fine. Can you sit up by yourself?"

Alexis finally managed to stand. Her legs felt shaky. "Thank you for doing that. I feel horrible. Any news on Pauto?" Alexis became restless. She wanted to know if Pauto was conscious and wondered about the extent of his injuries. She demanded answers.

"I witnessed the Healing Warlock and his team take him off the field. I believe they moved him to the Manor. Let me speak to one of the judges. Stay here, please," Andreh insisted, using a stern voice.

Reluctantly, Alexis stayed where he left her, but she remained unsteady on her feet, much like someone intoxicated. A few minutes later, Armbruster returned with Andreh. They both had a serious demeanor. Immediately, Alexis felt panic. Did she kill Pauto by accident? *'Oh, God, no! Please let Pauto live!'* she pleaded silently.

Andreh stepped back, allowing Armbruster to take the lead. He grabbed her right hand and pulled her toward him. "Sweetheart, we should head to the Manor. The judges request your presence. Come on. Andreh and I will help you!" Armbruster said, urging her to move.

"NO! I am not going anywhere until someone updates me on Pauto's health. Is he okay? Stop the bullshit. My head is hurting, and I can barely think. Tell me now!!" Alexis screamed at the top of her lungs. The noise of her own shrill voice hurt her head badly. She bent over in pain and puked.

"He is going to be okay. He regained consciousness right after the Healing Warlock cast an *Awaken Spell*. He is sore, bruised, bleeding, and probably feeling the same as you! So, let's head to the Manor so you can change and speak with the judges. You can also see him for yourself, okay?" Armbruster was not asking. Instead, he was demanding. Armbruster picked her up. Miraculously, she did not resist. Armbruster carried Alexis in his arms all the way across the field to the Manor. Andreh followed silently. The crowd cheered as they watched the Queen exit the Colosseum.

Five minutes later, she sat on a cot in the assessment room, her feet dangling off the side. She saw Pauto across the room, sitting up. Aerianna was by his side, crying. He looked over and managed a smile, trying to let Alexis know he was okay and not mad at her.

"I am so happy to see our warriors have received medical attention," Steffani Vonderfill, the head judge, remarked. "The Battle Rounds are now complete. Alexis is the winner, but Pauto, you put on a heck of a show! A huge thank you to both participants for your efforts. You are worthy opponents. I will see you both tomorrow at the Awards Ceremony!" Steffani began leaving the room, but Alexis stopped her.

"What about the Battle Races? It is my final chance to race against my sister. We have planned this race for months. You cannot take that way!" Alexis screamed. She was furious that they wanted to cancel the event.

"My Queen, if you wish to race against Zandorah, you may do so. However, no one else will be racing. We have had enough drama for one event," retorted Steffani. She was surprised the Queen refused to quit.

"The race is on. Let the other judges know. I will be ready in an hour. Let us finish this once and for all."

"Fine, but we are amending the race," she adamantly insisted. "There will only be one. See you later, My Queen." Steffani hurried off to find the other judges to discuss the changes.

"Alexis, are you sure you have enough energy to race? We can postpone it until tomorrow. There is no hurry. The W3s will understand. No Clan member wants to see you suffer," Armbruster said, watching her facial expression. She still looked unsteady.

"I am ready. Someone, locate Zandorah and inform her of the new plans to race. Andreh, please check on Elannah, my Torrin, and prepare her for racing. I will meet you at the stable in thirty minutes." Andreh left speedily to find Essten and confirm that Elannah was ready to race.

Alexis curled up on the cot, closing her eyes. Her head still ached. Nonetheless, she was eager to finish the last competition of the day. She could rest later and sleep the remainder of the night.

As Alexis rested, Pauto and Aerianna left the building and returned to the Palace. Neither wanted to stay and watch the race. Pauto was hurting, and Aerianna was furious with Alexis.

Andreh and Essten discussed Elannah. "So, you feel she is ready, Essten?" Andreh inquired.

"Yes, I pinned her wings when I heard the Queen planned to race. You may escort her to the race track if you wish." Essten explained with a smile.

"Thank you, Essten. I will take her. Why don't you relax? I will have someone bring Elannah back to the stable after the race. Please ensure she is washed, placed back into her stall, and secured later this evening."

"Of course, Andreh," responded Essten. He nodded and returned to his office to await the return of the royal Torrin.

Andreh made his way back to the Manor, eager to talk to Alexis before her race against her sister. He intended to persuade her once more to either delay or call off the event. He was convinced that she wasn't physically prepared to compete, especially after suffering significant injuries during the Fight or Flight segment of the battles. Despite his concerns, he was aware that she would likely dismiss his request and proceed with the race solely to assert herself as the ultimate warrior.

CHAPTER 15

Armbruster helped Alexis change into a different outfit—a much lighter version of her battle uniform. It consisted of stretchy black pants with leather patches on the knees, butt, and inside of the thighs. The shirt, a flexible material in dark purple, was tucked inside the waist of the pants. She also wore long black riding boots, which were comfortable and sturdy.

Alexis had also washed her hair and pulled it back into a ponytail to eliminate the blood that had been caked all over her head. She stared at the full-length mirror, noticing the cut on her head still looked dreadful. Carefully, she touched the wound, checking it, and the pain radiated, causing her to flinch. It had turned a dark plum color. The gash was mainly closed but still oozed little droplets of blood. The cut on her arm was less severe. She was covered in bruises on her thighs and buttocks. Her right breast ached, probably from falling and landing roughly onto Trixxie earlier.

"Your Majesty, it is time. We must head to the race track," announced one of the helpers. He bowed before the Queen.

"Fine. Thank you. I will have my husband escort me to the race track," Alexis clarified. Armbruster took her hand. The two exited the building. The sky was overcast, and there was a brisk breeze. It made Alexis shiver, producing goosebumps. It was autumn on Alstromia, and she wished for the warmth of her room and fireplace back at the Palace. Instead, she would race seven laps around the race track at the Colosseum, attempting to defeat her sister, Zandorah.

Earlier in the day, Zandorah had been given the dreadful news. She would be forced to compete against Alexis in the Battle Race.

Zandorah had hoped Alexis would drop out or insist the event be canceled—no such luck. Zandorah wondered how Alexis would be able to compete with her wounds.

Alexis moved forward and challenged her to meet at the track at 4 o'clock. It was getting dark. The tall old-fashioned lamps illuminated the path to provide adequate lighting, but it was still less ideal for racing at nightfall.

Zandorah knew the race was not about anything but Alexis asserting power over her. At this point, Zandorah didn't care. She wanted to finish the race. It would be the last time she planned to compete against her sister. She decided this was her final Battle event.

Zandorah and Shawnatar had been discussing starting a family. So, now Zandorah's priority was to take care of herself, Shawnatar, and the kingdom of Iriss. Hopefully, soon, she would have a baby, and then her life would be complete.

Alexis and Armbruster arrived at the race track and were escorted to the stalls at the other end of the arena. Elannah was with Andreh. He spoke to her, reminding her she was a champion.

Armbruster excused himself, feeling awkward with Andreh nearby. He informed Alexis he would be watching from the Royal Box. Alexis nodded, acknowledging the information, turning to speak to Andreh.

"You look rough, Alexis. I was just on my way to the Manor to see you. Are you sure that you wish to follow through and race? You can still back out. Everyone will understand. You completed a fierce battle against Pauto." Andreh wanted her to know he supported her. He also did not wish for her to reinjure herself. Maybe this time, she could sustain more severe injuries. The idea made him cringe.

"No. I will not back out. I plan to proceed. The race will begin shortly. Help me get on Elannah's back, please."

Andreh bent down, allowing Alexis to use his back to straddle the Torrin. Once seated, she thanked him and trotted off to the starting line. Andreh followed. He stationed himself at the end of the track by the finish line. Andreh prayed Alexis was energized enough to make it through the entire race. He heard a huffing noise and turned around.

It was Zandorah on her restless Torrin. She gave him an awkward smirk and guided her Torrin toward the starting line to meet up with Alexis. Zandorah managed to line up next to her sister. Her hands were clammy, and she could barely catch her breath from her heart beating so fast.

"Hello, Alexis. You look like crap! Are you sure you want to race today? Everyone would understand if you prefer to postpone until tomorrow. I do not feel good about facing off against you under these circumstances," Zandorah stated.

Alexis contemplated her words but planned to race just to make a point. She could push through the pain to prove herself no matter what, flaunting her abilities.

"Absolutely. This race is happening today. Ready or not. You don't look so well yourself, Zandi," Alexis knew her sister was unprepared. She could see it on her face. Zandorah had sweat beads forming on her forehead. She also trembled, barely able to maintain control of her Torrin.

"Okay. I am fine. Let's get this done. I want to head back to Iriss as soon as possible," Zandorah added, rolling her eyes.

The judges were seated, facing the track. The gong would be heard at any moment. Andreh stood by the finish line, tapping his foot with impatience. Armbruster sat in the Royal Box with Lorthana by his side. He was wringing his hands with worry. This race determined more than just a race victory. Yarlen sat beside him, looking down at his lap, trying to remain calm.

Alexis previously informed Armbruster she would decide at the end of the race if she wanted to declare war on Iriss and Zandorah. The sisters were still in disagreement over the kidnapping and Gardone's involvement.

Alexis could not accept that her sister took her father's side, assuming Alexis was somehow partially responsible for her kidnapping. It was absurd. The time had arrived. Would Alexis declare war? Could she forgive Zandorah and make peace? The answers were about to be revealed in a matter of minutes. The crowd was relatively calm and much smaller than before. The few remaining spectators yelled and clapped with anticipation. The majority of W3s left the venue after the last Battle, opting to celebrate in the village.

Alexis wrapped the reins around her hands and hunched down, anticipating the loud gong noise. Zandorah remained perched on her Torrin nonchalantly.

Steffani approached the gong and smacked it with all her might with the mallet. Immediately, Alexis took off with Elannah, racing around the track.

Zandorah stood still for a moment, frozen by panic. She heard voices chanting her name, bringing her out of the mental fog. She tapped her Torrin's side, pulling back on the reins, eager to catch up to her sister. It did not take long.

Alexis had slowed down on purpose, allowing Zandorah to catch up a little. She wanted the race to be memorable and was not about to win outright. She planned to coax her reluctant sister into competing. As Zandorah approached Alexis, she had sheer panic on her face. She began sweating profusely, her eyes stinging.

Alexis giggled, fueled by adrenaline, elated to see her sister struggling. Alexis extended her foot and kicked Zandorah's Torrin, causing it to stop abruptly. Her sister almost toppled off the beast, barely able to hang on. Furious at the underhanded move, Zandorah sped up, ready to kick some butt. She was mad, which is precisely what Alexis was hoping would happen.

The sisters raced around the track, bumping into each other, sometimes punching and kicking along the way. The crowd loved the show they were putting on. However, it was not as exciting as some had hoped.

Alexis was the first to begin the sixth round of seven. She was getting tired and was still sore from her battle before. Alexis forced herself to turn around briefly. Zandorah was close on her heels.

Relentlessly, Alexis pushed forward, hoping to outpace Zandorah. Her sister was having a difficult time keeping up with her.

Zandorah's Torrin lacked stamina. She was not used to competing. It was becoming apparent that her Torrin was beginning to slow. Zandorah feared she would not be able to complete the race.

Then, something astonishing happened, and Alexis slowed down. It looked as if she was in pain. Her head was low, and she leaned to the right, almost falling off Elannah. The spectators noticed, too. Some booed while others cheered, hoping to motivate Alexis to complete the rounds.

Armbruster stood up nervously. He watched as Zandorah overtook Alexis on the track. Andreh screamed Alexis' name, begging her to push through. He knew she was hurting by the way she attempted to stabilize herself on the Torrin. She did not look well.

The seventh-round began with Zandorah in the lead. Alexis wanted to win but knew it was not going to happen. She could barely breathe. Her chest ached, and she could not hold on much longer. Her hands were numb, and her head pounded. Alexis felt relieved. She would not be forced to throw the match to appease her mother and Clan members. She could lose outright, fair and square.

Alexis rode behind Zandorah, watching her force the Torrin toward the finish line. Alexis saw Andreh hysterically waving and screaming. Suddenly, she felt awful, coming to the realization she had to push through and beat Zandorah. She could not lose.

Pushing through the pain, Alexis caught up to Zandorah yards away from the finish line. She glanced at her sister's face and knew what had to be done. Alexis pulled back on the reins, smiling, feeling instant relief. Zandorah finished the race and came in first. Alexis followed, hearing the crowd clap and holler. Alexis had lost, and she felt okay with the result.

Zandorah approached the judges, still on her Torrin. She was sweaty and dirty from the track's dust and beyond exhausted. Finally, she dismounted, waiting for Alexis to arrive.

Alexis moved her Torrin to the other side of Zandorah, jumping down and almost losing her footing. She was worn out, feeling her body object to every move she made. Alexis grinned at her sister, who was now smiling ear to ear.

"Thank you, Alexis," is all she said to her sister. Zandorah walked away as the crowd now filled the arena. Spectators wanted to congratulate the winner and get a better view.

The judges shook Zandorah's hand. Steffani grabbed Zandorah's right arm and raised it into the air, declaring, "Everyone, please help us congratulate this year's winner of the Battle Race, Zandorah Snipperdoom!" She lowered her arm, giving her a quick hug before exiting the arena.

It did not take long for the spectators to get rowdy. Security escorted Zandorah off the field. Andreh shook his head as he finally managed to reach Alexis.

"Please tell me that you allowed her to win on purpose. There is NO way you could have lost. You were in the lead," Andreh screamed so she could hear him over the boisterous group. He became furious at the thought that she threw the race. It was not like her to give up such a coveted title.

"You will never know," she replied. "Help me get Elannah out of her, please," Alexis pleaded with him. She wanted to leave the area. The two made their way out of the Colosseum and walked toward the stable. Alexis was limping, dragging her foot.

Andreh noticed. "Do you need help?" he offered, frowning.

"I will be okay. I would like to return to the Palace. Will you ensure Elannah is placed back into the stable? I am planning to head home. I am in desperate need of a hot shower and clean clothing."

"Of course, Alexis. Take care. I will see you later," Andreh promised, taking Elannah's reins.

Alexis cast a spell and appeared in her chamber seconds later. To her surprise, Armbruster waited for her, sitting in the chair by the window.

"How are you?" he asked as he watched her undress.

"I am just peachy. I am sore and desperately require a hot and relaxing shower.

Why are you here, Armbruster? Can we please talk later?" she begged, shaking her head.

"I wanted to see for myself that you were unharmed from the race. I care about you. You know that. I love you. No matter what has happened between us lately, you are still the love of my life."

Alexis stopped walking. She spun around naked. "Why? Why would you still love me when you know what I have done? I do not understand." Alexis was perplexed.

"I fell in love with a stubborn, beautiful, powerful, and crazy Witch years ago. You, Alexis, will always be the one for me. I do not care what has transpired. We will always be husband and wife. Go shower. I will be here when you get out," Armbruster reassured her.

Baffled by his words, she shrugged her shoulders, unable to find the right words to say in response. She made her way to the shower, ready to feel the hot water on her aching and bruised body.

Andreh left Elannah in Essten's capable hands. Worried about Alexis, he returned to the Palace to check on her.

At the race track, Lorthana embraced Zandorah. "I am so darn proud of you!" her mother declared. "How did you manage to outmaneuver Alexis? I want all the details," she said. She had never thought it was possible that Zandorah would defeat Alexis.

Shawnatar gazed at his wife, beaming with pride, standing beside Lorthana. He would wait his turn, allowing his mother-in-law the first opportunity to speak with Zandorah.

A few minutes later, Zandorah snagged him by his shoulder and hugged him tightly. "So, hopefully now, Alexis and I will be okay with no more feud between us. She was gracious and allowed me to win. I know it. The Clans should rejoice. It means NO WAR!"

"You are assuming. We both know your sister. Let's wait to see what happens tomorrow at the Victory Celebration and the Awards Ceremony. I will hold my breath until then," Shawnatar remarked. He knew Alexis would not give in so easily. She may have allowed Zandorah to win the race, but that did not necessarily mean she would stop the war threats. Alexis was not one to forgive and forget. The sisters had a volatile relationship, and it frightened him.

Alexis emerged from the shower, wrapped loosely in a towel. She'd cast a healing spell in the shower to eliminate the leg and foot pain. It had become unbearable. Rather than suffer, she opted to heal herself using magic.

Armbruster was still in her chamber, as promised. He patiently waited for her in bed, which she felt was quite presumptuous. Rather than argue with him, though, she dropped the towel and jumped onto the tall bed. With a smoldering look on his face, he gently pulled his wife under the sheets, ready to ravage her body.

Andreh hesitantly approached her chamber. He wanted to surprise Alexis, but feared she might not be alone. So, he knocked quietly on the door. After two knocks with no response, he lifted the handle to open the door, but it was locked. Hearing a noise behind him, he jumped nervously, releasing the door handle.

"Sir, may I help you?" a security commoner inquired.

"No. I am here to see the Queen. I must speak with her at once," Andreh clarified.

"I have been ordered to keep everyone away. The King wants it so. He wishes to be left alone with the Queen. Sir, I must ask you to leave," the commoner insisted.

"Very well. Thank you," Andreh retorted, visibly upset. *'Armbruster is in the Queen's chamber alone with her? What are they doing? Oh, God, I hope they are not sleeping together,'* he said under his breath, feeling defeated.

Reluctantly, he headed toward his room at the other end of the Palace, pouting and deeply perturbed.

A few doors down, Aerianna whispered into Pauto's ear. "Are you sleeping?" He moved slightly. "Babe, are you okay?" she asked.

"Yes, Luv. I am fine. I need rest. Close your eyes and go to sleep," Pauto answered. He was more uncomfortable than he let on. His hips hurt, and his back ached profusely. Pauto figured the healing potion should have removed the pain and was perplexed as to why he was still not feeling better.

Pauto did not wish to upset Aerianna. She was already doting on him way too much, as far as he was concerned. He did not enjoy the extra attention. He preferred to rest and forget about the day. It had been a heck of a competition.

"Honey, please, don't lie to me. I can see it on your face. You are still hurting. What can I do? Should I summon the Healing Warlock again?" Aerianna was persistent. He gave her that.

"Do not be silly. I will be fine. Let's sleep, and tomorrow, I will wake up refreshed. I promise." Pauto rolled over, closing his eyes. He wanted to sleep.

Aerianna did not believe him, not for one minute. She curled up next to him. It did not take long for Pauto to fall asleep. He snored loudly on his side, facing away from her.

Worried about Pauto, Aerianna jumped out of bed and picked up her clothes on the way to the bathroom. She was determined to speak with Edwinn and find out why Pauto was still in pain.

★*.★*.★*.★*.★

The day literally began with a bang. Fireworks exploded outside Alexis's window, starting the day's festivities. It was still dark out, but the twin moons changed color and slowly became bright.

Today was the highly anticipated day—the Victory Celebration Day. It began with an outdoor breakfast in the courtyard of the Palace. Friends and family of the Royal Couple attended. It was a limited invitation event, followed by the Victory Parade.

Later in the afternoon and early evening, the Award Ceremony would be held at the Manor on Tullah Mountain. It was a long but fun-filled day. Alexis awoke feeling fabulous. Her body was not sore. Luckily, the spell she had cast the night before had done the trick. She glanced at the other side of the bed, admiring his muscular physique. Armbruster was still quite handsome. She felt herself getting hot for him, but knew it was time to get up. Plus, she felt awkward. Last night had been enjoyable, but it also felt wrong. The entire night with Armbruster, she fantasized about Andreh.

Alexis could not help but wonder what had happened to him last night. She was sure Andreh would have come to her for no other reason than to celebrate the end of the battles. She craved his body and attention.

Armbruster rolled over in bed and saw Alexis rush off to the bathroom. She was naked, and he saw a large number of dark purple and red bruises all over her behind. He felt sorry for her. Those had to hurt badly. He sat up in bed, looking out the window. It was a beautiful day, and he could not wait to eat. His stomach growled loudly.

When Armbruster heard the shower start, he was tempted to join Alexis. However, he did not want to act too pushy. After contemplating his options, he chose to dress and leave her chamber to shower in his room. Alexis would be present at the breakfast in a little while.

Andreh and Armbruster ran into each other in the hallway. Andreh was on his way to see Alexis when Armbruster came out of her chamber, looking smug.

"Good morning, Andreh. What a glorious day, right?" Armbruster declared triumphantly. "Well, have a good one!" He could see the defeated look on Andreh's face, and Armbruster reveled in delight. He walked off with a cocky grin.

Furious, Andreh opened the chamber door. He heard the shower running in the bathroom. Without hesitation, he pried open the door. Alexis was stepping out of the shower and spotted Andreh right away. She grinned, happy to see him.

"Well, hello there," Alexis started, acting coy.

"Hello there? That is what you say to me after you spend the night with Armbruster? Okay. I see how it is..." Andreh shrieked.

"Hmm, someone is not a happy camper. What is wrong, lover?" She teased, running her fingers from his chest down to his pants. She stared at him, trying to soften his anger.

"Stop it. I mean it," Andreh tried desperately to resist her touch and remain focused on his anger toward her.

"Oh, come on now. Let me make you feel better and forget about everything," Alexis continued, removing his clothes. "I could use another shower. As you know, I am a very, very dirty Witch."

"Yes, you are," Andreh agreed, watching her head for the shower. Finally, he would get what he desired. Alexis was about to make his day.

Armbruster entered the Command Center half an hour later with a broad smile. His day started the best it had in months. Rammadar was seated near the window, gazing out at the valley below. The moment he heard someone enter, he jumped out of the chair and spun around to face them.

"Oh, good morning, Sir. How was your night?" Rammadar inquired out of curiosity.

"It was fantastic. How are you, dear friend? Have you given any more thought to my offer? I would love for you to stay here on Alstromia on my staff. You have been an essential member of our team, and I appreciate you!"

"Yes, I have been thinking about our previous conversation for days. I am ready to give you my answer now."

"Great! Please, do not keep me hanging. What is your answer?" Armbruster hoped Rammadar would agree and stay on Alstromia as his new Second-in-Command. Armbruster felt for a while that it was time for Yarlen to step down. He was old and tired. Yarlen would serve the kingdom best as Head Seeier, focusing on teaching and working on new magical abilities.

If Rammadar agreed to take on the new position with the Security Command Team, Armbruster planned to announce the changes at the Award Ceremony in the evening. He stood facing Rammadar with impatience.

"Sir, I am honored you would consider me for the position. I gratefully accept your offer under one condition. I need a few hours to speak to Zandorah and resign my job on Iriss with her kingdom. I hope you understand!"

"How fantastic! You have no idea how delighted I am at the prospect of you joining our team. Thank you! Of course, you are expected to give your notice to Zandorah. I am sure she will understand. Without a doubt, she knows how much you have missed Alstromia and all your friends!" Armbruster declared, thrilled.

Now, the difficult part would begin for him. He had to hunt down Yarlen and give him the bad news. Yarlen would no longer hold the title of his Second-in-Command. Hopefully, Yarlen would agree it was in the empire's best interest to have someone younger on the staff.

"Thank you again, Sir. I will not let you down, I promise. I am excited about the move to Alstromia. I cannot wait to begin the new venture. May I leave? I wish to locate Zandorah and inform her of my decision." Rammadar was ready to begin a new chapter of his life.

"Yes, do what you must, friend. We will speak later. Good luck!" Armbruster grinned, happy that Rammadar agreed to join the team.

Rammadar gleefully exited the chamber, whistling. Finally, he would be back, living on Alstromia. He could not wait to spend time with friends, living his best life with those he cared for deeply. With any luck, Zandorah would be gracious and release him without a fuss.

★ *. ★ *. ★ *. ★ *. ★

Zandorah and Shawnatar headed to the courtyard to join others for the breakfast gathering. Both had slept well. Zandorah was on cloud nine after her victory against Alexis. She had not spoken to her sister since yesterday and wondered how she would conduct herself.

Lorthana greeted everyone and pointed out the seating area. Zandorah and Shawnatar chose to sit next to Armbruster and Lorthana. Alexis was still absent, but Rammadar scooted into the seat next to Zandorah, ready to share the news with her about his upcoming move.

"May I have a private moment with you? Please!" Rammadar insisted, with a guarded look on his face.

"Umm, right this minute?" Zandorah asked, confirming his urgent request.

"Yes, please. It will only take a minute. I promise."

"Sure, no problem." Zandorah stood up, and the two walked to a bench on the other side of the courtyard near a fountain.

"Zandorah, I am giving you my notice. I will not be returning to Iriss with you. I plan to stay on Alstromia. Armbruster has offered me a job, and I have accepted. It is an outstanding opportunity for me and my career! Plus, I have missed my colleagues here and wish to stay. I hope you understand. I have spoken with Juannah Ogarstan and asked if she would be willing to take on my job if you approve of the changes. She agreed and would be honored to fill the position."

Zandorah was left speechless. She did not expect Rammadar to abandon her. She realized he missed Alstromia but never believed he would resign his commission and leave Iriss.

"It seems like you have thought of everything. If you wish to leave, I will not stop you. It breaks my heart to see you go, but I wish you the best. Of course, I will trust your judgment. If you feel Juannah is ready, then she may take the position. That is okay with me. Let us chat more after breakfast, okay?" Zandorah felt deeply hurt and wanted to focus on other things. She was also hungry. It would be better to iron out all further details later in the day.

"Thank you, Zandorah. You truly are a gracious and kind ruler." He gently kissed her on the cheek, walking toward the table to share the good news with Armbruster.

Andreh dressed and watched Alexis as she tucked her wand into her belt. She looked gorgeous as ever. Today, she wore stretchy black pants, a white blouse with tall black boots, and a short black cape was draped over her shoulders. Her hair was pulled up, with little curls framing her face. Her eyes sparkled as she kissed Andreh on the lips.

"Come on, handsome. The breakfast will start shortly. Let's go."

"Maybe you should head out first without me. I am not sure it is a good idea for us to show up simultaneously."

Alexis agreed. She did not need the stares and drama. "Right! Well, see you there." She exited the chamber and headed down the hallway in a cheerful mood.

Andreh waited for a few minutes before following her to the courtyard. He thought about their time together earlier as he walked out into the yard, a naughty smile on his face. Aerianna greeted him. She pulled him aside.

"Listen, Andreh. I do not care what is going on between you and Alexis. However, today is a monumental day. Please, stay away from her and Armbruster. Let the royal couple do their job without your interference. I implore you!" Aerianna warned. She glared at him, visibly angry.

"Aerianna, stop it. Please release my arm. I do not plan to do anything but observe and celebrate the day, as everyone else will be doing. So, back off," he snapped.

"Fine. As long as you understand where you stand in this relationship!" Aerianna added before stomping off to be seated.

Andreh fumed but decided to let it go. Aerianna was right about one thing. Today was not the day to start drama. He planned to stay in the background as much as possible. There was no need for any kind of trouble.

The breakfast went by fast and was uneventful. Everyone seemed genuinely happy, eating, talking, laughing, and having a wonderful time. Alexis noticed Andreh looked glum. She wanted to speak with him, but felt all eyes on her, so she remained seated, pretending to be in a joyful mood.

Armbruster stood up, tapping his brew bottle. "Everyone, if I could have your attention for just a moment, please!" he loudly bellowed in a commanding voice. The group became quiet, eager to hear what he had to say.

"Friends, family…I have outstanding news. Today, we welcome a new member to our Security Command Team and the Royal Staff. Rammadar Ximberton has accepted the position as my new Second-in-Command. Yarlen is retiring and will now be teaching regularly. He will remain Head Seeier as well.

So, with that said, let us welcome Rammadar!! Also, let us thank Yarlen for his service!"

The W3s around the table appeared surprised. Yarlen looked away. Apparently, he was not happy about his new retirement. Sonia clapped half-heartedly, assuming he had been forced into retirement by Armbruster. It made her furious. She planned to talk to him later!

Alexis rose out of her seat and immediately congratulated Rammadar. "What a great move, Rammadar. Welcome! I am so pleased you will be here with us. It will be nice to have new blood in the Palace," Alexis joked as she shook his hand.

"Thank you, Your Majesty! I am honored and grateful." Rammadar spent a few minutes shaking hands with others around the table. He felt welcome and happy to be back on the planet permanently.

Zandorah shook his hand tearfully. She was still hurt but happy for him. "Rammadar, my dearest friend, please know you will be greatly missed. If you ever wish to return to Iriss, you have a job waiting!" Zandorah hugged him and walked away, crying. It was a horrible day for her. She would miss her friend and confidant, Rammadar, dearly.

Shawnatar quickly followed Zandorah, realizing she would need his support. Today was a bittersweet day for Zandorah.

She celebrated her victory over her sister, the Queen, but had to deal with the tragic loss of her friend. Shawnatar felt awful, and he hoped Zandorah would bounce back quickly from this hurt.

CHAPTER 16

War is not always predicted. At times, it begins quickly and unexpectedly. Other times, quarrels and long-drawn-out disagreements brew before war breaks out. Alexis sat in the Royal Observation Box, facing the cobblestone street, relaxing before the parade began. She loved observing others. The City of Miccay bustled, and the crowd was lively.

Clan members mingled and walked around with jugs of brew, laughing cheerfully. The Victory Parade was minutes away from starting. The AoE was about to showcase its formidable army by marching down the old streets in battle uniforms.

Armbruster joined Alexis. He wore his battle uniform, which was a rare event. It made him look powerful and handsome.

"Can you believe the Battle Rounds and Harvest Festival are ending? Another year in the books!" Armbruster announced.

"Armbruster, it has been a heck of an event. So much has happened this year. My mind is still spinning. You never told me you planned on offering Rammadar a job here. Why?"

"Alexis, I was not sure he would accept. I have been thinking for quite some time that Yarlen should retire. He is not the same. Everything is too much for him. This is the best thing for all of us. Rammadar will do amazing work for Alstromia, trust me."

"Oh, don't get me wrong. I am thrilled he accepted the job. Yarlen is not the same Wizzard he was a year ago. I believe he is better off not having so much responsibility to deal with daily. I wholeheartedly agree. Rammadar will become a great new addition to our staff. We need someone younger in the position," Alexis concurred. She was happy about the unexpected change.

Trumpet noise could be heard from a distance, indicating it was almost time. The parade was about to begin shortly.

Lorthana waved to the royal couple as she appeared with Zandorah and Shawnatar. Andreh, Aerianna, and Pauto arrived at the same time. Everyone took their seats along the parade route, ready to witness the AoE's appearance. Every year, the new graduates of the *Alstromia Magical Learning Academy (AMLA)* put on a special magical performance.

The trumpets blasted a second time, and the crowd's roar became thunderous. Alexis fiddled with her fingernails, wishing the parade was over. She was eager to attend the Award Ceremony. She worked hard, training for months to get into shape to be able to compete in the Battle Rounds. Some nights, she was bruised, beaten, and exhausted.

Andreh and Pauto both helped her immensely. It was ironic that she ended up facing off against Pauto in the end. He was a strong warrior, and she greatly valued him. She contemplated why Armbruster had not asked Pauto to fill the position he offered Rammadar. It was strange. Pauto should naturally have been given the job.

Alexis decided to question Armbruster about that decision later. It still bothered her. It was odd that someone outside the team was given the position. Alexis wondered if Pauto was hurt by Rammadar taking the job, bypassing him in the process. The job should have been Pauto's. He had earned it. Now, Rammadar would be in charge. Alexis hoped it would not cause issues between Pauto and Rammadar.

The parade was in full swing. The crowd evidently approved of the event. The town burst at the seams with W3s and commoners. It made Alexis happy to see how flawlessly everything had gone off so far. Aerianna did an outstanding job planning the event and deserved recognition.

Suddenly, the spectators went wild as the Army of Elite *(AoE)* appeared. The crowd clapped, shouted, and stomped their feet. Armbruster made the announcement.

"Please, welcome our Army of Elite (*AoE*), commanded by Steffen Starleight and his Second-in-Command, Sheillah Hexxon!"

The AoE marched down the street, holding their Ceptres. The crowd could not get enough. AoE commander, Steffen Starleight, stopped briefly in front of the Royal Observation Box, saluting the King and Queen.

Alexis jumped out of her seat, nodding to Steffen. Sheillah advanced, bowing before the King and Queen, smashing her Ceptre to the ground out of respect. It was quite a scene. It took almost five minutes for all the AoE and

Standard Army of Warriors (*SAoW*) to march past the Royal Couple and spectators.

The new graduates made their way down the street, showcasing magical abilities, levitating each other, casting spells, and more. One of the spells was highly applauded when a dark black cloud formed in the middle of the street, unexpectedly turning into a Draghoon that breathed hot pink smoke over the spectators.

The gifted graduate, *Cazzandra Whiddletoad*, invented the magic. She was also named the Graduate of the Year, allowing her to study directly under Yarlen in the Palace.

Not much impressed Alexis, but that performance did. After the parade, she immediately asked Armbruster to introduce her to the young Witch. Alexis was eager to learn more about her.

"My Queen, it is such an honor to meet you in person," gushed Cazzandra. "Thank you for allowing me a moment to speak with you."

"Your spell quite enthralled me. Did you invent it yourself?" Alexis inquired out of curiosity.

"Yes, My Queen. It is an original incantation I call the *Power Spell*. What I did not do here, in public, was the last part. The powerful magic is intended to be used during War or Battles. The Draghoon will breathe actual flames and shoot painful darts at the enemy. However, I toned it down for this occasion!" She proudly announced, beaming. It was such an honor for the Queen to notice her abilities.

"Yes, I would hope so," agreed Alexis, laughing. "I invite you to sit with me tonight at the Awards Ceremony. I want the opportunity to get to know you more," Alexis offered.

"Thank you, My Queen. I am flattered. See you then!" Cazzandra left quickly, not to wear out her welcome. It was exciting! The Queen herself wanted to get to know her! Cazzandra felt like she had just struck gold.

Andreh was in awe of her performance as well. He also found Cazzandra quite charming. She was a beautiful young Witch with the most mesmerizing bright green eyes. She had long, red hair that flowed past her bottom, which was braided for the event. She wore a figure-flattering black jumpsuit, accentuating her long, muscular legs. Her plump breasts peeked out of the top of her jumpsuit. Andreh planned to follow her. After all, he was a single Wizzard. He could date anyone he wanted, and he definitely wanted to get to know Cazzandra.

Andreh's wandering eyes did not escape Alexis. She saw the look on his face as he watched the young Witch. Jealousy took over. Alexis wanted to destroy the young girl, but she decided to give her a chance. Andreh would not be allowed near her. Cazzandra would be off-limits. Alexis would see to it, personally!

The crowd dispersed. Many of the W3s began celebrating. Most would not attend the Award Ceremony. Only those with special invitations would have the honor to be present.

The Village became lively as commoners, Blud-Trackers, and W3s mingled, enjoying the last day of the Harvest Festival. Henrii's BrewHaus was packed. It was a fun-filled night for many. Henrii, his wife, and workers would have their hands full, pouring brews, potions, and handing out snacks to a rambunctious lot of visitors and attendees.

Alexis entered her private chamber, ready to shower and change her clothes for the evening event. Karita, the chambermaid, had already laid out Alexis's outfit. It was carefully placed on the bed with matching shoes below on the floor. Alexis approved. It seemed as if Karita was finally becoming proactive, not needing constant reminders from her.

The fireplace roared with dancing flames, and the room was warm and cozy. There was a note propped up on the table by the fireplace.

Alexis picked it up. It read, ***"You are the most beautiful Witch I have ever known. I love you forever, Your loving husband, Armbruster."***

Alexis stared at the note. *'Why would he do this?'* It seemed strange that suddenly he was so attentive, with such a massive outpouring of affection! Alexis chuckled to herself, and she stripped off her clothes, eager to shower.

A few doors down, Armbruster admired himself in the mirror. He thought he looked rather dapper. His battle uniform still fit him well. He had not gained any weight over the years, choosing to stay fit and working out daily with Pauto. Now, he had to change into his Ceremonial attire. He planned to wear his crown, which he rarely did anymore. He wondered if Alexis would complete her outfit with the tiara. He had asked Karita to place it on the bed for her to see. Hopefully, she would get the hint and wear it.

The trumpets rang out once more from outside the Palace. Karita knocked on the chamber door and entered. "My Queen, it is time. Carmin has already brought Princess Lilah to the Manor. The child is dressed in her royal cloak and gown and is wearing her tiara, per your instructions. May I help you place your tiara on your head?"

"Did Armbruster put you up to this? Be honest, Karita."

"The King asked me to retrieve the tiara from the Tower and place it on your bed. I assumed he had already asked you to wear it for the evening."

"I see. No, he did not. Yes, please. Place and secure it on my head." Alexis sat down, allowing Karita to secure the crown on her head. It sparkled, completing the regal look. Karita smiled as she stepped away.

"You are ready, My Queen!" Karita shouted excitedly. She admired Alexis in all her glory.

"Thank you, Karita. You have done a fine job. I thank you!" Alexis walked out of the chamber and headed to the Landing Deck. She would fly in the Royal carriage to the mountain top, landing in the field by the Manor.

As she walked onto the Landing Deck, Armbruster met her there. He extended his hand, reaching for hers. "You look absolutely stunning, Alexis." He kissed her on the lips, helping her into the carriage.

Once they were both seated and secured, the carriage driver took off into the darkening sky as the twin moons glistened in the distance. It was a magical night.

Andreh changed into his ceremonial uniform, adorned with rows of medals. Andreh was a fierce warrior and competitor. He had a total of 21 medals attached to the left side of his chest. His pants were tucked into his boots, and he was ready to attend the Awards Ceremony. He held his Ceptre in his left hand, looking at himself in the mirror. He wondered if Cazzandra would speak to him.

He had been thinking about her all day long. Perhaps later, he could see Alexis in private. But, somehow, he doubted that would happen. Nonetheless, Andreh was excited about the evening and could not wait to see what would develop.

The Manor was active when the Royals arrived. Alexis jumped down gracefully from the carriage, holding onto Armbruster's arm. The Royals waved as they entered the Manor. Alexis spied Viollah Grackenbone, standing on the podium, holding the microphone. She was about to begin her performance before the actual ceremony.

Alexis and Armbruster entered the Ballroom, escorted by security. Alexis sat at the long table on the left side of the stage, watching Viollah belt out one of her favorite songs, *"Glory to the Victor, Glory to Alstromia."* Armbruster held Alexis's hand. He was not afraid to show his affection in public. Alexis gazed around the room, hoping to find Cazzandra.

Andreh entered the ballroom, looking sexy as hell. Alexis could feel a wave of heat run through her as she spotted him approaching. Then, suddenly, he stopped. Andreh turned his back. Alexis moved around in her seat, attempting to see what he was doing. When Andreh turned around again, he held Cazzandra's hand. He proudly guided her to the Royal table.

Alexis wanted to scream. *'HOW dare he!'* she thought. Andreh advanced, letting go of Cazzandra's tiny hand. "Your Royal Highnesses. May I present Cazzandra Whiddletoad of Alstromia?" Andreh bowed and moved aside so Cazzandra could curtsy before the Royals.

"Please, Cazzandra, sit next to me," Alexis offered, squinting her eyes. She was furious with Andreh. *'Is he flirting with Cazzandra to piss me off, or is he genuinely interested in the younger Witch?'* Either way, Alexis planned to discuss it with him later in the evening. She hated the way he acted around the younger Witch.

Cazzandra took a seat and placed her hands on her lap. She chose to wear a navy-blue gown with a sheer silver cape tonight. Her hair was pulled up into a loose bun.

The random ringlets of hair made her look spectacular. She only wore lipstick. She was a natural beauty and required nothing else to make her stand out from the crowd. Andreh found himself becoming aroused as he gazed at her. She was a stunner.

Alexis ignored his blatant gawking. It made her furious. She chose to chat with Armbruster instead, concentrating on the musical number by Viollah.

Twenty minutes later, Viollah walked up to the tall microphone to speak. "Welcome, everyone! What a spectacular scene! I see so many wonderful and familiar faces. I am honored to be your master of ceremonies tonight. We will begin the evening by singing everyone's favorite tune, *"Alstromia, Our Home!"* Please join me by standing." Viollah's voice was powerful and euphonious.

Once Viollah finished, she clapped, cheering on the audience for their participation. "Next, let us welcome our three judges, *Steffani Vonderfill, Korilyn Krater, and Marcus Waggerton.* Steffani Vonderfill, please join me at the microphone and make the announcements!" The crowd clapped, eager to finally witness the presentation of awards. Steffani took the microphone in her hand.

"Tonight, we are gathered to celebrate the competition's warriors. We have already handed out the smaller awards earlier in the day at the Colosseum. Now, we will hand out the final Trophies and Awards. We, the three judges, had a tough time deciding the overall winner. It was a fierce competition, and all the contestants fought hard for the *Victor of the Year* title. However, as you know, there can only be one! We will begin with Third Place – Zandorah Snipperdoom! Please come up on stage."

Zandorah jumped out of her seat and quickly headed to the podium. Steffani hugged her, handing her the bronze-colored trophy. Zandorah left to sit back down, beaming with pride. She was pleased with her placement at the event.

"Next, we will welcome our Second-Place winner, Alexis Snipperdoom!" Everyone looked around, confused.

"What? What did she say?" asked Alexis, not believing she heard correctly.

"Your Majesty, please come and accept your trophy!" Steffani insisted.

Embarrassed and confused, Alexis slid out of her seat. Reluctantly, Alexis headed for the stage, snatching the silver trophy from Steffani's hand. When Steffani attempted to hug her, Alexis pushed away, rushing back to her seat.

"Okay, now, the moment you have been waiting for…our First-Place winner and the *Victor of the Year* goes to none other than Pauto

Vexxorth!!! Congratulations, Pauto. Please come up here and accept your trophy," Steffani screeched excitedly. Aerianna jumped out of her seat, clapping, proud of her fiancé!

Like everyone else, Pauto was stunned. He had no idea he would win. He assumed Alexis would be the victor, but quickly managed to step up on the podium, and Steffani ceremoniously handed him the heavy gold trophy. He smiled, holding up for all to see, as the crowd applauded and called out his name.

Armbruster watched Alexis' facial expression. He knew she felt cheated. She should have won. Armbruster wondered why the judges chose to crown Pauto the victor. The rest of the evening would be miserable. He would be forced to listen to Alexis whine and complain about her stolen victory. It would be hell. Armbruster was no longer looking forward to the rest of the night.

At that moment, Armbruster decided he no longer wanted to remove Alexis as the Queen or ruler of Alstromia. He vowed to support and love her, no matter what. She deserved his respect. She had been through hell lately, and he was not about to add to her suffering. Enough was enough!

"Witches, Warlocks, and Wizzards, thank you for witnessing this yearly event. We had a record number of participants. It was an event we will never forget. Please do not forget that the WinterFrost Festival is approaching in a month. We hope to see you all then!" Steffani handed the microphone back to Viollah as she and the other judges left the stage and headed out of the building. They hoped to avoid Alexis Snipperdoom. The three judges realized she would question their decision, but voted unanimously to declare Pauto the winner. He had won over their hearts and battled admirably.

"Armbruster, I want to leave. Tell Carmin to take Lilah back to the Palace." Reluctantly, Armbruster agreed with her. He did not want to stay either. It was just going to get worse. The noise outside was louder than expected. Armbruster frowned and marched toward Pauto.

"What the hell? I thought we decided the fireworks would not begin until just before midnight, after the dance and party?" Armbruster bellowed.

"Sir, I have no idea. I will ask Aerianna. I will be right back." Pauto ran off to locate her since she was in charge of the event.

Suddenly, Rammadar ran toward Armbruster, followed by twenty Security Guard of Command team members. They held Mesmer Ceptres. "Sir, we must get you, the Queen, and the child back to the Palace. We are under attack. Someone has waged war against Alstromia! I have ordered the deployment of the AoE and the SAoW! Please, Sir, follow me," Rammadar screamed.

Alexis took off her high heels to run faster. She grabbed Armbruster's arm. "We have to get to Lilah, "Alexis screamed. "Oh my God, who would do this?"

Alexis looked outside and saw that the mountain was on fire. Fiery sparks rained down from the sky, illuminating the night. Screams were heard, followed by banging noises.

Andreh bumped into Alexis and Armbruster. "I have the Princess secured at the Palace in the basement. She is okay. I have also summoned Yarlen and his team. We are attempting to cast a spell to secure the planet. We have no idea who is attacking us or why."

Alexis looked around frantically. Suddenly, she spotted her running out of the building. Without hesitation, she ran after her, ready to kill if need be. Alexis withdrew her wand from under her gown. She never went anywhere without it. She caught up to her as they approached the carriage.

"Did you seriously believe I would let you get away with this? You are out of your damn mind, Zandorah. How dare you declare war! I hope you are ready to be annihilated. There will be no mercy. Rest assured," Alexis warned. She aimed her wand at her sister. "I could kill you now, but that would not be fun, would it? Get back to Iriss. I am ready to destroy you!"

"Alexis, I did not do this. You must believe me!" Zandorah yelled, hoping Alexis could hear her over the noises. Fearing for her life, Zandorah closed her eyes and transported herself to Iriss. She realized Alexis blamed her for the ruthless attack. However, Zandorah was not the attacker. She had no idea who had begun the war, but she planned to find out.

In the meantime, Zandorah planned to prepare her army for war. *'Juannah better be ready,'* thought Zandorah, entering the Castle of Zandor. Zandorah stared at her staff in the Royal Planning Chamber, feeling overwhelmed.

"By now, you have heard what has happened on Alstromia. We already know someone else has done this and is trying to pin this on me! Alexis will be bringing this fight to Iriss. Juannah, please prepare our troops. It will be a long and bloody battle!"

On Alstromia, injured W3s ran around aimlessly, confused. Blood was splattered on the ground as fiery bolts dropped from the sky, hitting innocent victims courtesy of an unknown enemy. It was a bloodbath. Alexis looked up, wondering who was truly behind this sneak attack. *'Can Zandorah be responsible?*

Did she lie about instigating the war? Who else could be behind the strike on Alstromia?'

Suddenly, Alexis saw Trixxie off in the distance. She was attempting to fly off, scared of all the noise and bombardment. Alexis rushed to her side to calm her down. That was when tragedy struck. Trixxie was hit by a giant, flaming boulder plummeting out of the sky. The ginormous beast loudly dropped to the ground, her eyes instantly closing. Alexis believed she was only hurt and attempted to lift the beast's heavy head, holding her beloved Draghoon.

In shock, Alexis did not even consider casting a spell to try to revive her. Trixxie tragically died in her arms, taking one last breath as blood ran down her giant head.

Andreh grabbed her hand. "Alexis, we must go NOW. Trixxie is gone. It is too late for her! Armbruster is already at the Palace with Yarlen. Come on. There is no time."

"NO, we have to help others. Look around you. They are dying," Alexis pointed to wounded W3s. Some were dead, sprawled in the street, covered in blood—others were missing limbs. The area looked like a war zone.

"We are under attack. Andreh, we have to do something. We cannot leave them," Alexis insisted desperately. She knew this could be the end. Then she spotted the AoE on their

Torrins, soaring into the sky. It gave her a brief hope and some relief.

"Okay, you are right. However, we must return to the Palace." Andreh squeezed her hand and slammed down his Ceptre. They vanished in the grey fog, quickly appearing in her chamber. The moment they arrived, Armbruster magically appeared. He was in his battle uniform, holding his Ceptre. His wand was also strapped onto his sturdy, black belt.

"Alexis, we need to discuss our strategy. Please join me and others in the Security Command Team Chamber. I will be waiting." He disappeared right after, leaving Andreh and Alexis alone. She allowed herself to fall into the chair, peering out the window. Much of Tullah Mountain was on fire. She could see flames shooting out of the Colosseum. The Manor was engulfed, and she could hear loud explosion noises that rattled the bedroom window.

"Alexis, what do you want to do?" Andreh asked.

Alexis chanted, and instantly, she was dressed in her battle uniform. She pulled her hair back. "Let us join Armbruster and the others. I want to hear what they know or suspect."

Minutes passed, and the two entered the Security Command Center. The group parted, allowing the Queen to enter. Alexis stood at the head of the large conference table, leaning onto its surface with her palms down. She was unsteady, angry, scared, and confused. Nonetheless, she would portray power and stability, reflecting her position as Queen and ruler of Alstromia.

"Today, we have been attacked by an invisible enemy, a group of cowardly weaklings. We will discover who is responsible and terminate them. Mark my words. We will not allow them to destroy our homes and planet. I have banished my sister, Zandorah, until we know if she had anything to do with this spineless act. We will rise up! Yarlen has already secured the planet with his students. There will be no more attacks today. We will hunt down the ones responsible and make them pay!"

Alexis made a fist, furiously waving it around in the air, screaming, "*Alstromia, our home! We will not forsake thee, our home, our refuge.*" Others joined in.

Andreh stood on a chair to gain everyone's attention. "To the Queen and the kingdom. We will be victorious! All hail Queen Alexis Snipperdoom!" The group cheered.

Alexis blushed, grateful for the powerful and supportive members of her security team. She smiled at Andreh, happy he had been by her side when the attack happened.

Alexis noticed Armbruster standing by Andreh. He acted stoic, saying little, allowing her the glory of attention. She realized her life was filled with love and support, and she felt appreciative. Alexis could not imagine this war ending her reign or life. Alexis closed her eyes, listening as the group applauded. Though it was a somber moment, Alexis felt relieved to know she had their backing. Together, they would save Alstromia.

Armbruster placed his hand on Andreh's shoulder. "Thank you for all you have done today. It means a great deal to me. What do you think about that incredible Witch?" Armbruster asked, pointing to Alexis, beaming with pride.

"I believe war becomes her, Your Majesty. She will prevail. The Queen is the strongest Witch I have ever met in my life. She will undoubtedly discover who is responsible and obtain her revenge. It is just a matter of time!"

FOR MORE INFORMATION ABOUT ALEXIS SNIPPERDOOM, BE SURE TO CHECK OUT THE OFFICIAL GUIDE

JD BROYHILL
POWER PLAYS
AN ALEXIS SNIPPERDOOM NOVEL
BOOK 1

JD BROYHILL
ENEMIES FROM WITHIN
AN ALEXIS SNIPPERDOOM NOVEL
BOOK 2

JD BROYHILL
ENTANGLED VENGEANCE
AN ALEXIS SNIPPERDOOM NOVEL
BOOK 4

www.ingramcontent.com/pod-product-compliance
Lightning Source LLC
LaVergne TN
LVHW100504110826
845146LV00002B/512

* 9 7 9 8 9 9 2 6 7 3 2 8 9 *